A MALI HOOPER THRILLER

#JUSTICE PREVAILS

KADY HINOJOSA

BOOK 2

Visit the author's website at *www.kadyhinojosa.com*

Note: This story is not suitable for persons under the age of 18.

Cover Design: Damonza.com

Editorial Services: Beth Dorward. Visit the editor's page
on Reedsy at *https://reedsy.com/#/freelancers/beth-d*

E-book ISBN-13: 978-1-7354976-2-4

Paperback ISBN-13: 978-1-7354976-3-1

To my husband, Jose:
You are my rock, my champion, my
supporter in all things, my best friend.
Thank you for all you do and all you are. I love you.

To my family and friends:
Thank you for being my cheerleaders and
for your never-ending encouragement.
I am grateful you are in my life.

CHAPTER ONE

Warren, CT
Sunday, August 9, 9:00 p.m.

WEARING AN A-LINE gray pin-striped skirt with white silk blouse, the composed woman stepped into the window-less building, wrinkling her nose in distaste as the stale stench of cigars assailed her senses. She paused, her eyes squinting to narrow slits as they adjusted to the dim lighting. Her breath quickened as she anticipated what was to come. Wasting no more time, she crossed the room, the click-click of her black stiletto heels echoing, occasionally muted by various Persian rugs scattered throughout.

"Big enough man cave for you?" asked the man as she approached, humor lacing his voice. "I'd go for a couple of those seventy-five-inch televisions. I don't think he'd miss two from the eight hanging on the wall."

"He won't miss anything much longer." She sniffed. "Are we ready to go?" She watched the shackled, rotund man inside. Although standing, he slouched from exhaustion. His arms were secured to a beam above his head making it impossible to sit down. He shifted from foot to foot as a heat lamp bore down on him. Sweat poured down his face and dripped off his double chin to his chest, continuing its descent to his underwear, the only clothing he wore.

She lit a cigarette and took a deep drag, holding her breath, relishing how the smoke felt in her lungs.

"Yes. Everything is ready."

She nodded as she blew the smoke out through her nose. Taking a few more puffs, she dropped it on the floor and ground it out with her stiletto.

"Let's begin." She walked to the door next to the one-way mirror and entered the room, closing the door behind her.

The door squeaked as it opened and closed. The man straightened and glared toward the sound. "What the hell am I doing here? Where am I? Let me go immediately."

"You're hardly in a position to make demands." The woman laughed, walking closer and perusing his body.

He swung his untethered right leg out to kick her, in the process pulling on his arms. He winced and scowled at her.

"Tsk, tsk." She moved to his side so the camera behind the mirrored window could view him, making sure to keep her back to it. "State your full name and your position."

"Go to hell."

"I can stand here all day. I can also walk out of here. You, on the other hand…" She paused and lit another cigarette, eyes narrowed as she watched him. She slipped the pack and lighter in her jacket pocket. "Now state your full name and position." The smoke from her cigarette curled up toward the ceiling as she waited.

"My name is Thomas Martin. I am the lead anchor and host for ABC's morning show, *Let's Get Going*." He stated each word succinctly.

"Thank you. Do you know why you're here?"

"So you can get your kicks ogling a celebrity?"

She laughed, delighted. "I've seen many more attractive and well-hung men than you, Tommy. You don't mind if I call you Tommy, do you? Good. No, you aren't here for me to ogle. Try again."

"I'm not playing this game, or whatever this is, with you. Release me. I'll make it worth your while."

She finished her cigarette and flicked it toward him.

"You don't recognize where you are?" She ignored his plea for release.

"I'm in a room with no windows and a light glaring in my face. How the hell am I supposed to know where I am?"

"Hmmmm…you have a point. Well, you're in the office of your man cave in Warren. We've modified it a bit, which is perhaps why you don't recognize it. Most of your furniture is gone and we added a one-way mirror."

His eyes widened. "You were in my house when I arrived last night."

"That is correct. We arrived on your property just after your staff left, and we waited for you to come back, tail between your legs."

His eyes darted everywhere, as though seeking a way out.

"There's no one here to help you. You instructed your lawyer to release your staff after your arrest, making sure they fully stocked your refrigerator and freezer before leaving. Planning to hide out here, Tommy?"

"I…I, this is my home, damn it. I don't need to have a reason to come here. And my lawyer brought me here."

"True. But you made it clear you did not want to be disturbed and you didn't want anyone to know your whereabouts. Not only that, you had your lawyer very publicly have your Manhattan apartment stocked so everyone would think you returned there. Nice diversionary tactic, I have to say."

"How did you—?"

"This place is certainly secluded." She interrupted him. "There's what…about fifty acres? And your house and this outbuilding, plus the other one across your very private road, are smack in the middle of it. Very quiet, no one nearby. Hmmm…"

She paused and lit another cigarette, watching him squirm as understanding dawned in his eyes.

"What do you want with me?" He breathed erratically and tried to break free of the ropes.

"Settle down, Tommy. You can't get away." She paused. "I simply want answers. The sooner you give them to me, the sooner this is over."

He stilled his movements as best he could. His nostrils flared as he brought his breathing under control. Calmer, he asked, "What do you want to know?"

"That's more like it." She dropped her cigarette on the floor and walked over to the only piece of furniture in the room, a long table with two drawers, nestled against the wall near the door. She opened the top drawer and pulled out a newspaper. Holding it up behind her toward the mirrored window, she then shifted it toward him. "This paper is dated three weeks ago. The headline is NBCs Shining Star Fired! It goes on to explain how three women and two men have come forward with claims you assaulted them when they were children. Their parents worked on your show, when you were just getting started eighteen years ago, and they regularly brought their kids to the set while filming. Any of this ring a bell?"

"That's bullshit! I didn't touch those kids. Never saw them."

"Really? Tina James explained in vivid detail how you would take her to your office on various occasions, for treats she said. She went on to explain how you fondled her and placed her hands on your genitals, telling her what a good girl she was and that her visits were your secret. The others have told similar stories."

"That's not true! They're lying to extort me. I'm taking them to court to show them for the liars they are and to prove my innocence."

"You're not taking them to court, Tommy. You've been indicted and they are taking *you* to court. I am giving you an opportunity today to set the record straight. Be honest, confess your sins, and you might live another day!"

"What!" He paled, his face drained of all color, as he began to shake. "Who are you? Why are you doing this to me? I have a right to face my accusers in court. I will prove my innocence!"

"You can call me…Justitia." She cackled at her private joke. "I am standing up for all children who have been abused by power-hungry pedophiles like you. Justice will prevail." Letting the newspaper fall, she reached into the drawer again and pulled out another newspaper. "This is yesterday's paper. Did you have a chance to read the headlines after your release yesterday afternoon? The article is about twelve more people who have come forward since their stories first broke to accuse you. Are they all lying Tommy?" She threw the paper at him and reached into her pocket for her cigarettes. Lighting up again, she shook her head. "I'm giving you a chance to be honest for once in your life, to confess your sins, and to save your soul."

Thomas hung his head. His body shook as tears ran down his face, merging with sweat and dripping off his jowls to the floor below.

Janet finished her cigarette as she watched him in disgust. "Ready to answer my questions?"

He met her gaze with anguished eyes.

"Was Tina James telling the truth?"

He nodded. "It didn't start out that way. She was such a cute little girl with her pigtails and freckles. I brought her up to my office to give her some candy. She was so excited, she jumped on my lap to hug me." He sniffed and stared at the ground. "She felt so good sitting there. Things just happened." He looked up, sobbing now. "I never had sex with her, just bounced her on my lap and had her touch me. That's all I ever did, I swear!"

Justitia's body was rigid, her jaw so tight she was sure it would snap. She walked closer as she glared at him. "And the rest of the girls?"

"Similar stories I suppose. I don't really remember."

"What about the boys, Tommy?"

He looked at her with shame and fear in his eyes while Justitia waited.

"I…I…"

"Go on."

"It was different with them. I liked watching them masturbate on my lap while I did the same." His sobs intensified as he repeatedly apologized for what he did, his words unintelligible.

Taking several deep breaths, she was surprised. She had not really expected his confession, certainly not this fast.

"Get a hold of yourself, Tommy."

He sniffed and hiccoughed a few times before looking up. "Are you going to let me go now? I've been honest and I realize I'll have to pay for what I did."

"You're right, Tommy. You do have to pay for your crimes. But it won't be in a court of law. Nor will you sit in jail only to be released in a few years for good behavior. That's not justice! The children, now adults, you abused throughout the years deserve better."

Panic set in. "No! You promised you'd let me go if I told you the truth."

"No, Tommy. I said you might live if you confessed." Looking at him, she tilted her head to the side and pursed her lips, seeming to consider her options. "After careful consideration, I've decided you don't deserve to live. You are the scourge of the earth. Taking advantage of children who can't fight back is beyond reprehensible. However, since you did confess, I'm willing to give you a chance to survive."

Justitia returned to the table, reached for something leaning against it, then turned and walked back toward him. "What is this?"

He squinted through the light, trying to see what she held. He paled when he recognized the weapon. "It's a Mark V DGR."

"It's *your* rifle, correct?"

"Yes."

"Did you use this rifle to shoot all of those beautiful animals now hanging on the walls of your man cave?"

"Some of them, yes."

"So you can appreciate hunting." She held the gun out in front of her to study it. "Well, it's only fair, for all of the children you abused and even for those exotic creatures you killed, that you now be on the other side of this rifle." Her eyes were on him as she finished talking. She didn't want to miss his reaction. He didn't disappoint.

"No! No! Please don't do this, Justitia." Cursing and struggling, he pulled on the ropes, tearing the skin on his wrists even more. His blood merged with sweat and trailed down his arms.

"Tommy, Tommy, Tommy, you should be grateful I'm giving you a chance to live. I would stop struggling if I were you. Conserve your energy. You're lucky because

I'm going to give you a ten-minute head start, which is more of a break than you gave any child or animal. If you can get off your property and to the authorities, you'll live. If not?" She shrugged. "Well, so be it. Now hold tight, we'll get this hunt underway shortly." She smiled as she turned and walked out, gaining satisfaction from the mixture of pleas for mercy and cursing her to hell that spewed from his mouth.

* * *

The bright light flashed off. He shivered at the sudden loss of heat. Feeling a rush of air and sensing a presence bigger than himself, his body went rigid in fright. He cried out in pain as his arms were jerked up, and cringed when he heard the swish of a knife through the air a split second before the cold blade slid against his arms and sliced through the ropes. His arms dropped to his sides, and he moaned as blood flowed from his shoulders down onto his fingers. He was shoved to the ground before the person moved away. With arms unable to support him, he cried out in pain when his face slammed into concrete. Blood oozed from his nose as he lifted his head. A woman's silhouette appeared in the doorway, the light behind her preventing him from seeing her face.

"Your ten minutes start now."

"Wait, what about clothes and shoes?"

"Nine minutes and forty-five seconds." She turned and walked away from the door.

He scrambled to his feet and stumbled to the door before pausing to look cautiously around the room. His man cave was in darkness except for one small light on at the far end next to the door leading outside. His eyes perused the length of the room before finally noticing to his right the shadow of a man holding his rifle. He was standing near what he now realized was a window looking into his office. Glancing at the video camera pointing into the room, he inwardly cringed.

Without further hesitation, he half-dashed, half-hobbled to the door leading outside, his legs weakened from his forced standing position. He made his way across the grass to the trees edging the pond. His one-acre pond ran parallel to a good portion of the dirt road leading off his property. His only hope was to make his way to the opposite side of the pond and stay hidden in the trees before turning toward the main road.

As one minute ran into the next, Martin's panic increased. His feet were cut and bleeding from the pebbles and twigs on the path. Smashing through brush and bushes, he was like a bull in a china shop. Silence was not a consideration or even a thought as he raced to survive. He was not even aware of the noise he made. Running around a tree, he tripped over a root and fell hard on his knees. Gasping for air, he pounded the ground with his fist as he cried. Martin had purchased this property for its seclusion, the privacy allowing him to have fun with his friends without any prying eyes. He cursed that seclusion now as he pushed off his knees, whimpering at the pain, and stood. Feeling woozy, he limped to the tree and leaned against it for support.

Looking around, he observed his pond through the

trees, the light of the moon reflecting on the calm water. Cattails edged it and waved gently in the breeze. He listened to the leaves rustling above and glanced up to watch them. The trees were singing their own tune. Late summer was a beautiful time of year here. The land was changing, preparing for fall and winter. Once green fields were now a golden yellow and the trees were just hinting at change with a few leaves at the top fading to a pale green. He wished it was daytime so he could soak up the serenity around him—watching the trees sway, seeing the family of ducks splash in the water, observing his horses graze in the paddock. How he would have enjoyed seeing the colors at the height of this season one more time. Funny how he never appreciated the sounds, colors, and smells of his property before. Not really. Oh, he was lauded by his friends on the beauty of his place and loved showing it off. He had lived for those weekend parties he threw, and anyone who was anyone wanted to attend them. He was the talk of the town, king of the roost, and he had loved the attention. But in a moment of self-realization, perhaps because he knew he would not survive, he realized he had been on a treadmill his entire life, working long hours, partying when he wasn't working, drinking and the occasional snort, and the sex. Every waking moment was filled with something. He had never stopped to smell the roses, as it were. That made him sad because there was so much around him he had taken for granted.

He wasn't sure how long he had been leaning against the tree pondering life but when he looked up, the man was standing in front of him, about ten feet away.

His eyes were full of regret. "Those kids were so sweet. I only wanted to love them."

Martin watched as the man lifted the rifle and took aim.

CHAPTER TWO

FBI Field Office, Federal Plaza, New York City
Wednesday, August 12, 7:10 a.m.

"Good morning, Mali Hooper speaking."

"Did I beat her morning call?"

Mali giggled, shaking her head. "Good morning, Jake. Yes, for the third straight morning you've beaten Kirsten's call."

"Hah! Be sure to tell her."

"You two! When did it become a competition to be the first to call me at work?"

"I plead the fifth," Jake stated with a smile in his voice. "But it's a no-brainer to catch you at work early."

"Are you saying I'm predictable, Agent Black?"

He chuckled. "Not at all. We just both understand how much you love your work. The FBI is lucky to have you." Changing subjects, "Are you finished with your analysis on the Watson case?"

"Finished it last night. It's on Frank's desk. What about you? When will you be back from DC?"

"Tonight. We're still getting together on Friday for dinner with dad and Heather, right?"

"Absolutely."

"Great. I'll call you tonight and we can talk details."

"I look forward to it. Thanks for calling, Jake. I'm glad you'll be home soon."

"Me too." The line went dead.

Mali was smiling as she hung up. She and Jake had been dating for a little more than three months, having met five months ago on a case that still gave her sleepless nights on occasion. They got off to a rocky start but ended up working very well together, becoming closer during the case and after Jake led the team that rescued her when she became the target of a game.

Jake lived in New Jersey with his daughter, Heather, having moved in with his dad, Jerry, after Jake's wife passed away a few years back. A Lieutenant Colonel in the Army, he retired early when his wife became ill, and joined the FBI so he could be around more for his daughter. Mali adored Heather and enjoyed Jerry's company whenever they got together.

Setting aside her thoughts of Jake, Mali turned on her favorite news livestream, WABC, on her second monitor and continued to read e-mail on her primary monitor. She loved coming in early to listen to the news and prepare for the day without interruption, Kirsten, and now Jake, being regular exceptions. She smiled at that.

"An update on Thomas Martin, KNBC's weekend morning show host. Three weeks ago, three women and two men came forward and accused him of sexual assault when they were children, all between the ages of six and eleven. This allegedly occurred eighteen years ago when Martin was working at a local station in upstate New York. The accusers were children of production workers. Charges were formally filed last week, and Martin was arrested and taken into custody. He spent one night in jail and made bail as soon as it was posted after his arraignment on Friday. William Stack, his attorney, said his client was innocent and requested privacy for Martin, who returned to his penthouse in the Upper East Side after his release where he plans to stay until his next court date. This morning, four more women came forward with their own stories, adding to the twelve additional accusers who joined the case last week. That makes a total of at least twenty people who have come forward since we first reported this story. Martin was fired from KNBC after the story broke, citing a no-tolerance policy and a lack of confidence in him. We will provide you with more details as we receive them." The reporter shook his head. "A shocking development for sure." He paused and touched his earpiece before continuing. "Our weather forecast with Gina Smith follows after this short break. Stay with us."

Sitting in her cubicle on the twenty-third floor, Mali stared at the screen, still stunned by this news. She watched Thomas Martin's show most weekends and enjoyed his reporting and sense of humor. To think him capable of abusing children made her skin crawl. She shivered as her thoughts turned inward.

Sighing, she turned her head and looked outside. She had worked hard to get where she was in life, despite her privileged upbringing, maybe in spite of it. As a member of the Hooper dynasty in Philadelphia, Mali's life had been sheltered, no hardships. Growing up 'in society,' the expectation for her had been clear: marry the "right" man and be a show wife who could throw good parties, raise perfectly behaved kids, and look good for her husband. Her two older sisters had done just that, but Mali had always wanted more than being eye candy on a man's arm. She smiled when she reminisced about her rebellious years, including eloping with a football player she met in college and divorcing him after three months of marriage. Her parents barely spoke to her throughout that fiasco, which she readily admits was indeed a disaster, but her father had come through and made her marriage and divorce disappear as if those two events never occurred. She had no idea how he did it, but she was not surprised. Her father had tremendous influence given his position in society.

When she first began working for the FBI in Chicago and even later after she transferred to the city two and a half years ago, there were some who believed she was just a pretty face with wealthy parents. She had paid her dues with that first job in Chicago and here, arriving every day before anyone, except perhaps Frank, leaving after everyone else and even working on weekends. Her friends half-teased, half-chided her for working so much and not taking time for herself. With her unusual gray almond-shaped eyes, high cheekbones, auburn tresses, perfectly manicured nails with matching lipstick, and toned body, her friends told her she could have been a model. While that profession had its own share of challenges and required dedication and hard work, it was not the life she wanted. She wouldn't trade her job for any other, despite feeling as though she had to prove herself to her colleagues.

That is, until the Hunter case three months ago. She was not only a primary contributor in solving the case, but she also survived the game. Team members and others in the force looked at her differently now, with more respect and confidence she knew what she was doing. The day she realized that was an incredible day for her.

While that was a head rush like no other, the lasting impact of the game, for her, was the realization that social media, even with its obvious benefits, seemed to have the negative effect of numbing people to their surroundings. FaceTime, Instagram, Twitter, Snapchat, Tinder, YouTube were just a few of the multitudes of venues available. There were games and apps for everything. People were so busy playing video games, texting, posting selfies and videos, and living their lives through their phones and devices that the world went by unnoticed. Quite a few people were more apt to pull out their phones to record something happening rather than helping to stop it. She nearly died during the game, all while people watched and rooted for a unique way for the assassin to kill her. It was incomprehensible to her and something she still struggled with three months later.

Fortunately, it was over, the guilty parties were either dead or in jail, and life had returned to the routine she craved.

The phone rang, shaking her out of her thoughts.

Still looking outside, Mali picked up her phone. "Good morning, Mali Hooper speaking."

"Did I beat him?"

Mali laughed. "Not by a long shot, Kirsten. Jake called ten minutes ago."

"Damn! I knew he'd beat me today. My damn phone ran out of juice and then I got sidetracked with early morning issues."

"You two are loco, you know that!?!" Mali stated, a smile in her voice.

"Hey, are you available for lunch today? We haven't really spoken since you started your analysis on that case a week or so ago."

"Yes, the Watson case. I just finished it last night. Can't do lunch today. I have a meeting with Frank to discuss what's next. He said he'd call in lunch for us."

"Rats. Okay, well let's plan lunch soon. Gotta go. Toodles."

"Later."

That evening, Mali was lounging on her balcony enjoying the sights of the Hudson River when her phone rang. After glancing at the name on the screen, she answered it with a smile on her face and in her voice. "Hey, you made it home."

"Hey to you as well. Yes, I arrived about two hours

ago, just managed to get Heather to bed." He laughed. "Her eyes were drooping, she could barely stand up without swaying, and yet she didn't want to go to bed."

"Awwww. She missed her dad."

"I know. I believe there's a part of her that's worried I'll leave her like her mom did."

"As young as she was when Christa passed away, there's still a hole. She's lucky the new taskforce you're heading up allows you to be home more."

"I'm grateful for that. I'm excited about this program. Social media murder crimes, such as the Hunt-edLives game, are becoming more prevalent today. After Hunter Inc collapsed and we seized all assets, including the patent to Hunter's GPS-Satellite system that powered the game, The Hunted Ones, our first task has been to deal with the data and technology. It's massive. We're still assessing it all to determine if and how all of it can benefit us moving forward."

"It sounds really interesting, Jake, and I'm glad you're enjoying it. Has your team been able to analyze the GPS-Satellite system Hunter developed?"

"In progress. I'm meeting with Joe and his team on Monday to discuss their latest findings. He said he knows what Hunter was trying to do with that last game he was working on."

"Wow, I'm intrigued."

"So am I."

"How was DC?"

"Interesting. Maury Jackson, an agent and leading expert in the Counterterrorism Division, and Sally

Baker, who heads up the Cyber Crime Division attended the meetings with me. Did you ever provide analysis for them? Maury's team handles issues related to internet and social media terrorism, groups with extensive presence online, among other things. Sally and her team deal primarily with malicious cyber activity like identity theft, espionage, fraud, child pornography, things like that."

"I worked with Maury and his team on Ken's analysis regarding that terrorist cell in San Francisco. I've never worked with Sally."

"Ah, of course."

"While there may be overlap in some of our cases, my team will be responsible for solving murders in the social media world, including the use of app games. That's why Maury and Sally went with me. We met with the higher-ups at headquarters to discuss how we could work together, and to better delineate lines between our programs. We'll work well together, and I look forward to tapping into their expertise as we need it."

Mali smiled. "I can hear the excitement in your voice, Jake, and I'm happy for you."

"Thanks. While it will be nice to have relative autonomy and a separate budget, the best part, of course, is that I'm home more for dad and Heather…." He paused. "And for you."

"I like that part too," Mali said in a soft voice. As she was about to say something more, a yawn and sigh escaped. "Oh, excuse me."

Jake laughed. "You sound as sleepy as I feel. Get

some rest and I'll see you on Friday evening. I'll pick you up from work at four-thirty."

"Great. Have a good rest and I'm sure I'll talk to you in the morning."

"Count on it, and before Kirsten calls."

Mali was laughing as she hung up the phone.

* * *

Weehawken, NJ
Friday, August 14, approximately 5:30 p.m.

Mali and Jake walked into Jake's home to the delighted screams of his daughter, Heather. An active six-year-old, her curly ebony hair was contained this day in a long braid, and her deep blue eyes sparkled as she looked at her dad. She was three feet of energy, barely stopping to sleep at night.

"Daddy, it's been hours and hours since I last saw you," she exclaimed as she launched herself into his open arms.

Laughing, Jake hugged her. "I saw you this morning, squirt, when I dropped you off at school."

"But you were gone for days and days before so that made today seem like hours and hours." Heather squealed when Mali pulled her braid. Not giving anyone time to make sense of her logic, she squirmed out of Jake's arms and ran to Mali, wrapping her arms around her waist and squeezing as hard as she could.

"Hi Miss Mali! I'm so glad you could come to dinner. Papa has made barbecue chicken and scalloped potatoes, my favorite. I helped him with the salad."

"That sounds delicious! And you helped him? I'm sure it will taste extra good tonight. How are you, Sweetie?" Smiling down at her, Mali brushed a few tendrils off Heather's forehead.

"I'm awesome. School is lots of fun and I'm learning lots and lots. Today, I learned how to skip when we played outside. Do you want to see?" Without waiting for a response, Heather skipped around the family room, weaving around the sofa, leather chairs, and tables, humming the entire time.

Whenever Mali came to Jake's house, she felt welcomed because of his wonderful family. The home was full of life, bright and sunny during the day, cozy at night. Children's books littered the coffee table, and a doll was lying in a mini-crib in front of the fireplace, which was cleared of wood and ashes this time of year. The fireplace was the focal point, its facade sporting the same red brick as the house and reaching from floor to ceiling. The wooden mantle was graced with family pictures as well as a ballerina trophy, and above it was a large print of Jake, his dad, and Heather.

Mali looked at Jake and smiled.

At the swoosh of a door, both turned toward the kitchen.

"Mali, it's good to see you again," said Jerry as he walked in and gave her a hug. "You look lovely, as always."

"Thank you, Jerry. Dinner smells delicious." She smiled as she looked between the two men. While both were tall, lean, and shared matching dimples when they smiled, as did Heather, their similarities ended there. Jake's jet-black hair curled below his collar, his eyes were a deep blue that could cut you like a knife or melt you like butter, and a barely noticeable jagged scar trailed from his left eyebrow back to his ear. Mali remembered thinking Jake was intense when she first met him. She still believed that. Jerry, on the other hand, was jovial with kind brown eyes and hair that was a mix of sandy brown and gray.

"Thanks. We should be ready to eat in a few minutes. Hello Son," he said, patting Jake on the shoulder as he looked at Heather. "Time to wash up, young lady. Dinner is almost ready, and I need my sous chef to finish helping."

"Okay Papa." Heather didn't miss a beat and, after rounding the sofa, skipped to the kitchen.

"Can I help?"

"No, no. We've got everything covered. Get a drink and have a seat at the table."

There was the usual hustle and bustle of getting drinks and placing food on the table. Chairs made a scraping sound as everyone sat. After a prayer, serving dishes were passed around and silverware clinked as the adults served their own food. Jake put smaller portions on his daughter's plate. As a young lady with much to say, her non-stop chatter entertained the adults throughout the meal.

"Mali, Jake tells me you're working on a new analysis. I've never asked before but I'm curious...what exactly does an Intelligence Analyst do and how long does it take you to complete an analysis?" Jerry picked up his glass of wine and took a sip, looking at her.

"Good questions. There is no set amount of time to complete each analysis. It depends on the case and what's involved. My days usually consist of a lot of reading and research on the internet, on state, federal and international databases, sometimes interrogating people, and asking myself and others a lot of questions. I also take information collected by special agents and fill in the gaps, as needed. I'm a tactical analyst so my work is directed more toward specific threats that are active or have already matured. Oftentimes, I assist in preparations for a specific mission."

"Like she did for Ken, dad, when he went to San Francisco to infiltrate that terrorist cell last year. And she was instrumental in solving the Hunter case a few months ago."

"That case was unbelievable," he said, shaking his head. "And to think—"

"No need to go into those details, Dad," Jake interrupted, shifting his eyes to Heather.

"Oh, of course, of course. But that case led to your new taskforce, right son?"

Jake nodded. "The best thing about that is I'm working locally, most of the time, and can be near this squirt." Jake leaned toward Heather and tweaked her nose which sent her into a fit of giggles.

Jerry beamed with pride.

Mali laughed. "There was so much data from Hunter Inc they had to set up Jake's office in a warehouse." She smiled at Jake. "Of course, it has all the latest computers, technology, and gadgets. Kirsten, my good friend in IT who helped us with the Hunter case, joined his team and is in hog heaven."

"What is hog heaven? Is it a special heaven for hogs?" Heather asked.

"It means Mali's friend is very happy," Jerry explained.

Heather frowned in confusion. "That's weird." An instant later, her frown cleared as she stated, "Well, I'm in hog heaven because Miss Mali is here." She attacked a bite of chicken and munched on it with gusto.

After dinner, Mali announced the ladies would clean up and pushed the men into the living room. Multiple trips were made from dining room to kitchen as the silverware, plates, and other dishes were carried in for cleaning. Mali opened a lower cabinet next to the sink and looked inside.

"What are you looking for?" asked Heather.

"Something to put the leftovers in." Mali opened another cabinet.

Heather skipped to the other side of the island, climbed onto the counter, and opened a cabinet. "They're in here," she said, pointing inside.

Mali thanked Heather, then picked her up and swung her around. Heather shrieked with joy as Mali set her down and continued with the cleanup. Placing all the leftovers in the refrigerator, she loaded the dishwasher, and washed and dried the pans, while Heather wiped down the counters.

When they finished, they joined the men in the living room. Heather pranced to the fireplace to play with her doll in the crib, and Mali sat next to Jake on the sofa. She curled her legs up when Jake pulled her close, keeping his arm around her shoulders.

A little after eight, Jake looked at Heather. "Time for me to take Miss Mali home and for you to get ready for bed, Heather."

"Why can't Miss Mali just have a sleepover?" she asked without looking up from her doll.

Mali blushed, Jerry chuckled, and Jake smiled.

"That's a very nice offer, Heather," Mali finally responded, "but I already have plans for tomorrow." She uncurled her legs and stood. The men followed her lead.

"Darn it." Heather pouted as she looked up. She hopped up and ran to Mali. "We'll have to plan it for another night."

Mali laughed, picked her up and squeezed her in an affectionate hug. "Until next time, kiddo." She set Heather down then turned and hugged Jerry. "I had a great time. Thank you."

"As did I. Now don't be a stranger."

Jake held her coat open, shrugging into his own as she buttoned hers. They headed outside. Jake held the passenger door open for Mali, then walked around to the driver's side and curled himself into the seat. The engine roared to life, and they waved to Heather and Jerry as they pulled out of the driveway. The drive across the Hudson to her apartment was made in contented silence.

When Jake pulled up to her entrance, he turned off the engine and faced Mali.

"Thank you for a wonderful evening. It was the perfect end to my week. I'm glad you're back in town."

He smiled and kissed her gently on the mouth. "Me too."

She raised her hand and brushed his hair back, cupping his face with her palm while they kissed again.

"Good night, Jake. Call me sometime this weekend." She got out of the car and walked to the entrance of her building. Looking back at him, she was comforted by the knowledge he always waited until she was safely indoors before leaving. She punched in the code, opened the door, and disappeared inside.

CHAPTER THREE

Mali's apartment
Sunday, August 16, 8:20 a.m.

MALI WALKED INTO her apartment, kicked off her running shoes, and reached her arms above her head before bending at the waist to stretch her hamstrings. She preferred to stretch in the privacy of her apartment after her morning run. Standing up, she looked around her home with a contented smile.

Her one bedroom, one-and-a-half bath apartment was on the ninth floor of a complex that was nestled right on the Hudson River. She was fortunate to find this place when she moved to New York and appreciated the trust fund left by her grandmother that made the purchase possible. She loved how warm and inviting her main living room made her feel. The overstuffed sofa, oak table and chairs, cow hide stools, and earth tone rugs scattered across the hardwood floors appealed to her rustic preferences. The warm countryside landscape paintings on her walls complemented the feel. The kitchen, with its large island and antique white cabinets, completed the open space.

Heading to the kitchen, Mali was just turning on her coffee machine when the phone rang.

"Mali, have you watched any news this morning?"

"Good morning to you too, Kirstin." Mali smiled.

"Turn on your television. Thomas Martin was murdered. They said he was shot."

"Oh my God!" All humor was erased from Mali's face as she rushed to the coffee table, grabbed the remote, and turned on WABC. She sank to the sofa, eyes glued to the television, phone clutched to her ear.

"...and he never went to his penthouse on the Upper East Side but traveled directly to his ranch in Warren, Connecticut. William Stack, Martin's attorney, said his client decided to go there for privacy. He had his kitchen stocked with food and supplies and instructed all staff to take a vacation. He insisted on being by himself. His body was only discovered when Stack arrived for a meeting last night. When Martin was not found in his house, Stack searched the grounds and found him in one of the outbuildings Martin had converted into what is being described as a massive man cave. He had evidently been shot." The reporter paused. "State police will hold a press conference at eleven o'clock with more details." He shook his head. "We'll be right back after this short break."

"Wow!"

Kristen piped in. "I know, right!?!"

"I always liked watching his show. It was hard to

believe he could be capable of what his accusers said… but to be murdered. Geez, no one deserves that."

"Do you think one of his accusers killed him?"

"Who knows, but I've lost my appetite."

They spoke for a few more minutes then said their goodbyes. Mali set her phone on the coffee table, turned off the television, and stood. Returning to the kitchen, she poured herself a cup of coffee then proceeded into her bedroom. Her mind was still trying to process what she had learned about Tom Martin so, without conscious thought, she crossed her bedroom and opened the sliding door to step out onto the balcony. Her balcony overlooked the Hudson River, and it was her favorite place to go when she wanted to contemplate life, relax. The Hudson could calm her like no other place. Watching water ripple against the bank, listening to boats chugging back and forth, enjoying the sun sparkling like diamonds on the water, or being mesmerized by the moon rays reflecting off the waves…it all filled her with peace and serenity.

Mali had no idea how long she sat outside but when her cell phone rang in the bedroom, she stepped inside to answer it.

"Hi Jake," she said, returning to her chair outside. "Did you hear about Thomas Martin's murder?"

"You heard?"

"Kirsten called awhile ago. Murdered in Connecticut. Unbelievable." She shook her head. "There's a press conference soon."

"That's not the worst of it. Joe just called me. Martin

was hung on his wall like one of his trophies. A picture was posted on Twitter."

A chill ran down Mali's spine and she shivered, despite the fact she was sitting in the sun. "Oh my God. #HuntedLives?"

"No. Joe says #HuntedLives is not active. This is tagged as #JusticePrevails. The press conference was pushed back to one o'clock so we can participate. Frank wants us there with him. We're meeting with him here at ten-thirty. I'm going to shower then head in. I've texted Joe and Kristen. We're all going to meet at ten. I can pick you up on the way in."

"No, I'll meet you there. I want to stop by the office to pick up a few things."

"Okay. See you soon."

Mali didn't waste any time. She pulled her shirt and sports bra off as she walked into her bedroom. The walls were painted a pale rose and her bed was covered with a white quilt with small red roses embroidered along the hem. It was the only area in her apartment she considered girly. She didn't notice any of that, though, as she hopped from one foot to the other to remove her socks before kicking off her running shorts. She shoved everything into the corner by her closet door and rushed into the bathroom to shower and get ready. Twenty minutes later, she walked out of her apartment.

* * *

Special Unit Warehouse
Undisclosed Location
Sunday, August 16, 9:45 a.m.

EXITING THE SUBWAY, Mali walked four blocks to reach the warehouse district. It was a quiet day and Mali reached the warehouse just before ten o'clock. From the outside, the building looked like any other in the warehouse district. A small camera was mounted above the only visible entrance, a single metal door. Mali pressed the buzzer next to the door, pulling it open when it clicked. She glanced at the camera and smiled then walked into a small receptionist area that had four chairs backed against the wall to the right of the door, a small thirty-six-inch television mounted near the ceiling in the opposite corner, and a fake palm tree below it. A long counter ran the length of the room with a small opening for access for the receptionist and to enter the interior of the building. The room was stark and the only art on the wall was a Henderson Deliveries sign behind the receptionist's chair. The television was silent today as Mali walked toward the interior door. Another camera was mounted above it and the door clicked as she approached.

Mali walked through the door, down a nondescript hallway passing two doors on each side. At the end of the hallway, she turned right and was just about to ring a buzzer on another door when it opened and Jake ushered her in. Closing the door behind her, he turned around and, now facing an elevator, pressed the down button.

"Thanks for coming. Joe and Kirsten are here and ramping things up," he said.

Mali nodded as she stared at the elevator numbers. Neither said anything as the elevator moved down three floors. It opened into a large open space. There was a conference table with eight chairs and multiple white-boards around it to the left. On the right were two restrooms and some vending machines. Four security monitors were located on the right side of the room just above a long table with two rolling desk chairs where the exterior and interior of the building could be monitored. Large screens were mounted high on the back wall, three across and three down for a total of nine screens, and four computer tables with two monitors on each table were situated in the middle of the room. All faced the back wall toward the nine screens. The center area was an IT specialist's dream. Positioned before the computer tables was a long, white high-standing table. The top of the table was the technical control center, a computer with controls that were easy to manipulate on top of the glass. All technical equipment was managed by this center and could be controlled, if needed. The user could swipe anything seen on the tabletop to any of the nine screens on the back wall. All nine screens could also be used as one large screen.

Joe was at the control center working his magic and talking to Kirsten. When Jake and Mali walked in, they turned and greeted them.

"Hey, Mali," said Joe.

"Hi Joe, Kirsten."

"I'm bringing #JusticePrevails up now." Swiping his finger up, Twitter displayed on the middle screen. Seconds later, all screens flickered, and Twitter displayed as one large screen. Under the title, #JusticePrevails, a picture was displayed.

The picture was of a large, rectangular room with multiple sitting areas, a bar, large screen televisions on one wall, a glass enclosed room against another wall, trophies of exotic animals throughout, and what looked like an office at the end.

"Wow!" exclaimed Mali.

Jake nodded. "The man sure lived large."

"How horrible!" exclaimed Kirsten. "How could anyone kill those beautiful animals?"

Joe zoomed in toward an African elephant. As the camera view neared the elephant, Mali asked, "Is that what I think it is, just beyond the elephant?"

"Yes," said Joe. When he stopped zooming in, they observed the side view of the lower half of Martin's body.

"Oh my God!" exclaimed Kirsten.

Joe scrolled down to a second picture.

It was a full frontal of Martin. Wearing only bloodied underwear, he was pinned against the wall next to the African elephant. Two metal stakes pierced both shoulder muscles from behind, protruding out the front of his upper chest. Two wood two-by-fours were secured below each armpit to add support for his body. An elk head was positioned below Martin and his feet were resting on the back of the elk's neck, behind its antlers. His body hung on the wall like one of his trophies, head tilted down as though looking toward the floor. His body was covered with scrapes and dirt. Blood appeared to drip from the metal stakes that pierced his body. There was a thin trail of blood running down his legs to his feet. A pool of blood had soaked the elk's neck and spread out around him on the floor. Resting near his feet was a white feather.

The only sound in the room was the soft hum of the computer as everyone stared in horror.

"Christ," said Jake, rubbing his neck. "I only see one bullet hole, on his forehead. How did he get all those scrapes, and why is he so dirty? What caused the bloody underwear? Zoom in, Joe."

Joe's eyes widened as he looked at Jake.

"Just do it." Jake rolled his eyes, shaking his head.

Joe zoomed in on Martin's underwear. Although a little blurry and covered in blood, they easily identified the bullet hole.

Mali shivered and rubbed her arms.

Kirsten grimaced. "So he was shot in his groin and also hung on the wall like one of his trophies. Was he killed for his alleged crimes or for hunting exotic animals? #JusticePrevails could apply to both."

"Hmmm. Given the timing, I tend to believe it's due to the indictment," said Mali. "Are there any comments, Joe?"

He nodded and scrolled down the screen.

"Wow! He looks better now than when he was alive. Ha ha."

"How could he shoot that beautiful elephant? He deserved what he got."

"A fitting end to a sick bastard."

"I didn't like the guy, but he didn't deserve that."

"He got what he deserved. Justice definitely prevailed."

The comments went on and on.

"Geez, has nothing changed in three months?" Mali's lip curled in disgust.

Jake signaled Joe, who turned off the screens. "Let's go to the conference table and get organized before Frank arrives."

"I want to write some questions down on the white-board." Mali headed to the center board and picked up a pen.

"Of course you do." Kirsten and Jake said simultaneously, then both laughed.

"Yeah, yeah, yeah." Mali scrunched her nose at them then turned to the board as everyone else sat.

On the left side of the board, Mali wrote Unknowns. Beneath it she wrote the following bulleted points: Who killed Martin? What weapon was used? Why is he so dirty? How did he get all the scrapes? What does the feather mean? Is #JusticePrevails a reference to his indictment or for being a trophy hunter (i.e., motive)?

Mali turned to the others.

Jake said, "He was supposed to be in his penthouse here in the city. Did he go to Warren of his own accord or was he taken there by whoever killed him? Did he know his killer or killers?"

Kirsten piped in, "A man like that would certainly have staff maintaining his property? Where were they?"

"Who posted the picture?" Joe asked.

Mali added all questions to the list then stood back.

"Thanks Hoop," said Jake as he stood. "We should get a few answers when Frank arrives. In the meantime Joe, find out who posted the picture. If it's like HuntedLives, as I suspect, someone's account was hacked…we need to verify that. And check other apps to make sure #JusticePrevails isn't trending anywhere else. Kirsten, save all the information then have Twitter remove it. Let's hope this is a one-time occurrence under that tag."

Joe and Kirsten left the conference area to do as Jake asked.

Mali looked at Jake. "This is unbelievable."

"Jake, I just buzzed Agent Grant in."

"Thanks Kirsten."

When Frank Grant stepped out of the elevator, his eyes scanned the room until he found Jake and Mali, who both stood as he approached. Special Agent in Charge Frank Grant had been Mali's boss for more than two years. While some underestimated him because of his lack of technical aptitude and his rotund appearance, not to mention the salt-and-pepper beard he now sported, Mali knew otherwise. He was a hard-hitting agent, fair, honest, and he had more integrity in his pinky than most other people had in totality. Despite his calm demeanor, Mali could tell by his stiff walk and scowl that he was angry.

Walking past them with only a nod, he slammed the manila folder he had been carrying onto the conference table then sat.

"Did you see the picture and comments on Twitter?" he asked.

Jake nodded. "Not all of them but enough. Kirsten and Joe are contacting Twitter right now."

"Damn it! I thought we were done with this abusive use of social media with the deaths of Hunter and his sister."

"Do the police in Warren consider this a copycat scenario?" asked Mali.

"Warren doesn't have a police force. State police provide law enforcement services, but they are not equipped to deal with this. Given how it appears similar to HuntedLives from a social media perspective, the FBI will take over this case. The New Haven field office services Warren via their Meriden satellite offices." He paused to thank Kirsten for the bottle of water she handed him. "To answer your question, they're trying not to speculate on that, but I wouldn't be surprised if the question is asked at the press conference. I would prefer to address it before they do." Frank looked at the whiteboard and the list of questions. "Interesting list. I can answer a few of those right now."

Mali walked to the whiteboard.

"The weapon was a Mark V DGR rifle." He paused. "It was his own weapon and he was shot twice, once in the forehead and once in the groin. According to his lawyer, Martin wanted to disappear for awhile so they created the illusion he was staying in his apartment. Evidently, Martin was so intent on privacy, he ordered the staff at his property in Warren to stock up then get lost. He didn't want anyone around."

Mali wrote the answers next to each applicable question with an arrow pointed from each question to the corresponding answer. While writing, she asked, "How did the killer know Martin had left the city?"

Frank shrugged.

Mali added that question to the growing list.

Frank continued, "That's all state police are aware of at this point. Everything else is supposition."

"How do you want to handle the press conference?" asked Jake.

Looking at his watch, Frank said, "Troop L of the State Police oversees Warren. They will begin with a description of how he was killed, weapon used, etc., then will turn the meeting over to us. I want the two of you to make a bullet list of how things went down with HuntedLives, just the highlights. I want to be able to refute any questions or comments suggesting this is a continuation or a copycat." He glanced at his watch again. "It's ten-fifty. You'll have to make the list in the air. We fly out of Teterboro in twenty-five minutes. Tom Overly, Special Agent in Charge at the New Haven field office, is en-route to Warren and will meet us at the property at noon. We'll have time to talk with him as we walk through the building before the press conference starts, which will be held at the entrance to the property."

"I'll grab my laptop." Capping the pen she used for the whiteboard, Mali spoke with Kirsten and Joe and picked up her things, then joined Frank and Jake at the elevator. She was worried this had something to do with HuntedLives, as she recalled the game while creating the bulleted list with Jake.

Just when she thought it was over....

CHAPTER FOUR

Thomas Martin Property
Warren, CT
Sunday, August 16, 12:15 p.m.

"GOOD GRIEF! I'VE been trying to convince Carol to let me convert the office in our house to a man cave. In my wildest dreams, I'd never come up with something like this, not that we have the space." Frank looked around the outbuilding they had all just entered.

The room stretched the length of a football field. Various hunting trophies—an African elephant, a gazelle, a Jacob four-horned ram, and a black rhinoceros—were mounted on the walls. Two full-size taxidermy zebras were strategically positioned with a bobcat and a young male East African lion. Black leather sofas and chairs were situated for easy conversation, and a temperature-controlled glass room housing a floor-to-ceiling wine collection dominated the wall opposite the eight mounted televisions. A twelve-foot bar situated beyond abutted a commercial-size refrigerator.

"The picture I saw online doesn't do it justice. I

couldn't pick my jaw up from the floor when I first came in here," joked Tom Overly. He cleared his throat. "The body was found just beyond the elephant." He led the group down the room.

Mali stopped to peer inside the glass room, recognizing the La Chapelle and Montrachet bottles, among others, on display. "My parents would be jealous of this wine collection."

After studying the area where Martin was discovered, they continued to the room at the end of the building.

"We believe this was an office that was converted into an interrogation room of some sort," said Tom. The outward-facing wall had been modified to include a one-way mirror, the observer could look in but anyone inside would only see a mirror.

Jake walked inside to examine the room more closely. "Do we have a timeline for what happened here?" he asked when he joined the others.

Tom shook his head. "We're working on it. We only know that he was killed somewhere outside and brought here. We don't know if he made the changes to his office or if someone else did."

"It doesn't seem likely that he did." said Mali. "Why would he? He came here to hide out. Prior to the news breaking, he was a happy-go-lucky guy, on top of the world."

Tom shrugged. "There are more questions than answers at this point."

"Whoever did this was a professional and very

thorough." Frank looked at his watch. "We need to go. The presser is about to begin."

State Trooper Redding stood at the podium. Behind him on his right stood two other state troopers and Martin's lawyer, William Stack. On his left side were Tom Overly and two of the Meriden resident agents, plus Frank, Jake, and Mali.

He held up his hands to silence the press. "Good morning. My name is Jeremy Redding, and I am a State Trooper with Troop L of the Connecticut State Police. I will give you a brief statement and then we will answer a few questions. At approximately eleven-twenty last night, we received a call from William Stack who identified himself as Thomas Martin's attorney. He said he found Thomas Martin dead in an outbuilding on his property. Upon arrival, we found the victim in what others have described as a large man cave. He had been shot twice, once in the forehead and also in the groin. In addition, Martin's two shoulder blades had been pierced with metal rods secured in the wall, with additional supports below his armpits to support his body. The weapon used was a Mark V DGR rifle, belonging to said victim. We want to thank the FBI for their involvement, and we will assist them in every way possible. Questions?"

Hands shot up and multiple reporters shouted questions.

"One question at a time, please." He pointed to a woman in front.

"Kay Elder with Connecticut News Fox 61. So

you're saying he was hung on the wall? Was he hung there before or after he was shot?"

"According to the coroner, Martin has been dead for at least five days, and it is unknown if he was shot before or after…" Redding trailed off, not knowing if he should reference Martin as being hung on the wall. He pointed to a man in the back.

"Thanks. Josh Smith, Associated Press. When did Martin come to Warren? He was supposed to be at his penthouse. And why is this only being reported this morning?"

William Stack stepped up to the podium. "I'm William Stack, Tom's attorney, and I'll answer those questions. Tom told me he wanted privacy that he knew he would not receive if he stayed at his penthouse in New York. Groceries and other items were brought into his penthouse and the staff were released. We also simultaneously had his staff here in Warren stock up on enough food and sundries to last two weeks after which they were released. I drove Tom here last Saturday evening, the eighth. We arrived here at approximately seven. I did not stay, Tom wanted to be alone." He took a deep breath before continuing. "We were supposed to meet at eight o'clock last night. I have a key and when he didn't answer the door, I entered and began searching for him. It took me awhile to find him…" He stopped speaking, looking down and shaking his head.

State Trooper Redding leaned into the microphone. "To answer your last question, it took time for forensics to arrive and begin investigating the murder. This press conference was pushed from eleven this morning until now to give the FBI time to arrive."

"Why is the FBI involved?" shouted a reporter.

"I am Special Agent in Charge Frank Grant. I operate out of the New York City office," said Frank after walking up to the microphone. "We are taking over this case due to the high-profile victim as well as what some have suggested is a copycat murder of those that occurred three months ago." He pointed to a man a few rows back.

"Thank you. Jarrod Smith with the New York Times. You're referring to the #HuntedLives real game. How are you so sure this isn't a copycat murder?"

"Anthony Hunter and his sister, Janet Simpson, are dead and Hunter Inc. is out of business. They were the masterminds behind the live hunting game. We have no reason to suspect this is a copycat, despite the new hashtag and comments about the picture that was posted."

Mali's eyes widened when she felt the vibration of her phone in her pocket. From the corner of her eye, she noticed Jake had placed his hand in the right pocket of his jacket glancing at her and realized his phone had done the same. Neither moved to answer but continued to look straight ahead.

"Well, what about the man who was arrested…" Smith looked at his notes. "…uh, Drake Butcher? Wasn't he released shortly after that last game? Is he still a suspect or have you found the assassin?"

"Yes, Butcher was released. His lawyer said it was a matter of his client being in the wrong place at the right time. There was nothing to tie him to the game, no evidence. For every murder in the game, he had an alibi. We had to release him. And before you ask, we do not have any leads on who the assassin was but there is no reason to believe he or she has any involvement in Thomas Martin's death. If you'll recall, in the game, the assassin did not make any moves without specific instructions from the players. He didn't even take a shot at the target unless instructed to do so." Frank pointed to a woman four rows back.

"Jean Taper, CNN. Do you have any leads yet, or a motive?"

"No to both questions. This is an on-going investigation, and we will explore all possibilities. I'll take one more question."

"What about the video that was posted in #JusticePrevails?" shouted a reporter.

* * *

Frank drew in a deep breath and slowly let it out. He scrutinized the sea of reporters, their gleeful faces betraying their excitement about the prospect of catching the FBI unaware. He took them to task. "Let us not forget that, regardless of what he may or may not have done, Thomas Martin was brutally killed." He paused, shaking his head, staring each reporter in the eye before continuing. "With this social media craze, one of our biggest challenges is being able to watch more than two hundred and fifty social networking services like Facebook and Twitter. It's just not possible. I can only stress how critical it is, and how reliant we are, on the community to provide us with tips. Thank you for bringing this to our attention. We will look into the video to verify its veracity. That's all." Amidst a chorus of shouted questions, he turned away from the podium, nodded at the state trooper, and strode up the drive to the waiting vehicle that would take them back into the property and waiting helicopter. All agents followed.

Mali hung back a few strides with Jake. As soon as the reporters were out of earshot, they both pulled out their phones and, by tacit agreement, Mali called Kirsten while Jake called Joe.

As soon as Kirsten answered, "Tell me about the video."

"It was posted on Twitter less than ten minutes ago under #JusticePrevails. It's more than four minutes long and shows Martin's confession. He's standing in a room in his underwear with his arms tied to a beam above his head."

"Is there anyone there with him?"

"Someone walks into the room to interrogate him. The face is never revealed, and the voice is altered via voice alteration software. Mali, Martin confesses and then he's hunted down, although the hunt isn't shown in the video."

"My God!"

Frank, who was standing next to the vehicle and talking to Tom Overly, glanced at Mali, eyes narrowed.

"Send it to me, Kirsten, and get it off Twitter." She hung up as Jake joined her, having just ended his call with Joe.

Frank nodded his head toward the car. "We'll talk

about what you've learned when we get up to Martin's man cave. I want to look at that space again as we talk."

Silence on the short drive. Frank strode inside first with the others shuffling in behind him.

"How the hell are we just now hearing about the video?"

Jake answered. "According to Joe, it was posted seven minutes ago, just before the reporter asked the question. Joe and Kirsten texted Mali and I, a minute or so prior to that last question. In fact, both of our phones," his eyes moved to Mali who gave an imperceptible nod, "vibrated but neither of us looked at our messages."

Mali jumped into the conversation. "Kirsten is sending me the video. I should have it by now. Give me a minute to find and open it." Not waiting for a response, she rushed to the bar and pulled her laptop out. The others followed at a more leisurely pace. Accessing the internet via a hotspot from her phone, she opened her email and found the attachment.

"I've got it." They watched as she clicked the play button.

Martin was sweating profusely because of the spotlight trained on him. "I wonder how long he's been standing there. He looks exhausted and weak, despite the defiance," Mali noted.

Jake nodded. "Look at the abrasions on his wrist. Obviously, he pulled on the ropes. But the steady trickle of blood down his arms suggest he's been there awhile."

"Any way to identify the woman?" Frank asked. "I'm assuming it's a woman because of the clothing."

"Nicely dressed, slight build, long blonde hair, slender well-manicured hands, but never more than the back of the head. I agree it's a woman," noted Tom Overly.

Mali looked over her shoulder at him with a small smile.

"What? I notice things. And while there is never a side view of her face, breasts were clearly visible when she turned to walk toward him."

Mali said nothing, just turned back to the video.

There was a collective gasp as Martin confessed.

"Christ," exclaimed Jake.

"Oh my God," whispered Mali.

"What kind of sick bastard would do that to a child," this from Frank, shaking his head in disgust.

No one spoke immediately after the video ended.

Rubbing his forehead, Frank grimaced. "Justitia? Hunting someone down? Actually thinking vigilante justice is justice? I'm getting too old for this." He sighed. "Let's get back to the city." He looked at Tom Overly. "You'll call when you have details on where the hunt took place?" At Overly's nod, Frank thanked him as Mali closed her laptop and prepared to leave, and Jake excused himself to make a call.

On the return flight, Jake told Frank his team would be there when they arrived to discuss steps moving forward.

"Good. And, Hoop, I'm moving you to Jake's team. You can provide any necessary analysis real-time."

Mali's eyebrows shot up as she looked at Jake. "Is this a permanent move and what about the Harris case I was just given?"

"To be determined later if the move will be permanent. Pass the Harris case on to Agent Hopkins. Move your things to the warehouse on Monday morning."

"Yes sir."

"Jake, stay in close contact with Maury and Sally. I have a feeling we'll need their resources."

"Yes sir."

Mali spent the remainder of the flight thinking about what they had learned from the scene of the crime, the press conference, and the video. Her mind was swirling with thoughts of what happened to Martin and what happened three months ago. What would she do if this turned out to be another game?

When Jake and Mali arrived at the warehouse, the remaining team members were already there. Mali walked to the conference area, pulling the whiteboard with the questions she had written plus one that was blank, to the control center where they were meeting. She handed a thumb drive to Kirsten as she walked by.

Jake wasted no time getting started.

"Thanks for coming in on such short notice. First of all, Hoop is joining our team. She's up to speed on everything and will provide analysis for this case. You can introduce yourselves later."

There was a chorus of hellos. Mali returned the greetings and smiled when Kirsten gave her two thumbs up.

"Kirsten, bring up the video. We'll save the pictures on the thumb drive for later. Joe, what did you find out about the Twitter account that posted the picture?"

"As you suspected, it was hacked. The owner had reported it as soon as he realized he was hacked. Still looking into the second account that posted the video. No doubt it's been hacked as well."

"How were they able to post it using the JusticePrevails tag? Didn't we have it removed?"

As the video appeared on the top middle screen before flickering to life on all nine screens thus becoming one very large screen, Kirsten added, "Accounts can be deleted, and tweets for a particular hashtag can be deleted, but not the hashtags themselves."

"Damn. So I can go to Twitter under this tag and nothing will be there right now because you just had it all deleted. But I can go back to Twitter tomorrow and there may be something new under that tag?" When Kirsten nodded, Jake rubbed his face before looking up at the screen. He changed the subject. "Has everyone seen the video?" Everyone nodded. "Good. When we view it now, look for details we may have missed. Is there any way to identify the woman, for starters?"

The team spent the next thirty minutes studying the video repeatedly. There were no visible marks on the interrogator's hands, nothing distinguishable about the clothing, and no inflections in the altered voice that could have suggested knowledge of one of the victims Martin admitted to assaulting. The only thing they could confirm with absolute surety was the interrogator was a slender woman with shoulder-length blonde hair who smoked.

"Is she one of his victims?" asked Felix, one of the team members. "And what's with her name?"

"Hard to say. He didn't seem to know who she was but that's not an indication one way or the other. We need to find out," replied Jake.

Mali walked to the blank whiteboard to log new questions and next steps.

Joe jumped into the conversation. "I googled Justitia. She is the Roman goddess of Justice and was portrayed as evenly balancing both scales and a sword, often wearing a blindfold. Lady Justice."

Kirsten asked, "What about the cigarette she smoked. What brand is it? Are there fingerprints on the butts she dropped?"

"There were no prints anywhere in the building or in that small office. And the cigarette butts had been removed," replied Jake.

Mali wrote all questions down, even if the answers were known. "What did the office look like originally? They obviously modified it since I doubt Martin had a one-way mirror looking *in* to the office. Where did they get that mirror, the rope, the spotlight?" She wrote everything down as she asked the questions.

"Good questions. And who is operating the video camera? It wasn't just turned on and left on because there were times the operator zoomed in on Martin."

"Who hunted him?" asked Kirsten. "And the woman said she was hunting him for his abuse against children but also because he hunted and killed the animals in the room. Are we going to consider the possibility this is a random nut who wants to fight for children and animals?"

Jake shook his head. "We're not ruling anything out at this point." He looked at his watch. Five forty-five. "It's getting late and we're not going to be able to get answers on a Sunday night. Joe, run your program all night to check social media in case something new shows up."

"Will do."

Jake looked at the team. "Obviously our priority has changed, and we'll have to table the Hunter data and GPS/Satellite project for now. Report here tomorrow morning at seven." He turned away.

"Excuse me, Jake?"

Jake turned back. "Yes, Joe."

"We can't table the project we were working on. In fact, our findings could help us with this case and others."

"How so?"

"The last game Hunter was working on? He was trying to create a ghost."

CHAPTER FIVE

AFTER A BRIEF break so family members could be called, Jake, Mali, Joe, Kirsten, and Felix had ordered pizza and were sitting around the conference table eating it.

"What is this ghost you're talking about, Joe?"

"Remember with The Hunted Ones game, the target and assassin can walk down a real street anywhere in the world. The businesses are real businesses, right?"

"That's correct."

"But there are no people on the streets, no cars. It's like a ghost town."

Mali frowned. "Remember when we had dinner at Frank and Carol's and first learned about the game?" She looked at Jake, who nodded. She explained to the others, "We asked their sons to show us the game with the action based here in New York City. I was astounded at how accurate everything was, the restaurants, shops, apartments, and other existing landmarks." Puzzled, she looked at Joe. "But there were people on the streets."

"Actually, no. What made the game cool was you could play in real locations you've never seen before. You could run by the Spanish Steps or Coliseum in Rome, jump off the Parthenon in Greece, or walk by your very own house. But there was no one else in the game except the computer-generated target and assassin."

"Wow! I never noticed."

"So what does that have to do with now and what do you mean by a ghost?"

His eye lit up, his words running together in his excitement. "Hunter was trying to take the application even further by making it completely real-time. He wanted the character in his new game to be able to walk down a street and see real people, cars, dogs, whatever, as well as inanimate objects. The character in the game would be a virtual ghost."

Mali's jaw dropped and she pushed forward in her chair. "So let me get this straight. I could be standing on a street corner and someone playing a game three thousand miles away could stand right next to me and watch me dial a phone number on my phone?" Joe nodded. "And a peeping tom could look inside the window of my house and watch me undress? That's despicable. What about my privacy? How is that even possible?" She rattled off her questions, staccato-style. By the time she finished talking, her hands had curled into fists on the conference table.

"And how would that even be legal?" Jake asked, equally stunned.

"First of all, he got close, but he wasn't successful. Secondly, no one would be able to look inside a building because the part of the program that seamlessly moved from real to computer-generated when a character walked inside a building was not changed. So no peeping toms, well, unless someone was skinny-dipping in a pool outside."

No one said anything as they digested all they had been told.

"Well, I'm certainly glad he wasn't successful," Mali finally stated, leaning back in her chair.

"But we were," stated Kirsten. "Well, almost."

Mali and Jake looked at Joe and Kirsten, both of whom had big smiles on their faces.

Joe nodded. "It's true. We have just a couple of things to tweak then we'll test it."

"Whoa, not so fast," exclaimed Jake. "This is a slippery slope you're…"

"But Jake," interrupted Felix, who had been silent up to this point. "Excuse me for interrupting. This technology can help the FBI. We can tail a suspect without him ever knowing, without even leaving our office. If we need to track a terrorist cell in Iran, we can do it from here without putting anyone's life in danger. Obviously, to take action against someone, we'd have to be there in person but consider the man hours that can be saved, not to mention the financial savings, especially early on in a case when we're just researching or doing basic recon." His gaze shifted to Mali. "This could even help in your research on various cases. The possibilities are endless."

Jake leaned forward in his chair, resting his elbows on the table, the pizza on his plate long forgotten. He rubbed his forehead and glanced at the clock. "It's seven-thirty and I need to think." He looked at everyone. "It goes without saying that nothing about this technology leaves this room and no one is to talk about it."

"We reiterated that when we discovered what Hunter was attempting."

"Good. Go home, get some rest. It's going to be a long week. I'll be in late. I plan to go to Frank's office first thing in the morning to discuss this with him."

Mali piped in. "I'll be a little late myself. I need to gather my things at the main office and bring everything here."

"I'll lock up, Jake," said Joe. Felix and Kirsten said they'd help clean up and leave with Joe.

Everyone stood and said their good-byes.

"I can't believe what I just heard," mumbled Mali as they made their way out of the warehouse.

"Nor can I. Hop in the car and I'll take you home."

"Just take me to the nearest station entrance and I'll ride the subway home." When he opened his mouth to object, Mali held up her hand. "No arguments, Jake. It's late and you'll miss tucking Heather into bed unless you go straight there."

Jake smiled and thanked her.

* * *

Mali's apartment
Monday, August 17, 7:20 p.m.

IT HAD BEEN a long day at work, the team making minimal progress. Mali was still trying to wrap her head around this ghost technology.

Opening the door to her building, she trudged to the elevator. She was mentally exhausted and wanted nothing more than to have a glass of wine and sit on her balcony. Thankfully, the doors opened right away when she pressed the Up button of the elevator. Entering her apartment, she flipped on the lights then dumped her computer bag and purse on the kitchen island. She moved into the kitchen and grabbed a wine glass from a cupboard, licking her lips in anticipation of that sweet nectar relaxing her. As she reached inside the refrigerator for the open bottle of Pinot Noir, her doorbell rang. Frowning, she closed the refrigerator door.

Tiptoeing to the door, she rested her hands lightly on its panel as she stood on her toes to lean in and peek through the peep hole. Dropping back on her heels, her jaw dropped open in astonishment. *It can't be!*

"I know you're in there, sweetheart! I followed you into the building."

Mali was at a loss. She just stood there, eyes wide, like a deer caught in the headlights of a car.

"Jaz, open this door. I've been waiting all day long just to see you." Annoyance had crept into his tone.

Mali slid the security chain on then opened the door as far as the chain would allow.

"Now, is that any way to greet your husband?" Daniel Matthews whined with a mock pout.

Mali met Daniel Matthews at a frat party while in college. He was the star of the football team, the quarterback, gorgeous with hazel eyes and flaxen hair down to his shoulders, and an arm to rival that of Aaron Rodgers.

He swept her off her feet and they eloped three months after their initial meeting. Her parents were furious with her. As a member of Philadelphia's Hooper dynasty, she was expected to marry 'the right man' as her two older sisters had. They were appalled when she divorced him less than four months after saying 'I do'. She never told them why, that she had caught him with a cheerleader, and they had never asked. But her father had taken care of everything and made the entire marriage disappear.

Studying her ex-husband now through the crack in the door, she noticed his good looks had sagged, and his toned body had softened into pudginess. The hair she used to love running her fingers through hung limply past his shoulders, grease and dirt from lack of washing weighing it down.

"Ex, Daniel."

"Whatever. Open this door, unless you want all your skeletons left out here for anyone to see."

Mali breathed in and out of her nose, fuming. She released the chain and opened the door, stepping back to allow him entrance.

With a big smile, he walked in, studying her apartment with a calculating eye.

Mali shut the door and turned, watching him as he prowled around, feeling violated with every step he took.

"Nice place you have, wifey. You've spent your trust fund well."

"What are you doing here, Daniel? And stop referring to me as your wife."

Daniel glanced over his shoulder and smirked before

continuing his perusal of her place. "When I returned from Puerto Rico two months ago and read you were almost killed, I had to find you…to make sure you're alright, of course. It's taken me quite awhile to discover where you live." He walked back to the front door where Mali still stood. Standing nose to nose, he took in a deep breath. "You smell good and you look even better than I remember." His voice deepened into a husky tone. "Your auburn hair is a little shorter than I remember, but I've never forgotten your mesmerizing gray eyes." His eyes roamed down her body. "You have the looks and body to be on the cover of Playboy. Instead, you choose to hide behind this geeky FBI costume?" He flicked the collar of her jacket. "Tsk. Tsk. Tsk. What a waste."

"I can't say the same for you. And you smell like stale beer." Mali pushed him away from her. "I've had a long day. What do you want?"

"I'm glad you asked. My business dealings in Puerto Rico didn't pan out, unfortunately, and I'm a little short on cash. I…"

Mali, interrupted, laughing. "Oh my God. You want me to give you money? Didn't my father give you enough all those years ago?" She paused and looked him up and down. "Well, however much you want, you're not getting it."

"I wouldn't be so quick to say no, Jaz!" Daniel's eyes turned hard as stone and his evil smile unsettled her. "I would hate for your boss and friends at the FBI to learn how you used me all those years ago to get away from your family, and how I caught you doing the bedroom tango with my best friend a mere four months after our marriage."

Mali gasped. "That's a lie and you know it!" Her hands balled into fists as she stood ramrod straight and shot daggers at him through her eyes. "What happened to you, Daniel, that you would resort to blackmail? Or maybe this is who you always were, and I was just blinded by your good looks and charming ways. My eyes were certainly opened after that football game, though. And here I thought you were just a philanderer all those years ago. Get out!"

"When I'm ready. Fork up twenty-five thousand dollars by Wednesday and I'll disappear."

"That's a laugh. Get out, Daniel!" Mali turned to the door and opened it.

He smiled as he sauntered toward her. He stopped a breath away from her and leaned down to whisper in her ear. "I'll be back on Wednesday for the money. You don't want to mess with me, wifey." He stepped out of the apartment and walked down the hall.

Mali shut and locked the door, then turned around, leaning against it. She wasn't sure her legs would hold her up. She was shaking and couldn't stop. She had no idea what she was going to do. *Breathe, just breathe.*

When she calmed down, she went back into the kitchen and poured herself that glass of wine. After gulping half of it down, she picked up her phone and called her BFF. Sara West was Mali's oldest best friend. They had known each other since they were ten years old, and Mali could always count on Sara's straight-forward and honest opinion.

"Mali, hi! How are you? We're still getting together with Kirsten and Jen next week, right?"

"Hi Sara! Um, yes, I believe so. How are my god-children?"

"They're fine. What's going on? You sound…distracted or upset. Bad day at the office?"

"Yes, it was a bad day but the day got worse when I arrived home twenty minutes ago."

"What happened?"

"Daniel showed up and is demanding twenty-five thousand dollars, in two days, or he'll go to my boss and tell them about us, well, his version of us. He plans to play the jilted husband using an elaborate lie."

"You're kidding! How did he even find you?"

"I don't know. He said when he read about the game, he tracked me down, wanted to make sure I was alright. What a joke." She paused and wiped her eyes, only then realizing she was crying.

"Oh hon. I'm so sorry."

"What should I do? My dad erased my marriage and subsequent divorce and by the time I applied for a job with the FBI I had convinced myself the marriage never even took place. I lied on my application and said I was never married. Lying is kind of frowned upon with the government. I could get fired."

"They're not going to fire you. You're too valuable." Sara paused. "You told Jake about your marriage a few months ago, right?"

"Yes."

"You need to tell him right away. He'll help you deal with the FBI as well as with Daniel."

Mali rubbed her forehead with her fingers.

"Things seem a lot worse than they are because you're tired, Mali."

Mali sighed. "You're right. I'm going to take a hot shower then try to sleep."

"Good. Get some rest and talk to Jake tomorrow."

"Thanks Sara. I needed to hear some rational thinking. My mind just turned off when I saw him."

"That's what friends are for. Feel free to call me again if you need to. I'll see you next week."

Mali nodded. "Give my god-kids a big hug and say hello to Tom for me."

"Will do."

Mali hung up and set her phone down on the nightstand as she walked past it into her bathroom. After a long, hot shower, she climbed into bed, tossing and turning, until exhaustion pulled her into a restless sleep in the wee hours of the morning.

CHAPTER SIX

Home of James Adams
Malibu, California
Tuesday, August 18, 6:52 a.m. CST

"MAKE THIS GO away, Jessica," he screeched at his attorney. Working in the movie industry for more than thirty years, no one dared trifle with James Adams. He was introduced to acting when he was twelve years old and had worked his way up through the ranks. He had lost his virginity when he was just thirteen, proud that he had taken the eleven-year-old co-star in his trailer between takes of a movie he was making. That movie had catapulted his young career and that of his co-star. Talk of the town was how well the two youngsters worked together, an 'undeniable chemistry for two so young' was what they had said. He never forgot that, capitalizing on it throughout his career. With his dark, moody looks, piercing green eyes, and well-muscled physique, James Adams was bad-boy attractive, and he knew it. With four Oscars under his belt, three for acting and one for producing, he commanded only the best roles and projects. He was known for bringing new, young and raw talent to the screen, many of whom owed James Adams their careers. He briefly considered them as he paced back and forth in front of his pool that overlooked the Pacific.

"It isn't going away, James," was the calm response.

"Damn it! I pay you good money to be my attorney and to fix things for me."

"James, two more women have brought your... indiscretions...to the District Attorney's attention, bringing the total to eight in the past four days. They have every intention of suing you for rape, sexual harassment, and..."

James stopped pacing, his unused hand curling into a fist. "Those bitches, all of them, owe their careers to me and this is the thanks I get!?!" He roared, fuming. "Any sexual relations I've had over the years have been completely consensual. I don't have to force myself on any woman, or man for that matter!"

"The complaint isn't about them today, it's about when they were teenagers, minors. They claim you promised them great acting careers if they performed certain...courtesies, shall we say, for you and your guests at your mansion."

"That's bullshit!" He walked into the house stopping at the bar, and opened a small black box. Pulling out a razor blade strapped to the inside of the lid, he set it on the bar. Next, he reached in and grabbed his snuff spoon, filled with white powder, and poured it on the bar, using the razor blade to cut a line. "Hang on," he said, dropping his left arm and holding the phone next to his leg. Leaning over, he grabbed a straw from the dispenser conveniently placed next to the box and, placing one end of the straw in his nose and holding it with his right hand, he moved the other end of the straw to one side of the line of powder. Inhaling through his nose, he moved the straw along the line of powder, sucking it up into his nasal cavity. Dropping the straw after he finished snorting the cocaine, he sniffed a couple of times before returning the phone to his ear.

"Better?" she asked, having gone through this before.

"Yes."

"Good. Given the age of #MeToo, this isn't going away. In fact, it's growing, which is why, as I've been told by a friend at the D.A.s office, official charges will be filed tomorrow. They are offering you the privacy of turning yourself in by nine a.m. without any fanfare. If you're not there at the appointed time, they'll haul you out of your house with cameras rolling. They also plan to execute a search warrant and will go through your home tomorrow. We need to meet as soon as possible to discuss how we're going to handle things in the morning and to strategize in general."

"Fine, whatever," was his sullen reply.

"James…"

"Jessica, I appreciate the heads up, and I do appreciate everything you do for me," he sighed. "Come to the house for lunch and let's talk."

"I'll be there at eleven thirty." The line went dead.

James stared at the ocean. Without warning, he

turned and threw his phone at the mirror behind the bar. Glass shattered and flew everywhere.

"Señor, are you alright?" a small Hispanic woman asked as she raced into the room. Her steps faltered and her voice trailed off as she took in her surroundings. Broken shards of glass littered the bar, stools, and floor, even reaching as far as the leather chairs facing the floor-to-ceiling windows. They sparkled like diamonds in the morning light.

"No, Belinda, things are not okay." He rubbed his neck as he, too, surveyed the room. "I'm sorry about this mess."

"No problemo, sir. I will clean it up, pronto."

"Thank you. Ms. Anderson is arriving at eleven-thirty for lunch. Can you prepare something for us?"

"Sí, sí. I will have something ready, Señor."

James nodded. "I'm going for a walk." Shoulders slumped in defeat, he turned around and walked past the pool and down the sloping gardens to the gate. Punching in the code, he passed through the gate and down the stairs to the beach. He walked to the water's edge, letting the waves lap over his toes

The beach wasn't crowded at this early hour. Looking to his right, he observed two adults and a toddler playing in the distance. A man was holding the toddler above the water, bouncing her up and down. Her delighted giggles as cold water splashed her chubby legs evoked a smile from James, despite his problems. A small dog was barking as it ran to the waves then retreated just as the waves reached its paws.

Turning left and sloshing water with each step, James ambled down the beach, deep in thought. He didn't pay attention to how long he walked but when he stopped and turned around, he realized he was much further than he had intended to go. He reached for the phone in his back pocket before remembering it was in a puddle of glass at home. He was going to call Belinda to say he might be late getting back and to have Jessica wait. Shrugging, he was about to head back when he noticed an approaching boat. It was a Hustler, forty or fifty feet in length at a guess. A man and a woman were on board, and the woman was waving to him.

"Excuse me, sir."

"Are you alright?" he called out.

"Yes," she gave a self-deprecating laugh as the boat pulled to the shallows, gently bouncing in the waves. "I'd be lying if I said we were lost. I told my boyfriend I wanted to cruise past Malibu to see if anyone famous was at the beach. You're James Adams, right?"

James smiled and nodded.

"Oh my gosh. I have never been so lucky as to meet a real star," she gushed. "I know it might be bold of me to ask, we obviously interrupted you, but would it be at all possible to get your autograph. It would mean the world to me. I have a pen around here somewhere," she mumbled, turning to dig through her purse.

Preferring to continue his solitary walk, he smiled when she triumphantly held up a pen. Splashing through the shallow water to the boat, he reached the side as she held up a small piece of paper as well.

"Oh my gosh, this is so incredible! Thank you so much for doing this."

"You're very welcome." He took the pen and paper from her hand. "Who should I make this out to?"

"Justitia," was the cold reply.

James looked up in confusion and froze. "Whoa, I don't have any money on me," he said as he looked at the gun the man was pointing at him.

"Get in the boat."

"What?"

"You heard me, get in the boat or you die right here."

* * *

Special Unit Warehouse
Tuesday, August 18, 8:40 a.m. EST

MALI WALKED OUT of the elevator holding a box with her purse sitting on top and stopped short. Even though she felt like she had been hit with a sledgehammer between her eyes, the headache she had been nursing since she woke up still pounded her temples, she could appreciate the buzz of activity that was missing when she was there yesterday. A matronly woman sat at the table monitoring security cameras. Kirsten and Joe were at the control center, heads bent down as they studied something on the screen, Felix was at his station near the front working on his laptop, and Jake was sitting at the conference table speaking with someone on the phone. The upper three and lower three screens on the front wall were not in use. The three middle screens had a layout of Martin's property, the beginning of a timeline of events, and a list with names on it, respectively from left to right. The computer screens on all desks and the larger screens on the front wall seemed overly bright in the low-lit room.

"Good morning, Mali." Kirsten did a double-take as she took a second look at her friend. "Ooooh, you look bad. Are you alright?"

"Gee thanks," Mali grimaced as she approached Kirsten, Joe, and Felix. "I've seen better days. How's it going so far this morning? And where should I put my things?"

"Set up next to my computer, middle row." Kirsten pointed to her left. "We're working on a list of suspects, that's the list of names on the right screen. Felix is building the timeline leading up to Martin's death."

"Hmmm." Mali stared at the list of names as she placed her small box of items on the computer table. Setting her purse in front of the monitor, she proceeded to unpack the box. Not much was in it, a few files, one notepad with thoughts written down on the top sheet, and an empty mug. The last item she pulled out was a five-by-seven frame with the lunch invitation Heather made for her a few months ago. It was a drawing of Jake's red house with green grass in front and black sticks that were supposed to be the wrought iron fence. Standing next to the house were two large stick figures and a small one in between them, labeled 'Daddy,' 'Me,' and 'Papa.' Written in sky blue crayon below the drawing was 'Can you come to lunch? Heather.' It was the sweetest invitation Mali had ever remembered receiving and she had immediately framed it.

"Good morning." Mali gave a start, not hearing Jake walk up to her.

She glanced at him as she set the frame on the table on the left side of the monitor.

His smile faded as he noticed the bags under her eyes and her pale face. "Are you alright?"

"Headache. I need to talk to you later," she responded, reaching in her purse for an aspirin.

"Alright." He touched her upper arm before clearing his throat and moving to the front of the room.

"Now that Mali has arrived, let's gather for a meeting." Chatter stopped and all eyes turned to Jake. He scanned the room. "Mali, you've already met Felix Johnson. Felix is fresh out of Quantico after graduating from Texas A&M with a Bachelor's degree in Computer Engineering and a minor in game design and development this past May. He was top of his class. The only other person you haven't met is Susan Walker. She's been with the FBI for, what, about twenty-eight years now?" At her nod, Jake continued, "She's a security specialist and is handling all security for us. Both are an excellent fit for our team. Susan, Mali is a Tactical Intelligence Analyst and was key in solving the HuntedLives case."

Hellos and other greetings were echoed around the room.

"Hey, you were also a target of the game, right?" asked Felix. "I remember hearing about it while at Quantico."

Mali nodded, taking a deep breath and exhaling through her nose.

Jake continued. "Based on my conversation with

Frank last night, I requested that Jeff Cink join our team. Jeff is a senior-level Electronics Technician who I worked with in the Army. He joined the FBI a year or so after I did and is currently working in a Virginia field office. He should arrive later today or tomorrow."

"So do we have a green light on creating the ghost?" Joe asked.

"Yes, I feel an expert in radio frequency systems, data networks, and circuitry, among other things, can round out the expertise we'll need for it, and Jeff is the perfect man for the job. There will be strict limitations, naturally. Once we complete our initial testing to make sure it works, we'll use it for recon on the above suspects as well as any leads we pursue. This will be a test of sorts. Can it help the FBI and, if so, how? We'll also determine if the ghost can help us with research." His eyes roamed the room as he stared at each member of the team. "This technology is not to be discussed with anyone outside of this room. Understood?" After everyone nodded, Jake said, "Joe and Kirsten, I want you to continue work on the ghost and bring Jeff up to speed when he arrives. Let me know when it's ready to test. Felix, take an hour or so to finish the timeline. It doesn't have to be absolute. We'll modify it as we learn more. Once you're done with that, review the comments from the tweeted picture as well as the Instagram video to determine if any user made multiple comments and/or comments on both. They may be leads. Be creative."

"I'll take the suspect list, Jake, remove those I can and add others," said Mali.

"Great."

"Excuse me, Jake?" Susan raised her hand.

Jake turned his head, raising his eyebrows.

"If I merge the camera views onto two screens, I can still monitor the security of the building and free up the other two screens allowing me to assist. From a security perspective, I can review and research the Martin property to try to determine how and when the attackers got onto the property. Perhaps even when they arrived."

"Great idea. From what the State Police said, there were multiple cameras around the property, but none were located inside the house or in the outbuilding. From the forty-eight-hour period before his arrival, all recordings ceased. Your expertise may find something they missed. If there are no more questions, let's get to work. I want to meet again at two o'clock with a status update."

At three-twenty, the elevator doors opened and a short, pudgy man stepped in to the room. He checked out his surroundings, stopping when his eyes fell on Jake. "Well, hell's bells! I never thought I'd lay eyes on you again, Pirate." Jeff Cink was not a quiet man. His voice boomed across the room.

"Damn, it's been a long time, Slick. How the hell are you?" Jake closed the distance between them in three strides and wrapped his friend in a bear hug. "And what's with all this hair?" He swished his hand across the bushy beard when they pulled away.

"Hey, at least I've got hair somewhere on my head."

Jake stood an easy fifteen inches taller, and they both laughed when Jake leaned down and blew air on his bald head before rubbing his forearm across the top, pretending to shine it…an old ritual between them.

Mock-punching him, Jeff smiled. "Some things never change." He checked out the room again, nodding his head in acknowledgement of team members who were looking on in curiosity. "Nice digs you have here."

Jake's carefree mood changed. "I wasn't really expecting you until tomorrow."

"Hey, I didn't have anything better to do so here I am."

"Well, I'm glad you're here." They turned and walked to the control center. Joe moved to the side so Jeff could view it.

Jeff leaned down to get a closer look and whistled in appreciation. "Fancy set up. I'm impressed."

"Everyone, this is Jeff Cink. Jeff, this is…"

Suddenly, the console beeped and flashed red. All nine screens at the front flashed.

"Whoa, I didn't touch anything." Jeff raised his hands as he backed up.

Joe quickly stepped up to the console. "It's an alarm I set up to go off whenever #JusticePrevails goes active on one or more of the social media sites we're focused on," he said as he pressed some buttons. "It's active on Twitter and Instagram. I'm bringing #JusticePrevails up on Twitter now." The nine screens blinked two more times, before Twitter appeared on all nine as one large screen.

All eyes looked up.

"Next sinner is ready. Download LadyJustice app. Join Justice community. YOU choose the weapon. You have 2hrs before poll disappears. Tick Tock."

CHAPTER SEVEN

4:00p.m.

THE HUM OF computers was the only sound in the room.

"Jesus!" stated Jake, shaking his head. "What is the LadyJustice app?"

"I just installed it and am bringing it up now," said Kirsten. She was typing something on her computer and swiped her finger from left to right. "Here it is, Joe."

"Got it." Joe, in turn, swiped up and Twitter was replaced with an app. The Home screen was very simple. Against a black background at the top was Lady Justice in red. Below were two links, About and Privacy. The Statue of Liberty was centered on the screen followed by Where Justice Always Prevails in large white letters. At the bottom was a Join Now button in blue and just underneath those words, a counter with the number five on it.

"Click the About link," said Jake.

Joe did so and everyone read: "Every year, thousands of children are abused—verbally, physically, sexually. The offenders have to pay. While the #MeToo movement shone a light on this problem, it has not gone far enough. Our justice system has failed. Even a guilty verdict in the courts is often not enough, especially for those with money. Well, Lady Justice is doing something about it. And you can too. By joining, you will have a voice in the weaponry used and, at times, the location or whether a sinner will live or die. It's time to take control and give our children a chance."

"Oh my God," whispered Kirsten.

"Well, there's our motive," stated Mali.

"So are we going to have to protect all pedophiles and sex offenders now?" asked Felix, a peevish tone in his voice.

Jake stood still, arms crossed, staring at the screen. "Joe, let's see what it says about privacy."

When Joe returned to the Home page and clicked Privacy, a list of Privacy statements displayed.

* This app is the most secret private community app on the market, surpassing messenger apps like Viber, Threema, Telegram, and Voxer
* All users are anonymous—no followers, friends, or user profile
* Letter-sealing, end-to-end encryption keys are used to ensure privacy. No one outside of this community can access comments or poll results.
* Completely untraceable
* All phone numbers are private, encrypted and will remain private

* Your comments automatically self-destruct after 15 minutes, can never be recovered and are not accessible by anyone, not even us
* Polling disappears after clock runs out; results display for a period of 15 minutes after

Jake looked at Jeff. "Is all of that feasible?"

"Yes, the messenger apps mentioned use various elements. For example, Viber has the self-destruct feature and Voxer is completely untraceable. Those apps apply to private messages and/or calls between individuals and small groups. I've never seen it applied to unlimited users in a community. That doesn't mean it isn't possible. I can research it if you'd like."

"I want to finish going through the app then we'll reassign duties. Joe, join it."

Joe returned to the Home page. "Whoa. Look at the counter now. It's more than twenty-five thousand and counting." Shaking his head, he clicked Join Now.

A screen displayed with two fields, The first was titled Name with a message below it instructing the user to enter any username desired, maximum ten characters. The second field was Phone Number. At the bottom of the screen was a note indicating the user would access the app using his or her phone number and the username would display next to any comments he or she posted.

"Pretty basic," said Joe as he entered 'Gonnafly' for the username. "What phone number should I use?" He glanced at Jake.

Mali responded. "We can't use any of our phones. We have no idea who is behind this. Even if someone uses a fake username like Joe is doing, the phone number is real and can possibly be traced or the owner identified by whomever is doing this. We need a burner phone."

Jake nodded. "I agree. But we don't have time. You read the Twitter message. The poll closes in two hours. That was fifteen minutes ago."

"There's a store ten or so blocks from here that sells burners," said Felix. "I can run there, buy a phone, and be back in less than an hour."

Jake reached into his back pocket and pulled out his wallet. Opening it, he removed two twenty-dollar bills and handed them to Felix. "Go."

Felix raced to the elevator and rushed inside as soon as it opened.

Jake turned to the rest of the group. "This is obviously bigger than the Martin case so we need to change and expand our focus. Joe, Kirsten and Jeff, we need that ghost up and running. We may be able to use it quicker than we thought. Right now, though, I want that tweet and those posts removed from social media."

"I'm on it," said Kirsten, and she turned away to make the calls.

"Joe, contact your associates in the Info Technology Analysis Team, in DC, Amy and Brad right?" At Joe's nod, he continued. "I want them to work with Felix and figure out everything they can about this app in terms of the privacy aspect we discussed as well as the network used. Can we remove the app similar to how Parler was removed?

Susan, continue with your task regarding the Martin property. Perhaps there's something that can give us more information on who's behind this. Start with what you can and we'll finish joining the app as soon as Felix returns. Mali, I need to speak with you." He moved his head to the right and they walked to the conference table as the remaining team members dispersed to work on their tasks.

Mali sat and, placing her elbows on the table, rubbed her temples.

"Is your headache back?"

She nodded. "I'll survive." She looked at the whiteboard that listed the questions the team originally documented. "I need to update that list."

"The suspect list we have may or may not hold merit. We won't know until the identity of the next person who was taken is revealed." He rubbed his forehead. "I need to call Frank and update him. This just got a whole lot more complicated."

"When this gets out, the public is going to say it's a copycat of HuntedLives, even though it's not specifically a game."

Jake sighed. "I know."

"I'm going to update the whiteboard while you contact Frank." Without waiting for a reply, Mali left Jake to make her changes.

5:45p.m.

An hour and half later, all activity stopped as Felix strode into the room, breathing heavily and sweating profusely.

"Sorry it took so long," he said, as he handed the package to Joe and the change to Jake. "The store was further than I remembered."

"I was getting worried," said Jake. "We have less than fifteen minutes. Kirsten, capture every screen and Jeff, capture the code behind each screen, if possible."

"We're ready to go," said Joe after he had removed the packaging and set up the phone. Returning to the console and the app, he entered the phone number and clicked Join Now.

Everyone read: "Welcome to the Justice Community where your voice counts. Any negative comments about our purpose will be deleted and the user blocked from the app. Scroll down to cast your vote."

When Joe scrolled down, there was an audible gasp from everyone. "The sinner who will have a chance to redeem himself is James Adams."

"James Adams, the actor?" asked Mali. "He's one of my favorites. What did he do?"

No one answered as they continued to read. "His atrocities will be revealed later. For now, cast your vote on the weapon to be used should he fail in his redemption. Your choices are: Crossbow, Steak knife, Strangulation. Select one. Majority rules."

"There's a countdown clock here as well. It shows there's six minutes and change until the poll closes. This is unreal," stated Joe.

"I'm looking through news articles in California and online news sources, and have not found any report of James Adams missing," said Mali. "I'll try to find a number for him or an agent, or someone."

"What happens when you vote? What's on the next screen?" asked Felix. "We can't vote, can we?"

That made everyone pause and look to Jake for the answer.

"Christ." He glowered at the screen. "We need to see what displays after the vote."

"But if we vote and that's the weapon of choice, we will contribute to…" Everyone understood Susan's whispered inference.

Joe interrupted. "Two minutes and counting."

Jake said, "Vote for strangulation."

"Jake…" Mali began.

He turned sharp eyes on her. "We have to know what is said and what happens. We won't if we don't vote. The selection is on me."

"One minute forty-five seconds…"

"Strangulation, Joe."

* * *

Joe selected Strangulation and clicked Submit.

The poll displayed with real-time results.

Joe read aloud while everyone checked the numbers. "The crossbow is ahead with strangulation right behind it. The steak knife is a distant third."

"Look how many people have voted. There's close to one hundred thousand votes so far." stated Mali in alarm.

The tally kept fluctuating between cross-bow and strangulation, the numbers were updating fast.

"Look at the comments," said Kirsten.

Below the running poll tally was a comments field followed by posted comments from viewers.

"Twenty seconds," said Joe.

"Capture everything you can." Jake ordered as the clock ticked down.

6:00p.m.

THE SCREEN TURNED black before a slow trickle of red dripped from the top of the screen down.

"Did anyone notice what option had the most votes?" asked Jake.

Heads shook as everyone waited.

In bold red letters, the screen flashed "Crossbow is the winning weapon!"

Mali glanced at Jake and watched him release a breath. When he looked at her, she smiled her shared relief.

The page scrolled up to display one final message.

"Eight o'clock tonight, eastern standard time, is James Adam's reckoning. More information to follow."

The screen faded to black.

"Tell me we captured screenshots and code."

Jeff and Kirsten nodded.

"Felix, analyze the code. Is there any way to identify the user or maker of this? Where is it broadcasting from? What's the network? Is there any way to kill this app? Joe will pass on Amy and Brad's contact info in DC. They will help you."

"I've spoken with them, Jake, and they have clearance to help. Do you want them to fly here?"

"Not right now. Send the code to them so they can work with Felix. We need answers pretty quick." Felix and Joe nodded. "Jeff, Joe and Kirsten, continue working on the ghost. I'm going to ask Becky to order pizza for us. If anyone needs a quick break to make some calls, do it now. It's going to be a long night."

"I'm happy to go topside and ask her," said Felix, smiling.

Jake chuckled. "Down Romeo. Get to work on the code."

"Jake, I've got the phone number for James Adam's lawyer. I'm calling her now," Mali said as she turned away from the group.

6:15p.m.

FIFTEEN MINUTES LATER, Mali searched the room for Jake and headed to the conference table where he was talking on the phone.

Seeing her approach, he spoke into the phone before hanging up as she sat.

"I just updated Frank. Needless to say, he's concerned and pissed. He'll be here at seven."

"I spoke with Jessica Anderson, Adams' lawyer. She said he went missing earlier this morning. They were supposed to meet at eleven-thirty at his home in Malibu to discuss his impending arrest."

Jake's eyebrows shot up.

"The D.A. is officially charging him tomorrow for rape, sexual harassment, and intimidation. They were giving him the opportunity to turn himself in before everything went public. Ms. Anderson told me his maid said he went for a walk on the beach after her phone call with him which would have been around seven-thirty pacific standard time. She waited for a few hours, getting increasingly worried, initially thinking he had taken his life by walking into the ocean and just swimming away. The maid informed Ms. Anderson what was going on when she arrived at his residence for lunch. She spent a few hours making calls to some of his friends and regular places he visited, to no avail. The police weren't called until about an hour ago."

Jake was shaking his head throughout Mali's entire report. "So he's been gone somewhere in the neighborhood of eleven hours. Jesus." Rubbing his jaw with his hand, he looked at Mali.

"I've called the local field office in the Malibu-Los Angeles area. They are meeting the police in Malibu and will call us as soon as they have more information."

"Good." He paused, breathing heavily. "Dammit, Adams could be anywhere. We have no clues, no leads, nothing to go on for either case. Who the hell is behind this?"

"We'll get our arms around it Jake."

"But how many more lives will be lost before we do?" was his response.

When Frank arrived shortly after seven, Jake called the team together again.

"Okay. We have one hour. Where are we?" He wasted no time. "Hoop?"

"I spoke with the local agents in Malibu. After Adams spoke with his lawyer, he told his maid he was going for a walk on the beach. He told her to have lunch ready for them at eleven thirty. He would have left for the beach around seven thirty. A couple who were playing on the beach with their toddler said they noticed him enter the beach but he headed the other way. No one else was on the beach. Beyond his house on the left are a number of houses that stretch for miles. They are still canvasing the residents to determine if anyone saw Adams. I cross-referenced the list of his accusers, that the D.A.'s office provided me, with Tom Martin's accusers. No one is on both lists. The only connector between the two cases, at this point, is they were both accused of sexual intimidation and harassment, and the rape of minors."

"So no real leads," Jake stated.

Mali shook her head.

"Felix, what can you tell me about the code, the network, how it's broadcast. Can we remove the app like Parler was removed?"

"There is a lot of code to cover. What we know for sure, though, is what was stated on the privacy page of the app holds true. Users, comments, the poll…everything is untraceable and will be removed. The next time we enter the app, nothing will be there except new stuff. That means there are no leads from the list of comments made. Users are unidentifiable." He paused. "Amy and Brad are still reviewing the code but I may have discovered something."

All eyes turned to Felix.

"I'm pretty sure they're using blockchain technology. Blockchain is not my specialty, but if that's the case, they're using it in a way I've never seen before."

"What is blockchain technology?" asked Mali.

"The most basic way to describe it, without getting into HOW it works, is that a blockchain removes the central authority governing the way we do business today. It does this by time-stamping records of data which is managed by a cluster, or group, of computers not owned by any single entity. Each of these blocks of data is bound to each other using cryptographic principles, stuff I don't need to get into. The point is these blocks of data are bound together to form the chain. Without a central authority, all data is transparent, there is no transaction cost, and it's safe. No one can hack it. It removes the middleman and can replace all business models that rely on charging a small fee for a transaction."

"So something like GoFundMe uses this technology?" asked Kirsten.

"That's the right idea but I don't believe GoFundMe is using it yet, I'd have to check. Finance has the strongest use case for using this technology, think cryptocurrency like Bitcoin. But it can expand to any industry. Let me give you an example. Take any service, the middleman that charges a fee to connect you to the right provider—Angie's List, Uber, Reedsy, Airbnb, to name a few. Let's take Uber. You search for a car ride from point A to point B. You're given a few cars that are in the area, select the one you want and you pay a fee. Uber gets the fee and pays a portion of it to the driver, keeping the rest. With blockchains, you encode that transactional information for the car ride, cutting out the middleman. The entire fee goes to the driver. No more Uber. We live in a peer-to-peer society, with all the social media and everything that exists today, so it's a natural progression. An early example of the use of this technology is eBay."

"Wow!" exclaimed Susan.

"I'm not completely following," said Jake. "Nor do I understand how that applies to the LadyJustice app. We weren't charged a fee to join."

"True. But the same principle could apply, just without a fee. If I'm right, everyone who joins is, in essence, part of the chain. That's why all their information is protected and untraceable. I believe the app itself is part of the chain, probably the start of it. Or it could all just be on a blockchain network. Bottom line, the app probably won't provide any leads whatsoever. Amy and Brad are working to verify if my suspicions are correct."

"Dammit. So with fifteen minutes to go, we are no further along in figuring out what the hell is going on!" Jake's voice rose with each word he spoke.

No one said anything.

"I do have some news," said Jeff. When all eyes were on him, he continued. "We're ready to test the ghost."

CHAPTER EIGHT

BEFORE ANYONE COULD respond, the alarm sounded and all nine screens blinked.

"#JusticePrevails is active again," said Joe, as Twitter opened.

"Justice is about to be served. Go to LadyJustice to observe."

Joe replaced Twitter with the LadyJustice app and entered his username, Gonnafly.

James Adams appeared on the screen in a livestream. He stood outside against a white background, arms tied to something behind him. He could only be seen from the waist up, his chest was bare. His eyes were squinting and his normally tanned skin was bright red.

"Can anyone tell where he is?" asked Frank.

"Wherever he is, he's been there for awhile," said Mali. "Look how…"

Kirsten interrupted. "Sorry Mali. Joe, give me one of the screens. People are already commenting on Twitter. Goes without saying I'll capture everything." She swiped her finger to send what she wanted on the screen to Joe.

Joe nodded and proceeded to add Twitter to the lower right corner screen.

"Good Lord," said Frank, as he read the comments.

"Is that really him?"

"Oh, baby. Come to mama!"

"This has to be an act, right?"

"Of course it's an act. He's an actor who's on his way out. It's just a publicity stunt."

"I don't know. Looks real to me."

"Real or not, this is exciting. I wonder if they'll really use a crossbow on him."

"He deserves it if he did what they're saying."

"Good riddance to the pedophile is what I say."

"He's hot."

"You right about that!"

"No, I'm mean wherever he is, he's hot. Look at the sweat pouring off his face and it's really burnt. That's going to hurt later."

"He won't care later."

"Ha ha…good one."

The comments continued.

"Unbelievable," said Jake.

"No one deserves what he's going through," agreed Mali.

The backside of a woman entered the picture, wearing a white shirt and khaki pants.

"State your name, please." The voice was altered as with the Martin video.

Adams turned his head to the right to look at the

woman and camera behind her. "You know who I am," he spat out.

"That's pretty arrogant of you to assume everyone who is watching this knows you. I will ask again. What is your name?"

Breathing heavily, eyes narrowed, his stance defiant despite his circumstances, he replied, "James Adams."

"And you have worked in Hollywood as an actor and producer for decades, correct?"

"Yes."

"You are scheduled to be arrested tomorrow and charged with statutory rape, sexual harassment, and sexual intimidation. Is that true, Jimmy?"

"It's James. And, yes, although none of it is true. Any sexual relations I've had have been consensual, and enjoyable by both parties, I might add." His lip curled into a smirk as he looked directly at the camera.

"Including your eleven-year-old co-star, Jenna Langley, in your first movie when you were just thirteen? Or how about any of the other seven women who have come forward saying you forced them to perform various sexual acts on you and your friends when they were minors on the promise of successful acting careers?"

"I have never forced anyone to do anything they didn't want to do. If they chose to participate to get ahead quickly, that was on them."

"So you admit you and your friends had fun with minors."

His eyes widened, and his facade slipped, as he realized what he had said.

"No, that's not what I meant."

"Terry Sampson, your latest discovery and a rapidly rising star, said two years ago, when she was just fourteen, you and five friends cornered her in your pool cabana during a party and forced her to have sex. She went on to describe in detail what all of you did to her in your drunken haze."

"That's a lie! She came on to me, said she'd do anything for a part in my movie."

In a hard voice, she continued, "You are doing yourself no favors by continuing with your lies and arrogance. She was a child and you took advantage of her, period. Admit it. Confess your sins and release your soul from the bonds of misogyny."

"You're nuts! I love women, always have."

"Really, I've noticed all the girls you've abused have similar features, petite, long blonde hair, green eyes. Hmmm. Perhaps you're right. Maybe you don't hate all women, maybe it's just your mother. She has those same characteristics. Did she abuse you when you were young, Jimmy?"

Beneath his sunburnt face, Adams paled. "How did you…? That's not true," he whispered.

Voice softening, she asked, "Have you been taking out your hatred of your mother on all those girls?"

"No. I love them and only want them to succeed." He paused, looking up toward the sky before returning his pleading eyes to hers. "Please."

"Please what, Jimmy? Free yourself from the shackles that bind you. Face your past so you can make amends."

Tears rolled down his cheeks and his chest began to shake.

The woman lit a cigarette, smoking in silence as she watched him.

"Oh my God," said Kirsten. "How does that woman get all this information, an upcoming arrest, abused as a child? My heart almost goes out to him. Others think so too. Look at the comments."

"What a lost soul."

"He just needs a hug."

"Oh, poor man. I feel so sorry for him."

"Who knew behind that sexy face lay such a tortured soul."

"Give me a break, ladies. He's a pedophile and he's an actor. He can turn on the tears easier than I can take a piss."

Frank said, "We are helpless here. How can we stop this?"

No one answered as Adams started to speak again.

"My dad left us when I was ten years old. According to my mother, that made me the man of the house, in every sense of the word. She pushed me into acting when I was twelve, said I was so handsome. In those early days, she brought the girls to me. She told me my acting would be more believable, the relationships more real on camera, if I had sex with them. She was right. I won an award for my first movie and so did Jenna. After that, I wanted to continue the glory and I didn't see any harm. There was glory for them too. Every person I've been with has had a great career. They have ME to thank for that. I can't believe anyone is complaining."

The woman tossed her cigarette toward the ground and straightened, her body rigid.

"The lack of remorse for what you've done, and the way in which you justify it, is appalling. You are a pedophile, the lowest of humans. You have used your position to intimidate and coerce girls into sexual situations. You don't deserve to live." She paused. "Do you recognize where you are?"

He shook his head. "Los Angeles is below us in the distance, we're in the hills somewhere."

"That's right. It's only fitting your life should end as you lord over the land." She stepped sideways out of the view of the camera.

"Wait! Don't do this!" he shouted. "No! No! No!"

Pfffft! A bolt was released from an unseen bow. It slammed into James Adams, hitting him squarely in his chest.

There was a collective gasp from everyone in the room as blood spewed out from Adams' mouth, the force of the bolt pushing his body back. They watched shock cross his face before the light faded from his eyes and his head dropped to his chest.

"I'm going to be sick," said Kirsten. Hand covering her mouth, she turned and raced to the restroom.

The camera drone zoomed out and out and out until the famous Hollywood sign was visible, Adams a mere speck on the first L. Justice Prevails flashed on the screen seconds before the livestream ended.

CHAPTER NINE

Mali's apartment
Wednesday, August 19, 8:00 a.m.

MALI DIDN'T RECOGNIZE the person who stared back at her from the bathroom mirror. Her eyes were sunken in their sockets with dark circles beneath them, their usual brightness dulled from lack of sleep. Thoughts of Daniel and his threats plus this case had taken its toll. Her face was so pale she looked like a ghost. She laughed at that. *Makeup isn't going to fix this.* While she felt a little more human after showering and preparing for the day, she feared the perpetual frown she wore would give rise to early wrinkles. Walking into the living room she turned on the news, only to cringe as she flipped through the channels. James Adams' murder was splashed everywhere. There was a mixture of sadness, outrage at what Adams had done, demands for the FBI to take action and find justice for him, and even many who suggested justice was already served. Mali turned off the television with a sigh and strode in to the kitchen to make coffee. She was exhausted and the day had barely begun.

At five minutes to nine, she rode the elevator downstairs and prepared to leave her apartment building, having agreed to be the test subject for the ghost. She reached the door leading outside and paused. The ghost was supposed to be waiting somewhere out there and would track Mali to work. Taking a deep breath, she pulled it open and stepped outside.

Honking horns blared in the distance and boats of assorted sizes chugged by on the Hudson. Birds chirped in the trees. A squirrel scuttled past her to jump on the trunk of the nearest one and race up its branches. Her eyes roamed the area, taking everything in. Life going on as usual, only this wasn't a usual day.

She jumped and placed a hand on her fluttering stomach when there was a rustle in the bushes along the wall. Turning her head, she took a deep, calming breath when a black cat crept from its depths. Shaking her head, she shrugged and headed to the subway. *I need to get a grip.*

As she waited for a red light to turn green, she absently swatted at something buzzing around her head. She was startled when someone tapped her on the shoulder.

She turned around. Daniel stood there with a big grin on his face.

"What are you doing here, Daniel?"

"Hey, baby," he cooed, grabbing her hand and squeezing. "Is that any way to greet your husband."

Mali's jaw tightened and she shoved him away. "Let go of me!"

"I'm just here to remind you I'll be by for my money later tonight. Don't forget. And remember, I'll call your boss if you don't have it."

Her heart was pounding and her nostrils flared, fisted hands resting on her hips, as she glared at him.

"What are you going to do? Hit me?" he laughed as he looked her up and down.

"Stay away from me!"

She turned and fled across the street, ignoring the honking horns, Daniel's laughter trailing after her.

By the time she reached the stairs to the station, her erratic breathing was under control. She pulled out her phone and called Jake.

"What was that all about?" Jake asked in alarm as soon as they connected.

"I guess I don't have to ask if the ghost is here."

"It's standing right next to you, on your left side."

"Really?"

"Yes, and it has been with you since you stepped outside your apartment."

"Can everyone hear me?" She looked to the left and didn't notice anything out of the ordinary. Raising her arm to her side, shoulder-height, she waved it up and down.

"You put your arm right through it."

"That is downright spooky. What am I wearing?"

"You're wearing your usual suit with white tennis shoes. I'm assuming your heels are in the black bag hanging on your shoulder. And, no, no one can hear you. Answer the question."

"This is creepy." She ignored his question. "I'm headed to the subway. I'm assuming the ghost won't be able to follow me."

"That is correct. We'll see you when you exit the subway station." Jake hung up.

Mali turned her head to the left again and stuck out her tongue before jogging down the steps into the station.

When she exited a few blocks from the warehouse, she decided to take a long route to try to lose the ghost. Instead of turning left, she turned right and picked up her pace until she was jogging. She cut across the street and ducked into an alley, picking up the pace and racing around the corner to the next street. She continued down the street for a few blocks at a brisk walk then circled back to the warehouse and entered, waving to Becky as she walked past her. Upon exiting the elevator, she was greeted with cheers and jokes about being afraid of ghosts.

"Nice try, Hoop," said Joe, adding, "I like how you took care of that clown who was bothering you."

"Did you really think you'd outrun the ghost? A ghost never tires, by the way," joked Jeff.

"Sticking out your tongue was the kicker, though," laughed Felix.

Jake stood silent, feet apart, arms folded across his chest, glowering.

Kirsten was also silent, concern etched on her face.

"You guys have no idea how strange and unsettling it was knowing a ghost was following me, and witnessed everything I did. Good thing I didn't pick my nose or anything."

Everyone laughed, as she intended, except Jake and Kirsten.

"Did the ghost work as designed?" asked Jake, without taking his eyes off Mali.

"For the most part, yes. There were a couple of spotty moments when we lost Hoop and shouldn't have. Fortunately, we added a recording capability that automatically turns on when the ghost appears and then turns off when the ghost disappears. We need to review the tape and assess this first test run."

"Go ahead and review it now. Hoop and I have to talk. We'll all meet in twenty minutes to discuss your findings plus I want to update the team on our conversation with the local field office in L.A. last night, the fallout that has begun, and assign tasks."

He turned and strode to the conference table, placing two whiteboards between the table and the rest of the room so there would be a semblance of privacy.

Finally sensing something wasn't right, and looking from Mali to Jake and back again, the chatter ended and everyone returned to their work, one-by-one.

Mali sighed then, chin up, turned and followed Jake.

"Who was that?" he asked without preamble as soon as she sat.

"That was Daniel, my ex. He showed up at my apartment two nights ago and is threatening to go to the FBI with some lies if I don't fork over twenty-five grand tonight. What you witnessed was a reminder from him."

The air deflated out of Jake, taking his anger with it. "Jesus. Why didn't you tell me?"

Mali sighed. "I was going to yesterday but then everything happened with James Adams and the case. Honestly, I was too drained to bring it up."

Mali's hands were clasped together on the table, knuckles white and nails digging into her skin. Jake placed his hand on top of both, the warmth seeping into her hands and through the rest of her body. She looked down at their connected hands and blinked rapidly refusing to let her tears fall.

"Before everything happened, you said we needed to talk. You were going to tell me then?"

Mali nodded, still looking down.

"You've seen my records, Jake, and had no clue I was married until I told you. I could be fired for lying on my application."

"You're not going to be fired. We'll go together to talk to Frank after we meet with the team."

She closed her eyes then removed one of her hands and placed it on top of his, squeezing. Opening her eyes, she looked up at him. "Thank you. I've been so worried."

"I can see that." He lifted his other hand and wiped away the single tear that had escaped. "Come on. Let's have that meeting then go to Frank's office."

* * *

Mali's apartment
Wednesday, August 19, 10:32 p.m.

THE MEETING WITH Frank went much better than Mali expected. He said he understood and, no, she wasn't being fired but a mild letter of reprimand would be added to her file. He also instructed Jake to return home with Mali and arrest Daniel when he showed up for attempting to extort money from a federal officer. The relief she felt had poured off her in waves.

Jake had returned home with her and they had been waiting for Daniel ever since.

"He didn't say what time he'd be here?" Jake asked as he took a bottle of water out of the refrigerator.

"For the umpteenth time, he gave no timeframe, just told me to be here with the money." Mali leaned back on the sofa and closed her eyes. "Maybe he watched you enter with me and decided not to come," she stated without opening her eyes.

"That's possible. He may have realized the gig is up and he's not getting a penny."

Lips pursed, her only response was "Hmmmm…" Her breathing slowed.

When Jake put his hand on her shoulder, she jumped.

Smiling, he said, "He's not going to show. We're both exhausted. Go to bed, I'll sleep here on the couch."

"You don't have to stay, Jake. You're right, for whatever reason, he's not coming."

"I'd feel better staying. I'll get up early and head

home so I can shower and change then get Heather off to school."

Mali nodded. Smiling her thanks, she went into the bedroom and returned with towels, sheets, a pillow, and a blanket. When she walked up to him, he pulled her into his arms, everything squished between them, and leaned down to kiss her. Nuzzling her nose, he smiled down at her.

"You look much less stressed. Will you be able to sleep?" His eyes turned laser hot as he stared at her. "If not, I'd be happy to help." Voice thickening, he pulled her even closer.

Mali gave herself over to her feelings, shoving the bedding from between them so she could embrace him fully. She moved her hands up and around his neck, playing with the hair at his nape, as she closed her eyes and breathed deeply. His scent intoxicated her.

Jake moaned, moving his hands down to her buttocks and squeezing them before yanking her against him so she could feel how much he wanted her. His kiss this time was not platonic. His tongue delved into the sweetness of her mouth, sucking on her tongue like it was nectar. She groaned, her body moving of its own accord seeking its mate.

Unbidden, an image of Daniel and another popped into her mind, dousing the flames threatening to overtake her. She pulled away, first removing her hands from his neck and placing them on his chest, then ending their kiss and pushing against his chest until they stood a foot apart.

Both were breathing heavily, trying to catch their breath. Mali peeked up at him, wincing when she saw his stony look.

"I…" She cleared her throat.

"You know I want to take our relationship to the next level, right?"

Mali nodded. "Jake, I…"

Jake rubbed his neck, his look softening. "I get you're not ready, although I'm not exactly sure why. But I can wait. I just need to know you want more at some point as well."

Mali's face softened as she reached up to cup his cheek, her eyes liquid silver. "I do want that, Jake." She paused, looking down at his white shirt. "There are things I need to tell you about my past I'm not yet ready to discuss." She gazed back into his eyes. "I appreciate your patience, more than you know."

The disappointment in his eyes was unmistakable but it was fleeting, replaced by understanding and something more. He took a deep breath, kissed her on her forehead, then pulled away.

"I need a cold shower." He leaned down and picked up the towel, walking into Mali's bedroom without another word. He didn't notice Mali's blush.

After taking a few more deep breaths, Mali made a bed on the sofa for him with the bedding that had fallen on the floor. After that task was completed, she walked to the kitchen, grabbed a glass and filled it with water, gulping it down.

She had just placed the glass in the sink when Jake

walked out of her bedroom, wearing his pants but no shirt.

Mali gulped, ogling his chest.

"Keep looking at me like that and we will continue what we started," he growled as he sauntered to the sofa.

Mali jumped, blushing as she walked briskly toward her bedroom. "Yes, well…Thank you, again, for your help."

"Mali."

She stopped as she was about to escape into her bedroom.

"It's okay to ask for help. I'm here for you."

She turned to look at him. "I know, that means so much."

"I'll be gone before you wake up. Get a good night's rest and I'll see you tomorrow."

Mali nodded then walked into her bedroom, closing the door behind her.

* * *

Kirsten and Jen's place, Greenwich Village
Saturday, August 22, 11:05 a.m.

A cacophony of noise greeted Mali as she knocked on Kirsten and Jen's door. Today was the monthly get-together with her three BFFs, Kirsten, Jen, and Sara. They rotated locales, and today it was Kirsten and Jen's turn to host.

Jen and Mali were college roommates, back in the day. Mali had introduced Jen to Kirsten at a Christmas party a few years back and they'd been together ever since. She had always believed they were a good fit and complemented each other. Both loved their jobs and worked long hours, Kirsten was somewhat laid back and introverted whereas Jen was a complete extrovert and very colorful both in her personality and the clothes she wore. On the other hand, Mali had known Sara the longest. They had met at summer camp when they were ten years old, felt an immediate kinship and had been inseparable as friends ever since. Of the four of them, Sara was the only one who was married and she had three kids, all of whom were Mali's godchildren. She loved being a mom and wife and focused all her energy on them. Mali always counted on Sara's down-to-earth viewpoint and her honest assessments.

Jen answered the door holding a scrap of a chihuahua, still barking quite ferociously. "Mali, hi! I'm so glad you're here. I'd give you a hug but Marco might bite your nose," she said with a laugh.

Mali laughed as she walked past her and the little terror. "I haven't forgotten the last time I was here and that beast nipped my fingers."

"Hey Mali." Kirsten walked over, a growling bundle in her arms that looked more like a toy than a chihuahua. She took Marco from Jen and headed to bedroom. "I meant to have Marco and Polo hidden in the bedroom before your arrival. Sorry about that." She disappeared around the corner.

"I'm always amazed how two such small creatures can make so much noise. And they don't like anyone but you two." Mali chuckled, shaking her head as she hugged Jen then moved further into the room.

"Whew! They're a handful but we love them," said Kirsten when she returned.

Mali admired their place. The contemporary, sparse home was so different from her own. Everything was gray, black and white except for the splash of red cushions on their sofa. No knick knacks. No pictures, except for three prints hanging on the wall above the linear fireplace. Their place always reminded Mali of a futuristic world, which somehow suited them given Kirsten's IT background.

"Something smells good," said Mali as the doorbell rang.

"A spinach and cheese quiche is in the oven," Kirsten said as the door was opened and Sara sailed in to a round of hello's.

"What can I get everyone to drink?" asked Jen as Sara and Mali settled on the sofa.

"Water for me right now," said Sara. "Tom and I had friends at the house last night and I drank two glasses of wine. I'm paying the price today."

Everyone laughed and ribbed Sara for being a such light-weight.

Mali said, "White wine sounds delightful. It's almost twelve o'clock, right?" She smiled.

"You look so much better today, Mali." Kirsten stated when they all had their drinks in hand. "Between the case and Daniel showing up, I was really worried."

Mali reached over and squeezed Kirsten's hand.

"Thank you. I am feeling much better. While the case is at a standstill, for all practical purposes, Daniel never showed up on Wednesday."

"Showed up for what?" asked Jen.

"Yeah, what do you mean?" asked Kirsten. "We haven't had a chance to really talk since Wednesday when we saw him."

"You saw him?" asked Jen, eyebrows raised as she looked at her partner.

"Um...not in person, but I couldn't say so." She shrugged. "Sorry."

"Daniel found me earlier in the week and tried to extort twenty-five thousand dollars from me. He said he'd go to the FBI with some elaborate lies unless I gave him the money on Wednesday."

"Oh my God!" exclaimed Jen. "What an asshole! I hope you put him in his place."

"Not at first. Seeing him really threw me for a loop. But he approached me on Wednesday morning and I told him a thing or two then." She shrugged. "I told Jake about it," at which point Sara smiled, "and we both met with Frank. All is good on the work front. Jake stayed at my place Wednesday night, just to be safe. But Daniel never showed. We figure he realized his threat had gone south and split. Good riddance is what I say." She shrugged.

"Whoa. Back up. Jake spent the night at your place?" asked Kirsten, eyebrows raised, a naughty smile on her face.

"He slept on the couch and I was in my bedroom."

"Well that's no fun," said Jen with a laugh when she noticed Kirsten rolling her eyes.

Everyone laughed.

Changing subjects, "Jen, how did your big charity police fundraiser event go? From the news report, it sounded like a tremendous success."

Jen's eyes lit up. "It was amazing, Mali! We raised more than one hundred and sixty-five thousand dollars between the price per plate and the silent auction. Thank you, by the way, for suggesting that AND for the donation from your parents of a two-night stay at The Ritz including dinner for two. That brought in five thousand alone."

"My parents enjoy giving to a worthy cause. I'm so happy it was a success."

"What a coup for you," added Sara.

Kirsten wrapped her arm around Jen, who was sitting, cross-legged, next to her on the floor by the coffee table. "People have finally taken notice of Jen and her abilities. It's about time, I say."

Jen smiled and blushed. "Awww, shucks, you guys." Laughing, she stood. "Lunch is about ready. Head to the table while I get the quiche. Kirsten, grab the fruit salad from the refrigerator."

Lunch was a mixture of jokes, laughter, and appreciative noises from everyone for the delicious, yet simple, meal.

They were just finishing dessert when Mali's phone rang.

"I'm sorry guys. I forgot to silence it." Mali stood

and walked to her purse. As she reached for the phone, it stopped ringing. She picked it up anyway to silence it, noticing Jake had called. "That was Jake. I'll call him when I get home," she said. As she was sitting back down at the table, she frowned when her phone buzzed again.

"Go ahead and answer it, Mali. If it's Jake calling again, it might be important," said Kirsten.

Mali smiled her thanks and walked back to her purse.

"Hey, what's up?" she asked as she looked out the window.

"Daniel Matthews is dead. I'll be at Kirsten's in ten."

CHAPTER TEN

MALI SANK INTO the nearest chair, her phone dropping to the floor unnoticed.

"Mali!" Sara jumped out of her chair and rushed to Mali, Kirsten and Jen right behind her. "What is it? What happened?"

Mali raised a shaky hand and brushed a tendril of hair away from her pale face. "That was Jake. Daniel is dead," she whispered.

"What? How? When?" asked Kirsten.

"I don't know. Jake's on his way here." She stared at them. "I couldn't stand him and was furious with what he was trying to do, but I would never wish him dead."

"Of course not, hon," said Jen, rubbing her arm.

Her friends were still consoling her when the doorbell rang, setting off a round of vigorous muffled barking from Marco and Polo back in the bedroom.

Jen went to the door and opened it, saying, "Hi, you must be Jake. I'm Jen."

"Nice to meet you, Jen." Jake stepped inside, his roaming eyes stopping when they landed on Mali, who was now standing with Kirsten and Sara.

Jake walked over to her. "Are you alright?"

Mali took a deep breath and nodded. "I will be." She looked at Sara then back at Jake. "Jake, this is Sara. Sara, Jake."

"It's nice to meet you, Sara. Mali has said many good things about you, about all of you," he said, as he looked at everyone. "I hate to break up your monthly get-together but Mali and I need to discuss a few things."

"Of course," said Kirsten.

Mali picked up her purse and hugged everyone, promising to call them later.

When Jake pulled away from the curb, Mali turned to him. "How did Daniel die?"

"He was shot outside the Show Palace, listed as a John Doe because he didn't have ID. His identity was released a couple of hours ago."

"My God. He was murdered? What is Show Palace?"

"It's a gentlemen's club in Long Island City, about ten minutes outside Manhattan."

Mali shook her head. "Why am I not surprised."

At the next red stop light, Jake watched her. "Daniel was shot at around ten minutes to nine...Wednesday evening."

Mali's jaw dropped. "That's why he was a no-show."

Jake nodded.

"Why didn't he have his ID? He would have needed it to get into a place like that, wouldn't he?"

"The Show Palace said he showed his ID to enter and at the bar. It's mandatory. The bartender remembered him because he was the first to arrive when they opened at seven and he ordered a couple shots of whiskey then handed him a card asking him to keep an open tab. The police said his wallet was not on him when they arrived at the scene."

"So it doesn't have anything to do with JusticePrevails? It was a robbery?"

"Apparently so. That's how they're classifying it."

A thought struck Mali. "Where did you get this information?"

"I made a few calls on Wednesday night after you went to bed and asked some contacts of mine to keep their ear to the ground. One of them called me this morning. I confirmed it with the police and coroner."

When the light turned green, Jake continued down the street. "I contacted Frank with an update. He said to put that chapter behind you and carry on. I agree."

They didn't say anything for the remainder of the drive to Mali's apartment, each lost in their own thoughts. When Jake pulled up to her entrance, he placed the car in park and turned toward her, arm resting on the back of the seat.

"I'm sorry I interrupted your day but I wanted you to hear the news from me."

"I appreciate that, thank you. This is all so unreal."

Jake nodded.

"Do you want to come up for a little while."

"I can't. Dad and I are taking Heather to the movies and McDonalds this afternoon."

Mali smiled. "I bet that's her favorite kind of outing."

"She loves those chicken McNuggets." Jake turned serious. "Are you going to be alright?"

"Of course. Thank you for telling me and for bringing me home. I plan to sit on the balcony a good part of the afternoon contemplating life." She smiled.

Jake leaned in and kissed her gently. "Try to get some rest."

Mali nodded, saying good-bye as she exited the car.

After setting her things down, Mali poured herself a glass of iced tea then went out to the balcony, sinking into her favorite chair and putting her now bare feet on the railing. The Hudson was busy this Saturday, as it was most days actually. She observed a tanker in the distance slowly making its way out to sea. Numerous sailboats, sails fully extended, passed by as well as a few speedboats that were weaving between them. There was even a pontoon chugging along. The choppy water splashed the sides of the boats and sometimes the occupants. She chuckled when she caught sight of a woman, who was leaning a little too far over the side of a pontoon, getting drenched by a passing speedboat. Mali couldn't hear what was being said, but from her erratic arm movement and body language, it was obvious the woman was angry.

Feeling calmer, Mali called her mother.

"Jasmine, how nice of you to return my call from four days ago."

Mali rolled her eyes. Her relationship with her parents was much improved after nearly being killed a few months ago, but some things never changed.

"Hello Mother. How are you and Father doing?"

"We're very busy preparing for your Father's upcoming business anniversary. Thirty years is a long time. As you know, we are planning a week of activities starting the first week of September, culminating in a dinner party on September Fifth, the date they officially opened. While I understand you can't participate in everything, I expect you to attend the dinner party on the fifth. It's a Saturday."

Ugh. "Mother, I can't promise to be there. We are involved in a tough case and I'm not sure I can get away."

"Jasmine Suzanne, you are entitled to a break from work. You haven't seen your father's partner in years and he always asks after you. It would be an insult not only to him but to your Father as well if you don't attend." Her mother's tone brooked no argument.

Willow was a force to be reckoned with. Mali closed her eyes and rubbed her face, knowing she was stuck.

"I expect you to arrive on Saturday morning. Plan to spend the night. You can bring Jake, as well as his father and daughter, if you'd like. We'd enjoy meeting them."

"I'll talk to Jake."

"Excellent!" Willow exclaimed, her tone much brighter. "The color scheme is rose and antique white. It's a formal dinner so plan to wear an appropriate dress in a rose color. Your sisters, naturally, will do the same."

Naturally. The Hooper sisters always dressed similarly. It was expected.

"I've got to go, Mother. I'll call you later this week to confirm."

After they hung up, Mali went back inside, her peaceful mood shattered.

Mali had just finished a light dinner of taco salad with guacamole when her doorbell rang. Not expecting anyone, she frowned and walked to the door. No one was there when she looked through the peep hole so she slowly opened it. A small brown package sat on the doormat. She looked to the left and then to the right but the hallway was empty. Curious, she reached down and slowly picked it up, noticing there was no return address. She sniffed it and shook it gently before going inside and closing the door. Setting the package down on the dining table, she walked into the kitchen and poured herself a glass of white wine. Returning to the dining table, Mali looked at the package as she stood sipping her wine.

When her glass was empty, she placed it on the table and reached for the package, first smelling it again then tearing one side open. Wrapped in delicate pink tissue was a silver tin box. She lifted the lid off the tin and gasped. Her breathing quickened as she stared at the card, HER card, from the HuntedLives game. The card had an outline of the New York City skyline and an image of a Swastika-shaped Shuriken. She dropped down onto the dining chair never taking her eyes of the card. Her heart felt like it was going to burst from her chest. Taking a few deep breaths, she reached for her wine glass, frowning when she realized it was empty. Returning her attention to the card, she picked it up and flipped it over. WINNER was hand-written on the back.

Her phone rang, startling her into dropping the card. With a shaking hand, she answered.

"Agent Hooper! I trust you received my little gift. I thought you'd appreciate my gesture and the memento from your game."

"Janet!"

"Who else, darling? It's been awhile and I've been very busy, but I just wanted to congratulate you on winning."

Could this day get any more surreal and horrifying?

Straightening in her chair and strengthening her resolve, she decided to try for some answers. "Why did you kill your brother, Janet? Why kill Rebecca Smith? And what happened with Dr. Dubois?"

"Tsk, tsk. So many questions, Agent Hooper, questions I'm not inclined to answer. Besides, that's in the past. I'm much more interested in the present." She paused. "Are you enjoying JusticePrevails?"

Mali's headed snapped back as Janet's words sunk in. *Janet's behind the latest killings?*

Her mind awhirl with questions, Mali took the offensive. "Are you going after pedophiles because you were abused as a child? Is that why you killed Anthony? Did he abuse you when you were younger?"

Janet's voice hardened. "I said I'm not inclined to look backward. Only forward…as should you." Mali could hear a slight crinkling, burning noise of a cigarette as Janet inhaled the smoke.

"What is that supposed to mean?"

After blowing it out, she continued. "Everyone has secrets, wouldn't you agree?"

Mali didn't answer.

"Justice prevails in many ways, Agent Hooper. Take your ex, Daniel Matthews, for example. He is now dead which simplifies things for you, right? I took care of him so you, too, can move forward instead of looking back."

Mali's head spun. Black dots danced in front her eyes and her stomach churned. She wasn't sure if she was going to pass out or throw up.

"I'll be back in touch later. You can thank me then. Oh, and be sure to say hello to Agent Black. He really is quite delicious." The line went dead.

Throw up, yep, she was definitely going to throw up. Racing to the bathroom, she reached the toilet just as she emptied her taco salad into the bowl. She heaved repeatedly, the taste in her mouth and the odor emanating from the toilet urging her on until her empty stomach ached and she sank to the floor. Tears flowed from her eyes as the ramifications of all Janet told her sank in. She wrapped her arms around her legs and squeezed hard, trying to stop shaking.

Mali had no idea how long she sat on the bathroom floor but she finally pulled herself up using the vanity for support. Splashing her face with icy water and rinsing her mouth, she turned and stumbled back to the dining room. She grabbed her phone, avoiding eye contact with the card, and shuffled back to her bedroom. Sitting down on the bed, she placed her hand across her stomach, lightly rubbing it, and dialed Jake's number.

"Hey beautiful."

Mali glance at the clock. *Nine twenty.*

"I received a little gift, if you can call it that." Her laugh bordered hysteria.

"What's going on?"

"The card that would have been left on my chest had I lost the HuntedLives game was on my doorstep. And I got a phone call. Janet Simpson is alive."

CHAPTER ELEVEN

Bay Ridge, Brooklyn, Frank's house
Sunday, August 23, 9:30 a.m.

AFTER MALI'S CALL, and ignoring her objections, Jake had immediately gone to her place. After studying the card, they agreed to table any conversation until the morning when they were with Frank. Mali had fussed that they would be interrupting Frank's weekend but Jake told her Frank insisted they come over.

Now standing at Frank's home, Jake rang the door-bell.

Carol Grant opened the door. Normally a jovial woman, she took one look at Mali and ushered them in, wrapping her in a motherly hug. "I haven't seen you since that horrible game ended and now this. How are you holding up?" she asked as she guided them into the living room.

"It's all a bit unsettling but I'm doing alright. Thank you, Carol. It's really good to see you." She smiled at Carol then looked around the room. Theirs was a happy home. The warm color tones, all the family pictures on the mantle, the various farm prints on the walls in honor of Frank's childhood, all spoke of love. Returning her attention to Carol, she asked, "How are the boys?"

Frank and Carol had two sons, Kevin and Josh. They were active pre-teens, Kevin heavily involved in sports with Josh focused on chess. During the past two years, Mali had enjoying getting to know them and had even attended a few of Kevin's baseball games. While she wasn't a very good chess player, she had accepted Josh's challenge, losing both times. The boys were instrumental in helping Mali and Jake discover the HuntedLives game was a real version of The Hunted Ones game, a popular hunting app.

"The boys have had a great summer. They're currently in Florida with their grandparents. They've been gone for three weeks and have had a wonderful time at Disney World and the beach, but I've missed them and look forward to their return. Just four more days and my babies will be back."

"Don't get her started, Hoop, or she'll be weeping buckets." Frank laughed as he walked into the room.

"Oh you!" Carol sniffed and batted Frank's hand away. Turning to Jake and Mali, she added, "I'll leave you to talk with Frank. I have snacks prepared in the fridge. Make sure Frank pulls them out." With a wave, she grabbed her purse and headed out the door.

"Good morning, Jake, Hoop," said Frank as he urged them to sit down. "What can I get you to drink?"

"Water is fine," replied Mali.

"Same here," said Jake.

Frank disappeared into the kitchen, returning moments later with their water and a tray holding a large bowl of mixed fruit, three small plates, forks and napkins. He set everything down on the coffee table. Pulling the nearest chair closer, he sank into it, leaned forward and clasped his hands between his legs, all business now.

He looked at Mali. "Are you okay?"

She nodded.

"Did you bring the card?"

Jake pulled it out of his pocket and handed it to him.

Frank whistled, shaking his head as he studied first one side then the other. "And she said she killed Daniel Matthews?"

"Her exact words were that she had taken care of him for me, sir."

He looked up, eyebrows raised.

"So I could move forward instead of looking back."

"How did she know Matthews was your ex? And could she have possibly known he was trying to extort money from you? If so, how?"

"I don't know."

"Did you tell anyone about his threats, other than Jake and myself?"

"Yes, my good friend, Sara. But she wouldn't tell anyone. She didn't even tell Kirsten and Jen."

"Kirsten Bellows?"

Mali nodded. "We've known each other since training, Jen was my college roommate."

"Simpson also said she's behind JusticePrevails?"

"Yes, I asked her if she was killing pedophiles, and if she killed her brother, because she was abused as a child. She didn't answer but got angry."

Jake added, "She plans to contact Mali again."

"Hmmm…." Changing subjects, "Knowing she's alive, can we use the ghost to find her."

He shook his head. "The ghost can't find, only track, and that's only outside of buildings."

"Do we know where she is?"

"No clue, but we might be able to trace her call the next time she contacts Mali," replied Jake. "I'm also wondering how she got Mali's number. You changed it after HuntedLives, right?"

"I changed my entire phone."

Jake frowned. "We have a lot to figure out, including how to find Janet. I've called everyone in, we're meeting at one."

"Good. Keep me informed."

Three hours later, after Jake gave a watered-down version of what had occurred, respecting Mali's privacy, he was sitting at the conference table with the rest of the team answering their questions while Mali wrote them on the whiteboard. Any question without an answer was followed by a question mark.

"So, we've identified who's behind this but we have no idea where she is or who her next target is," said Joe.

"That's correct."

Felix asked, "So why kill this Daniel Matthews person? He wasn't a known pedophile, was he? There was nothing about it on #JusticePrevails or the LadyJustice app."

Jake looked at Mali, leaving the decision to give more details up to her.

Drawing a breath, her eyes went around the conference table, before landing on Jake. She slowly let the air out of her lungs and responded. "Daniel Matthews was my ex-husband. He was trying to extort twenty-five thousand from me, threatening to go to the FBI with some lies."

Susan's mouth formed a perfect O, Felix whistled, Jeff said "Wow," all gawking at Mali, who shrugged.

"Sounds very personal and very creepy, especially if she plans to contact Mali again. How will she do it now that Mali has a different phone?" asked Susan.

"We don't know."

"Is Mali in danger? Simpson knows where she lives and is making this personal," added Kirsten, concern in her voice.

Mali shook her head. "We don't know that she's making this personal, Kirsten."

"You're kidding, right? She sends you your death card then kills your ex and you say it's not personal?" Kirsten's voice had risen with each word.

"I appreciate your concern, but even if this IS personal, I don't believe I'm in imminent danger. If Janet wanted me dead, she could have easily accomplished that since, as you pointed out, she knows where I live."

"I agree with Hoop...for now. And like it or not, Hoop is our only link to Janet." He stared at Kirsten first then Mali. "Which brings up my first task," said Jake. "We need to take steps to keep Hoop safe. I want the ghost to be positioned outside of Mali's entrance. Record everyone who goes in and out, and let's run each down. Follow Mali wherever she goes and watch for suspicious activity. We have an advantage in that Janet has no idea a ghost exists."

Joe said, "I'll take that."

"Good. Jeff, finish working any kinks out of the ghost. I want it fully operational today. I also want you to determine if we can have more than one ghost operating at a time. Can we place one or more ghosts with high-profile and/or wealthy people with active pedophile cases and track them, for example?"

"Even if we can do that," interrupted Felix, "won't it be like searching for a needle in a haystack? Which pedophiles do we monitor? Not to mention the fact that Adams wasn't even on anyone's radar and they got to him."

"Good questions. I'm just throwing out possible uses of multiple ghosts. Right now, we need to determine if it's even possible." Mali wrote down the questions as Jake continued. "Felix, continue working with the DC team. Is the blockchain technology you told us about in play here? Regardless, is there any way to hack into the app, turn it off, discover Simpson's whereabouts, anything that can help us? What can we glean from it?" He looked at Mali. "Research high-profile celebrities, CEOs, anyone with money who is under investigation for pedophilia, sex trafficking, etcetera. Put a list together of who they are, where they are physically right now, and where their case is. Let's notify the local field offices for each and get them involved in surveillance and protection." Jake took a drink of water. "I also want hidden security devices inside Mali's apartment and at her front door. Once set up, I want you to monitor it, Susan, in addition to the security here. Kirsten…"

Before he could continue, the console beeped and flashed red. "JusticePrevails is active again," said Joe as he rushed over, closely followed by everyone else.

* * *

"Twitter is directing everyone to a location in North Carolina on Periscope. This will be another live event," he said as he maneuvered to Periscope.

"If I remember correctly, Periscope indicates where the live action is taking place. Won't it take us directly to them?" asked Mali.

As everyone looked at the big screen, Kirsten replied, "Theoretically."

When Periscope opened, there was only one dot in North Carolina, Chapel Hill. Joe clicked the dot and they were standing on the side of a tree-lined road. People were walking here and there, some were riding bicycles, others jogging, a few carrying back packs.

"Where are we? How are we viewing this? Is the person using Periscope wearing a go-pro camera?" Jake rattled off the questions. As he spoke, the user turned to the right.

"Hard to say if it's a person or a drone but it looks like they're on a campus," said Felix.

Mali, who had opened her laptop and was staring at her screen said, "University of North Carolina in Chapel Hill. That's the bell tower."

"Jeff, I want the ghost there now! Kirsten, call our nearest field office and send them out there. Alert campus police."

The user meandered down the street and past the bell tower. The street was becoming more crowded with students on bikes and walking.

"We're just past the Wilson Library, it was across from the bell tower," said Mali. "The Student Stores and Student Union are coming up on the left which may explain why it's so crowded."

Jeff stated, "The ghost is there." He swiped to the left. "Joe, give me the bottom right screen."

Joe nodded and the street displayed from a different perspective.

"What am I supposed to be looking for?" asked Jeff, as he turned the ghost left and right. "There are too many people, they all look like students."

"We can't say, exactly, but it looks like you're in front of whoever is on Periscope. You've reached the Student Union but our guy is just coming up to the Student Stores. Turn around," stated Mali.

Everyone was looking from the Periscope view to the ghost's view for anything suspicious.

"Campus police are on their way to the Student Union," noted Kirsten. "So are two agents with the local field office. An Agent Tanner said he'd call when they arrive."

"If the user goes inside a building, we'll be blind," reminded Joe. The urgency in his voice was palpable.

"It's that guy," Felix near-shouted as he pointed to a man wearing a hoodie with jeans and was looking down at a black gadget he was carrying in his hands. "He's wearing a hoodie and that looks like an iPad or something in his hands."

Mali glanced at Felix and shook her head, not quite sure how a hoodie made him a suspect.

Jeff moved the ghost closer to the man Felix pointed out.

"Is there a camera? Get behind him, Jeff and look over his shoulder," said Joe.

"It's not him," grumbled Jake. "Look at the Periscope app. Movement has stopped and it's looking around. Damn it, it could be anyone!"

"Look down the road," said Susan. "The police have arrived."

So, too, evidently did the person on Periscope for he made a sharp turn and entered the student union.

Kirsten said, "I'm on the phone with campus police and I'm directing them into the union."

As she uttered the words, two things happened.

They watched the officers enter the building.

The Periscope view changed to a close-up of a man lying on a child's bed in what appeared to be a girl's room, given the pink bedspread he was lying on. His wrists and ankles were tied, spread-eagle, and he appeared to be asleep. His thin, bony frame was apparent even under the jeans and white t-shirt he wore, his feet were bare. He sported a sandy-brown beard beneath a long, pointed nose and a thick mop of blond hair on his head. *He looks a bit like a weasel.*

"What the hell?" asked Jake. "Are we on an app? YouTube? Facebook?"

"Periscope is no longer being used," stated Joe. "I'm trying to figure out what happened."

Felix shook his head in amazement. "Whoa. I've read about this capability but I've never seen it in action before."

All eyes shifted to Felix.

"It jumped to the LadyJustice app, Simpson has evidently opened the app to everyone, at least for this livestream."

"How did it do that?" asked Kirsten. "I've never even heard of that."

"Think of it like transporting in Star Trek, only instead of people, a livestream was transported. It's new technology they've been working on for gaming, allowing cross-over between games with similar functionality."

"So you could be playing one game then jump into another with your character?" asked Joe.

"Exactly."

"Wow!" exclaimed Joe.

"Exactly."

"What was the point of being on campus in North Carolina?" asked Susan.

"I'm not sure."

The sound of groaning drew their attention back to the screen. The camera pulled out and they watched the man struggle as full awareness returned.

Smoke rings entered the view interspersed with a slim trail of smoke floating toward the ceiling.

"Janet Simpson is in the room," observed Mali.

"Is there any way to locate where they are?" asked Jake.

"No, he could be in any little girl's bedroom," said Joe, adding "There's no GPS tracking since we left Periscope."

"Let me the fuck out of here," shouted the man, bucking and twisting, pulling on the ropes, his eyes wild as he tossed his head from side to side.

Spotting the woman and the video camera behind her, his movements ceased. "Who the hell are you?" he sneered. "Getting your kicks by tying me up and videotaping me?"

Ignoring his questions, she demanded, "State your name."

"Fuck you!" He turned his head toward the wall.

"You are pathetic, Hank Hunter," she stated as she threw her cigarette on the ground, her voice still altered for the viewers, as before."

Hank's head snapped back to stare at her.

Tendons stood out on his neck, beads of sweat appeared on his forehead. "Wh...Wh...Who *are* you?" he whispered.

"My God!" Mali and Jake looked at each other, the implications sinking in.

Janet continued, "You may call me Justitia. And you don't deserve to live for what you did to your sister."

Hank paled and licked his lips. "Can I have some water?"

Janet stepped fully into the frame, her back to the camera, and picked up a stuffed bunny. She ambled over to him, shaking the bunny with each step, stopping at the end of the bed when she was two feet away.

"You don't recognize the room? I had to make a few modifications. Pretty accurate, right?"

Jake shifted his eyes to Kirsten. "Locate the address of where Hunter lived as a child. It sounds like she's returned to where they grew up."

Hunter's jaw dropped as his eyes roamed everywhere, recognition dawning. "Janie?"

"As I said before, you don't deserve to live." She tossed the bunny, which landed on the juncture between his legs.

Kirsten looked up from her console. "Jake, they grew up in a neighborhood in Trenton, New Jersey, called Franklin Park. Here's the address." She sent it to Joe.

"Get the police over there now! Jeff, I want the ghost at the front of the property in case anyone comes out. Kirsten, make sure the police cover the back as well, I'm assuming there's also a back entrance."

The ghost appeared at the front of what was probably at one time a lovely row house. Narrow and tall, the two-story house was in dire need of repair. A piece of plywood covered one of the two upstairs windows, the yellow paint was chipped and stained, the white front door now a dingy gray from years of smog and filth. Huge chunks of cement were missing from both steps leading up to the front door, and the bottom three siding panels at the bottom of the house were missing.

A hand appeared in the camera's view, three fingers held up.

The woman's head turned slightly and nodded. She leaned down and pushed up his jeans, exposing an anklet on his left ankle.

"Sadly, our time here has ended. It is only fitting that you die here, where all those atrocities occurred, and in the same manner as your dearly departed brother. My only regret is I don't have time to watch your life end." The hand reappeared in the camera's view holding a gas mask. To the screams of Hank Hunter and his panicked attempts to break free of his bonds, Janet could be seen placing the mask on her head. Holding up a remote for the camera to see, she pressed the red button.

Hunter gasped as he looked down at his leg, shaking it as best as he could, given the restraints.

"No, Janie, No! No, No, No!" Screaming his agony, he was soon coughing and spewing vomit, the seizures taking hold.

Justice Prevails appeared on the screen then everything went black.

"The police are thirty seconds out," said Kirsten. "I told them about the cyanide."

"That's going to be thirty seconds too late. Jeff, move the ghost to the back. Simpson will hear the sirens and leave another way. Joe, full screen for the ghost."

The nine screens flickered and the view was enlarged. As the ghost floated over the house to the rear, they observed two people exit, a man and a woman, walking quickly to a van. Neither were wearing masks. Tina maneuvered the ghost to the van and turned it around.

"That's Simpson but who is the man?" asked Jeff.

"Drake," said Mali and Jake simultaneously.

"Get the license plate and pass it on to the police. Jeff, stay with the van."

As the van pulled away, the ghost followed.

"Who's Drake?" asked Felix as everyone watched.

"We believe he was the assassin of the HuntedLives game." Mali responded, eyes still on the van.

"You don't say, wow!"

No one responded.

"One police car has remained at the house. They are waiting for hazmat to arrive so they can enter," explained Kirsten, still on the phone. "The second car is in pursuit of the van."

The van jolted forward, weaving between other cars on the road. Running a red light, it swerved to miss a truck, continuing down the street.

Everyone instinctively jumped back as the ghost passed through the truck.

"Whoa!" exclaimed Jeff, momentarily releasing the controls of the ghost.

Jake warned, "Don't lose them!"

They watched the van merge onto US Interstate 1 heading north, increasing its speed.

Phone still to her ear, Kirsten said, "Area police are joining in the pursuit, none have caught up with the van at this point. I've directed them to two entry points onto the interstate in front of them."

"Whoa!" exclaimed Mali as the van moved into the far right lane, almost side-swiping a Nissan Prius.

When a police car entered the interstate, just ahead of the van, they watched the van veer to the far left, continuing to speed ahead. The police car made its way across the lanes, dodging traffic as it made the crossing.

"Traffic is getting heavy with the onset of rush hour." Susan stated the obvious, no one responded.

With no warning, the van veered to the far right again and exited the interstate, the police car unable to get over in time.

"They're headed to the Quaker Bridge Mall!" said Felix. "I've been there before with friends."

"They just pulled into the mall and it's stopping in front of the Macy's entrance," said Jeff. "The ghost is blind once they enter."

Jake's hands fisted as he tensed, watching Simpson and Drake enter the building. "Damn it! This is the closest we've been to catching them. We're not going to lose them."

"The police should arrive there shortly but that mall is huge and has lots of exit points." As Kirsten spoke, they watched three police cars surround the van with multiple officers entering the building.

The only sound in the room was the squeak, squeak, squeak of Jake's tennis shoes as he paced back and forth.

Kirsten looked at Jake and shook her head. "The police lost them inside. They could be anywhere."

Jake stopped pacing and looked at the screen. Nostrils flaring, he flexed his fingers as his face turned red. "Damn it!"

"There's more."

Jake took a few deep breaths as he stared at Kirsten.

"Two other bodies were found in the house in addition to Hank Hunter's. Believed to be the owners, each was shot in the head once."

CHAPTER TWELVE

Special Unit Warehouse
Thursday, September 3, 11:30 a.m.

Two hours after Hank Hunter's murder, #JusticePrevails had gone active on Twitter and Facebook with multiple pictures of it. A short video clip had been posted to TikTok as well. Comments, such as 'He got what he deserved!', 'Serves the bastard right', 'We're rooting for you Justitia', 'How can we help?', and 'Get all those pedophile pricks', numbered in the thousands, and were disheartening to the team. There was no way to track down all users of the comments, they didn't even try, knowing it would be a waste of valuable time.

Agent Tanner had contacted them from North Carolina. A man in his twenties wearing a Go-Pro camera had been apprehended shortly after entering the Student Union. He was paid five thousand dollars to walk around campus with the camera and Periscope active, and was told to avoid the police. There was an ad in the campus newspaper he had answered for a short-term job offering good pay. The camera and cash were left for him at the bell tower with instructions. He didn't question the job because it was quick cash and he needed the money. Another dead end.

Mali's apartment had been outfitted with security cameras in her main living area as well as outside her front door, and the ghost was following Mali every time she stepped outside. Susan was monitoring her security while Jeff controlled the ghost. She felt as though she was living in a fish bowl and she was not happy about it.

Jeff had also determined that four ghosts could run at the same time without negatively impacting each other.

Mali had researched on-going pedophile cases involving high-profile individuals, and the remaining three ghosts had been sent to follow the top three, from their perspective, that were in various stages of resolution. Jeff and Joe were monitoring them.

Felix was working with the team in DC trying to figure out how they jumped from Periscope to Lady-Justice, and to determine if blockchain technology was actually being used.

In between all of that, the team was trying to determine how the LadyJustice app worked and if sound could be added to the ghosts. No luck on either count.

Now almost two weeks later, being unable to pick up the tracks of Simpson and Drake, no substantial progress on all fronts, and no word from Simpson herself, tempers were running short and frustrations were high.

On top of that, the business anniversary dinner of Mali's father was just two days away. Being a dutiful daughter, Mali would attend, even though she would rather not. Jake had agreed to go with her but said his dad and Heather would not be going. He felt it wasn't the appropriate event for everyone to meet. Mali agreed. They were planning to drive to Philadelphia on Saturday morning, returning on Sunday.

"You're wrong, Jenson, there's no way the jump occurs that way," groused Felix, listening on the phone before everyone heard him hiss, "We'll just see about that." He hung up, grumbling about know-it-all old agents.

"Joe, you're going to lose Ted Matters," a CEO he was assigned to watch, stated Jeff absently.

Joe complained. "Stop telling me what to do and worry about your own targets."

Looking up from what he was reading, Jake observed everyone. Rubbing his jaw, he stood and walked to the main area. "Can I have everyone's attention?"

Everyone stopped what they were doing and turned their attention to Jake. "I get that everyone is frustrated. It's been a long couple of weeks and we don't have much to show for it." He paused, staring at each team member. "Get out of here for an hour or so. Grab a bite, get some fresh air, and come back with the right attitude." He returned to the table to continue reading.

There were a few whispered comments but no objections as everyone departed, some taking the elevator and others walking up the stairs. Mali walked over to Jake.

"I was going to take a walk and grab a sandwich. Do you want to come with me?"

"No. Thanks," was his clipped reply. He closed his

eyes and shook his head before opening them to look at Mali. "I'm sorry. I'm being just as waspish as everyone else." He smiled ruefully.

Mali smiled back. "We're all frustrated, Jake."

"How about an Italian sub at that deli a few blocks down the road, everything on it?"

"You got it. I won't be gone long."

After lunch, Jake called everyone together after receiving a short phone call.

"I just received a phone call from the field office that covers Boston. Larry and Jed Hunter just turned themselves in. They're willing to talk and they want protection from their sister."

"Wow!" exclaimed Kirsten.

"I bet they do after what happened to Hank Hunter," joked Felix.

Jake shot Felix a stern glance before continuing.

"They said they'd only speak with Hoop and I. Becky is booking a flight to Boston and hotel rooms for us, as we speak. We'll drive to Chelsea and interrogate them in the morning, returning tomorrow late afternoon. Let's hope we glean something useful."

* * *

FBI Field Office, Chelsea, MA
Friday, September 4, 9:00 a.m.

DESPITE BEING THREE years apart in age, Larry and Jed could have been twins. Same height, both had pasty white skin, a mop of stringy brown hair, pale blue eyes, and their bodies were thin to the point of looking emaciated. The only visible difference, when looking at the two, were the wire-rimmed glasses Jed wore. Larry sat ramrod straight in the chair, his shackled arms resting on the table. Jed was sitting forward in his chair and bending down so he could nibble on his fingernails, occasionally spitting out nails or skin he successfully chewed off.

As Mali stared at the Hunter brothers through the windows looking into the neighboring interrogation rooms, she thought they were very unassuming men, the kind you don't notice when you walk past them on the street. From what they had read on the flight to Boston last night, the two lived three blocks apart and worked at the same auto dealership. Larry was divorced and had two boys, Jed was married with a daughter.

Special Agent Gina Smith briefed Mali and Jake as they observed the two.

"They arrived together at approximately noon yesterday. After identifying themselves, they stated they wanted protection and were willing to talk with federal agents. They waived their Miranda rights and don't want a lawyer. They said they would only talk to the two of you. We placed them in separate holding cells where they remained overnight." Her lip curled as she glared at the brothers. "I'm glad I skipped breakfast this morning." She shook her head. "I've seen a lot in my day but this type of thing always turns my stomach and gives me sleepless nights." Taking a deep breath, she said, "Well, I'll leave you to it. Sims is coming in to run the video camera. Personally, I think these sleezeballs deserve whatever they get."

"Who first?" asked Mali, when the door closed behind Agent Smith.

"Jed. He looks more nervous."

He opened the door leading into the room, closing it behind them. Jed Hunter jumped when the door opened, and glanced over his shoulder at Mali and Jake.

"This is Agent Hooper and I'm Agent Black," began Jake, as he and Mali sat.

"I...I...I have to take a piss."

"Tough. You came to us, now talk."

"My sister is crazy. I want protection."

"You're in a federal building. I think you're safe. Now talk."

"I...I..."

Mali said, "Don't know where to begin? Let me help. Did you sexually abuse your sister?"

He looked down, whispering "Yes."

"We need more information than that, Hunter, if you want to remain in our custody. We could always cut you loose and let Janet..." Jake stated, his voice hard.

"No, no, I'll talk." He licked his lips and peeked at Mali and Jake before lowering his eyes to the table. "Our parents adopted Janie when she was six years old. She wasn't the cutest girl, but she was so happy to be part of a family. She was fun to have around." The words spilling out of his mouth were softly spoken but his voice was steady. "About a year or so after Janie arrived, we started going to her room at night. Hank said we could have even more fun with her. That first time, I wasn't sure what he meant or what to expect. I was thirteen, hadn't even kissed a girl yet." He briefly looked up at them. "Can I have a glass of water?"

Jake glanced at the window and nodded his head. A short time later, the door opened and a woman brought in a glass of water, closing the door behind her as she left. Jed gulped down the water and bent down to swipe his mouth with the back of his hand. His throat worked as he swallowed repeatedly.

"I don't have all day," said Jake, startling him.

"Hank woke Janie up and told her to stand up on her bed." Tears slid down Hunter's cheeks. "She was sleepy when Hank woke her but had a huge smile on her face when she realized it was us. So trusting." He swayed from side-to-side, not realizing it as he continued to speak. "She had a pretty pink nightgown on, she always wore pink. Hank told her to take it off, remove her underwear, and lie back down. He was stroking himself as she took everything off, we all were. Hank...Hank was the first to take her. She screamed so he covered her mouth and told her to shut up. After he finished, Larry had his turn. Then they told me it was time to lose my virginity and to get going. I didn't think about what we were doing, I was hard and excited, and with them egging me on, I had my turn."

Mali felt sick. She glared at Hunter through tears she refused to let fall.

"How often did you rape your sister?" Jake asked, his voice dripping ice.

Hunter flinched, seeming to shrink into himself. "Every few nights, I guess."

"You haven't mentioned Anthony."

"Hank brought him into the room after the second or third visit. He said he was too young to join us but wanted him to watch and learn. Tony sat in the chair by the door every time, cried mostly."

"How long did it last?"

"About four years. By then, Hank was gone, and Larry and I both had girlfriends."

Mali cleared her throat. Speaking in a voice devoid of emotion, she asked, "You've been married ten years and your daughter is eight years old?"

"Yes."

"I guess it's a good thing you don't have sons who want to have fun with their sister."

Hunter gulped and paled. "Oh God." Burying his head in his hands, he sobbed.

"I've had enough." Mali shoved her chair back and stormed out of the room. She leaned against the wall, breathing rapidly in through her nose and out of her mouth. Agent Smith, who was speaking with another agent, did a double take when she saw Mali, then rushed over. Grabbing her by the arm, she shoved her into the nearest chair and pushed her head between her knees.

"Breathe deeply and slowly."

When the dizziness passed, Mali sat up, leaning her head against the wall and closing her eyes.

"Pretty brutal?"

"You have no idea." Mali choked out, opening eyes

full of anguish to look at Agent Smith. "How could anyone do that to a little girl? Not once, but repeatedly?"

"There are a lot of sick people in this world." She handed Mali a glass of water.

Mali was taking a sip when Jake stepped out of the room. Agent Smith walked back to her desk.

He squatted down in front of her. "Are you alright?"

Taking a deep breath, Mali nodded. "I will be. That level of depravity is beyond my comprehension."

"I know." He stood, pulling her up with him. "Let's take a walk outside and clear our heads before the second interrogation."

They walked out of the building and ambled around, nowhere in particular.

"Jeb Hunter couldn't provide any useful information. He never saw or heard from his sister after she left for college."

"No surprise there," was Mali's reply.

Thirty minutes later, they walked into the interrogation room where Larry Hunter waited. Now slouched in his chair, he didn't bother to look up when they entered.

"This is Agent Hooper and I'm Agent Black," began Jake, as he and Mali sat.

Larry looked up with a sneer. "You kept me waiting long enough."

"And we can just as easily leave and come back tomorrow," stated Jake as he moved to stand.

"No, no, let's get this over with."

Jake sat back down. "We just finished talking to

your brother. He said you were the leader of your nightly attacks on your sister."

"I'm the oldest."

Mali tensed. "That's your justification?"

Larry studied Mali without expression.

"You don't like me."

"No I don't. What you and your brothers did to your sister was despicable."

"We were kids, boys will be boys."

"Ahhh, so your boys are following suit too? With your niece, perhaps?"

Larry shot up and leaned toward Mali, palms down on the hard surface. Startled, she pushed back from the table.

Jake bolted out of his chair and shoved Hunter back down. "Do that again and we cut you loose. Hell, we'll even contact your sister and tell her to come and get you."

Breathing hard and glaring at Jake, Larry stayed put. He turned his heated stare toward Mali. "My boys are good boys. Leave them out of this."

"Like father, like son," she shrugged.

Nostril flaring and hands fisted, Larry fumed but did not move.

"We don't need to hear the details of what you did to your sister. In fact, I don't want to hear them. I want information about Janet that could help us. Were you ever in contact with her or your brother, Anthony, throughout the years?" asked Jake.

He leered. "Did Jed tell you about Anthony. I started

bringing him into the room after the first few times, he was too young to participate but I thought it would be a good learning experience for him." He chuckled. "The brat just sat in that chair and cried." He laughed. "Although after a year or two, he was enjoying it, jacking off in the chair. I should have let him have Janie."

Mali worked to keep her face impassive.

Jake repeated, "Were you ever in contact with her or your brother?"

"Janie? No. Tony, yeah, every once in awhile. He was very excited when Janie joined the firm. He was hoping to get her into his bed, admitted to me he wanted to all those years ago. I was surprised she wanted to work with him. I assumed she hated us all." His face turned sour. "I guess she did."

"Did he tell you about the live HuntedLives game?"

"No. He called when he wanted advice about sex or when he wanted to update me about Janie. He did say he finally took her, and from behind." Hunter laughed again. "I won't bore you with those details."

Jake looked at Mali. "We're done here. Hunter is not interested in helping us stop his sister, even if it could mean some leniency." Both he and Mali stood.

"Wait...Leniency?"

"I can't promise anything. It would depend on the information and whether or not it was helpful."

"A few days before she killed Anthony, he called me. Said they were leaving the country to enjoy a life in France together. He said they had purchased property a couple of hours outside of Paris, along the coast, and they planned to live there. I didn't ask why he was moving. I didn't care."

"The name of the town."

"Cocul, Concan, Canton. I don't know. Something like that." He paused. "Will that help me?"

Mali glared at him. "It may help us. It won't help you. You're going away for a very long time for the rape and sexual abuse of your sister, you sick bastard."

CHAPTER THIRTEEN

Mali's Family Home, Philadelphia
Saturday, September 5, 2:30 p.m.

As JAKE PULLED into the drive leading her parent's home, Mali gazed at the majestic oak trees with vibrant pink, white and blue hydrangea bushes nestled between them, gently waving in the breeze, welcoming those who entered. The sweeping expanse of grass leading up to the Victorian house that had been her home for as long as she remembered, resembled a velvet carpet of deep green, perfectly manicured of course. Deep red hibiscus plants lined the top of the drive, and were the cherries at the top of the cake. Mali usually found the serenity of the half-mile drive soothing.

Today was an exception, for two reasons.

First of all, a sleepless night had left dark circles under her puffy eyes. She had not bothered to wash her hair since she'd be showering before the party. Her auburn tresses hung limply from her ponytail. She wore shorts and a t-shirt with FBI and Proud of it emblazoned across the front. The entire look would be disappointing to her mother but she did not have the energy to do more before they left New York.

The second reason was she didn't want to be there at all. While her relationship with her parents had improved in the past few months, she detested her father's business partner. It was no accident she had not seen him in years.

Mali murmured, "It is so surreal to me that twenty-four hours ago we were talking to two pedophiles about what they did to their sister, and today we are here about to attend a fancy celebration."

Jake glanced at her as he navigated the winding road. "Your parents will appreciate that you came."

She looked at him, her left eyebrow arched. "My parents expected me to attend. No was not an option."

He pulled up to the front door and turned off the engine. Turning toward her, he brushed a few tendrils of hair, that had escaped her ponytail, off her face and tucked them behind her ear. Smiling, he said, "That doesn't change the fact they will appreciate you for showing up to support your father. It's just one night. We'll be headed back to this case of pedophilia, multiple murders, and a deranged woman in no time."

Mali chuckled. "Well, when you put it like that, being here is much preferred." She gave a slight nod to the butler standing outside her door. He opened it and helped her out of the car.

When she walked around to Jake, she stopped and they both looked up at the imposing structure. The dark red shutters framing the upper floor windows and match-ing double front doors gave relief to the otherwise stark gray brick walls. Multiple pointed spires reached for the sky, completing the striking, somewhat ominous, look.

As they stepped inside a large entry hall, Scott, Mali's five-year-old nephew raced up the hallway from the bowels of the house, passed them with nary a wave, and sprinted up the grand staircase disappearing around the corner. A frazzled older woman trailed after him, huffing as she tried to keep up. She nodded at them as she followed her charge up the staircase.

"Rose's son, Scott, and his nanny," said Mali.

"Ahhhh…"

"Jasmine, you're here, finally." From her perfectly coifed blonde hair and flawlessly applied makeup to the royal blue silk dress and matching heels she wore, Willow Hooper was elegance personified. As she approached her daughter, her eyes narrowed and her lips thinned as she stared at her.

"Before you say anything, Mother, we've had a rough few days at work and I didn't bother to do much this morning because I knew I'd be showering here in a few hours." The words fell out of Mali's mouth, one on top of the other, in her haste to explain how she looked before her mother could voice her disapproval.

Stopping in front of her, Willow reached out with a finger and touched the skin under Mali's eyes. "I was only going to say that you look tired, run-down." She then turned Mali's head to the side and moved the hair above her ear out of the way. "The scar is barely visible."

"You say that every time I see you, Mother." Mali leaned in for a hug, a real one, not the air hugs of old.

Releasing her daughter, she turned to Jake. "You're not overworking my daughter, are you Jacob?"

Taking bother of her hands in his, he smiled down at her. "I can assure you I have not, Willow, but it's been a stressful few days."

Willow smiled then cleared her throat, all business now. "I'm sorry your father and daughter could not be here but I understand it isn't the best time for us to meet."

"I look forward to the day they can meet you and Charles."

She's blushing! I've never seen my mother blush.

She squeezed Jake's hands before releasing them. "I must be off. There are still many details to attend to before tonight's party. You'll be in the green room as usual. Guests will arrive at seven, dinner is at eight. Plan to be downstairs no later than six." Without another word, Willow turned and disappeared down the hallway.

"Let's go for a walk before heading upstairs. I'd like to stretch my legs and breathe some fresh air before we get busy.

Jake took her hand in his, turned left and led her into the formal living room. Wood paneling lined the walls on two sides. The third wall, which faced the backyard, and Willow's pool and award-winning gardens, was lined with picture windows for easy viewing. The focal point of the room was the massive fireplace.

The room was set up for the party with various bar-height round tables sprinkled throughout, covered in rose-colored table cloths, each wrapped and tied to the center of the table to avoid any unfortunate accidents.

"How many people are expected tonight?" asked Jake as he stopped to admire the mantle with its intricately-carved scene of the Philadelphia harbor in the eighteen hundreds. "This mantle is exquisite," he murmured, running his fingers over the figures.

"Mother said seventy-fifty people are expected."

They continued through one of the arched entries on either side of the fireplace that led into the dining room, and walked out the french doors onto the patio overlooking the pool and gardens beyond. Strolling down the stairs and past the pool, they meandered through the gardens. A contented silence enveloped them as they enjoyed the hydrangea, azaleas, and other flowers nestled amongst the Japanese maple, and other trees. Butterflies flitted from one flower to another and the soft buzzing of bees could be heard as they, too, enjoyed the sweet nectar. Mali breathed in the delightful scents surrounding her, breathing out some of the stress she had been feeling. She could feel her shoulders drop as she relaxed.

They returned to the house and walked up to the green room, as Willow called it. In actuality, it was Mali's room growing up and had not changed. Painted a delicate pale-green, the eye was drawn to two expansive bay windows, each with a cushioned window seat below, that overlooked the gardens. The king-size bed rested against the wall on the right side of the room and it faced a large fireplace, The bathroom was just beyond.

"This room was my solace growing up." Mali said as they walked inside.

Their overnight bags were sitting on the bed, partially

emptied, as their evening clothes were already hanging in the closet. By mutual consent, they unpacked their bags then Mali showered while Jake called his daughter and then Jeff.

* * *

5:55 p.m.

"Have Jeff and Joe narrowed down the location in France?" asked Mali, glancing at Jake as she walked out of the restroom to the dresser. "I need your help with these buttons," she added as she looked at him through the mirror above the dresser while inserting diamond studs into her ears. After their interrogation of the Hunter brothers, Jake had tasked Joe and Kirsten with tracking down the coastal town in France to determine if what Larry Hunter told them panned out. If so, they would contact the local French police for their assistance in searching the property.

Jake walked up behind her and proceeded to button the small cloth buttons on her skirt, not losing eye contact with her as he did so. "Not yet. There are numerous coastal towns that start with a C and are located two to three hours from Paris. They're looking at recent high-end purchases in each town. It's going to take awhile." He moved to the buttons on her top, placing his hands on her shoulders when he completed the task. "You look stunning." He leaned down to smell her neck. "And you smell amazing."

The heat rose to her cheeks as she held his stare. "Thank you."

Stepping back from her, he turned her around to get the full effect. Mali wore a tea-length lace two-piece dress with exquisite appliqués and beading throughout. While the front of the short-sleeve top had a modest neckline, there was a low V in the back. The skirt was pencil-thin and sported a split back. Mali's bare mid-drift separated the two pieces. As she stepped into her rose-colored matching heels, she looked like a delicate flower.

"You look very handsome, and I love the rose-colored tie you brought with you. Thank you."

Jake smiled. "I aim to please." He gestured toward the door with his arm and they left the room just before six.

Mali and Jake halted at the entrance to the formal living room, the argument between her sisters, Lily and a very pregnant Rose, unmistakable. Mali's father and two brothers-in-law were standing near the mantle, their conversation momentarily halted by the unusually loud altercation. Willow was seated on the sofa, looking elegant, if not slightly irritated, in her antique rose gown.

"I don't care if you are pregnant, Rose. Quit being so bitchy." Lily glared at her sister.

Rose looked down her nose at Lily. "I merely said you looked like a plump piglet in that dress. Whatever possessed you to wear it?"

Lily shot out of her chair, hands clenched. "You bitch! It's better than looking like a sunburnt cow."

Mali's eyebrows shot up. She had never seen Lily, her normally quiet-as-a-mouse sister, so outraged. Her nickname was Minnie because she was usually quite reserved. She wasn't surprised by Rose's attitude, however.

Without raising her voice, Willow drawled. "Ladies, you are not displaying the genteel behavior expected in this household. Apologize to each other immediately." Her voice, though soft, was laced with steel and brooked no argument.

Mali cleared her throat as soon as the apologies were given and received.

"Jasmine, Jacob," Charles boomed as he strode to the entrance to hug his daughter and shake Jake's hand. "I'm glad you're here."

"Hello Father."

"Likewise, sir."

"Charles, call me Charles." He turned back to the room and led Jake to the mantle. "Darren, Robert, you remember Jake." They shook hands while Mali sat beside her mother.

"You look lovely, Jasmine."

"Thank you, Mother."

"Richard should arrive just before our other guests."

Mali tensed, not saying anything. She turned toward her two sisters. "Hello Lily, Rose. You're getting close to delivery, right?"

"A little more than a month to go. It can't get here soon enough." She sighed. "God, I need a cigarette."

Talk centered around the week's festivities until the arrival of Richard Thorpe was announced just before seven. Jake joined Mali as everyone stood when he entered the living room. A tall athletic man, Richard Thorpe was still attractive at sixty-one, despite the crop of gray hair. His blue eyes were still sharp and carried an intelligence that, combined with his good-looks that he used in every situation, inspired confidence and trust from his clients, especially the women.

Mali watched him as he greeted everyone. Charming on the outside, cold on the inside, is how she had always described him. After a cool greeting from her sisters, Richard turned toward Mali.

His eyes widened and a big grin split his face. He moved closer to give her a hug but Mali stepped into Jake's side and shoved out her hand. Her face was a mask. Jake automatically placed his arm around her waist.

If Thorpe noticed anything, he didn't say a word. He just took her hand and said, "It's been a long time, Jasmine. You are gorgeous."

Mali removed her hand from his. "Dick, this is Jacob Black." She smiled inwardly when he frowned. He hated being called Dick. "Jake, Richard Thorpe, my father's business partner."

Jake nodded as they shook hands. "Thorpe."

"A pleasure, for sure. And so nice to see Jasmine with a boyfriend. She should be married by now." He laughed.

Now it was Jake's turn to tense.

Charles interrupted them to hand his partner a whiskey. They strolled back to the mantle, where Charles typically held court.

"Do you want to tell me what that was about?" Jake whispered.

Mali shook her head. "Nope."

Soon the doorbell rang and the guests began arriving. The party had begun.

The patio had been decked out with a slew of tables, and white twinkling lights overhead, that overlooked the pool and gardens. The gentle breeze stirred the evening air. A pianist played the soft sounds of classical music down by the pool. Most of the guests were outside enjoying the ambiance.

Promptly at eight p.m., all were called into the dining room for a toast and dinner. The chairs had been removed so guests could easily fill their plates with the delectable food sitting on the table. Prime rib, lobster tails, jumbo shrimp, plus a variety of salads and vegetables filled every available space. Charles was standing at the head of the table with Richard to his left. On his right side stood Willow and his daughters, in age-order.

He tapped his glass with a spoon to gain everyone's attention. "Before we eat this sumptuous feast before us, I first want to thank my beautiful wife, Willow, for all of her efforts throughout the week culminating in tonight's celebration. None of this would be possible without her." He leaned down to kiss her on the cheek as everyone clapped. "When Richard and I opened the business thirty years ago, we had big dreams of helping people grow their investments so they could retire comfortably. We managed to do that and a whole lot more, growing the company to twenty-five branches with more than two hundred and fifty employees across the states."

Everyone in the room applauded. "We couldn't have done it without all of you, our vice-presidents from all of the branches. So give yourselves a hand." More applause from the crowd. "When you go back to your branches, celebrate with your employees and give everyone a one thousand dollar bonus, from the managers down to the janitors. I want everyone to know how much they are appreciated." Cheers interrupted Charles. "Here's to thirty more years of Hooper and Thorpe Investments. Now let's eat!"

The party was in full swing with lots of eating, drinking, and merriment. Willow, always the perfect hostess, was gliding from guest to guest ensuring everyone was having an enjoyable time. Mali and Jake were down by the pool chatting with a couple who had flown in from London. It wasn't long before the couple excused themselves and ambled toward the gardens.

"Would you like something to drink?" Jake asked.

Hearing a buzz near her head, Mali absently swiped at it. "Water would be perfect, thanks."

"I'll be right back."

Mali leaned against the rail overlooking the gardens. The persistent buzz was still near so she slid a few steps away from the lantern that was perched on the railing. When she heard footsteps, she stood and turned with a smile on her face. It quickly turned into a grimace.

"Now is that any way to greet your father's partner?" Richard Thorpe exclaimed, as he stopped right in front of Mali. His eyes roamed from her head down to her toes and back up again. He licked his lips and looked into her eyes. "You've grown into a beautiful woman, Jaz."

Mali thrust her chin up, her lips thinned. "I'm not the little girl you could bully and abuse all those years ago," she spat at him. "Now get out of my way."

"Whoa," he chuckled, arms spread out to his sides. "I'm an affectionate guy, what can I say. And I'd wager your ten-year-old self was curious and enjoyed our… encounters."

Jaw clamped tight, Mali glared at him for an instant before shifting to the side. As she stormed past him, she ground the spike of her heel down onto the top of his shoe and shoved him to the side.

"Argh," he grimaced, regaining his balance. "Bitch," he growled to her back as she walked away.

Jake, who was on the patio making his way to Mali with their drinks, witnessed the entire thing. She rounded the pool and was walking up the steps to the patio when he caught up to her.

"What the hell was that all about?"

"Nothing." She continued up the stairs.

Jake set the drinks down and grabbed her arm.

"Mali…"

She looked down at the hand holding her arm then turned her gaze up. "Let go of my arm."

Jake immediately released her arm and Mali continued up the stairs.

She found her mother in the living room, whispered something in her ear, then walked out of the room and up the stairs. Jake was not far behind.

Stepping out of her heels as soon as she entered the bedroom, Mali walked to the bay window and opened the side windows, allowing the cool breeze in. She straightened and wrapped her arms around herself, staring outside. She didn't notice the breeze and didn't move when the door closed.

"What did he do to you?"

Mali tensed then turned around to face Jake. He was leaning against the door, arms crossed. His expression was grim. She was reminded of when she first met him. His intensity fell off him in waves. She sagged under the weight of his stare and sat on the cushioned window seat.

Looking down, she whispered, "I was ten. It started as intimidation. He would get close to me, rub my shoulders, whisper in my ear. Nothing overt. But it made me uncomfortable. It went from there to brushing his hand across my chest, having me sit on his lap. He would kiss me now and then, on the lips, mostly when saying hello or goodbye. Again, it was nothing overt and mostly done in the presence of my parents and others. If I turned away, he'd pinch me."

She didn't realize Jake had approached until he sat beside her, taking her hand in his. She looked at their clasped hands then up into his face. Her face was resolute.

"I couldn't tell my parents he made me uncomfortable. He was my father's partner and their business was thriving." She paused. "There was just one instance when he tried to get me alone in a room. We were in

Lake Tahoe on vacation staying at his summer home. I was able to get away and I stayed close to my mother the rest of the time. From that point on, I avoided him at all costs. I vowed then that no man would bully or intimate me again."

"And he didn't, from the looks of things." He smiled without humor. "You should be proud of yourself."

Mali smiled. "I hope I broke a bone or two in his foot."

Jake barked out a laugh. Sobering, he stated, "I could beat the pulp out of him for you, for me actually."

"A kind offer to be sure, and tempting, but no." She shook herself, like a cat shaking off water. "It was a long time ago. I spent a lot time with a therapist in Chicago when I worked there, working through a number of things. Dick upset me tonight, yes, but I was still able to handle the situation and come out better on the other end. I am proud of myself." She reached up and feather-kissed him on the lips. "Doing or saying anything to him wouldn't make a difference. He'll be gone tonight and we'll never be in the same room with him again."

"So why did you marry Daniel? You were in college, long before you went to Chicago with the FBI and started seeing a therapist."

"He was handsome, he paid attention to me, and I knew my parents would be furious. I can't really blame him for seeking…entertainment…elsewhere. I was more interested in my studies than in my marriage, and I didn't care for the physical side of our relationship."

"I understand so much more now," he murmured.

Squeezing her hands, he pulled them both to a stand then wrapped his arms around her in a bear hug.

Mali sighed. "I needed this hug. Thank you, Jake, for listening, for understanding."

He rested his cheek on the top of her head. "We've had a long day, and we have an early start tomorrow. The team is meeting at the office at eleven so we can have the latest information ready for Frank ahead of the press conference at three."

Mali nodded without moving, his steady heartbeat soothing her.

Jake's chest rumbled beneath her ear. Turning her around, he unbuttoned the same buttons he had buttoned earlier then gently pushed her toward the bathroom.

"You go first. I'm going to call dad then I'm going for a walk."

"Tell him I said hello." She walked into the restroom, closing the door behind her.

CHAPTER FOURTEEN

Special Unit Warehouse
Sunday, September 6, 12:00 p.m.

AFTER AN EARLY snack of toast and coffee, Mali and Jake had left Philadelphia for New York, arriving at the office at ten-thirty, just before the rest of the team rolled in.

Status reports had been given and everyone was just discussing what to grab for lunch when Susan's phone rang. On weekends, the receptionist's phone line was transferred to Susan.

"Excuse me, Mali? The call is for you."

Mali, who was updating the whiteboard at the conference table, said, "Thanks. Patch it through to the phone here please." She picked up the receiver on the first ring.

"Good afternoon, Agent Hooper speaking."

"Hello Agent Hooper. You really shouldn't be working on a Sunday."

Mali snapped to attention at the sound of Janet Simpson's voice. She tapped the table to get Jake's attention.

"Janet."

Jake was up in an instant. He rushed over to Joe and whispered something to him, signaling the others to silence.

"Happy to hear from me, darling?"

Jake slid a piece of paper to Mali telling her to stretch out the call. Joe was trying to trace it.

"Larry and Jed turned themselves in after you killed Hank."

Janet laughed in delight.

"They told us everything they did to you when you were younger." She paused. "I feel sorry for the child you were."

"I don't need your sympathy," she snarled, her voice harsh and implacable.

"It must have been horrendous for you. I can understand why you are the way you are."

Jake's eyebrows drew down in question. He mouthed, "What are you doing?"

Janet didn't answer immediately. Mali heard the hiss of a match igniting and assumed she was lighting a cigarette.

She wrote "She may get careless if angry" and showed the note to Jake.

"You have no idea who I am, Agent Hooper."

"But I do have an idea. You were viciously abused for three or four years. You're obviously very smart. You planned what you did to Anthony for years and years, adapting as needed. You molded yourself into a chameleon and brutal killer."

"Go to hell!"

Now it was Mali's turn to laugh. "You called *me*, Janet."

Janet breathing in and out harshly, rapidly, was evident to Mali.

"Don't hyperventilate," she said, chuckling. Turning serious, she soothed, "Your oldest brother is now dead, your other two brothers are in custody and will remain in jail for the rest of their lives. There's no need to continue with the murders."

Mali listened to Janet clap. Her voice was back to its derisive tone. "You think you can play me, Agent Hooper?" She snickered. "As Justitia has told her followers, this won't stop until all pedophiles and child traffickers are dead or in jail. We've only just begun."

"Vigilante justice never works."

"It already has, darling." She paused. "Now, I hope you are ready to show your appreciation for what I did for you."

"What are you talking about?"

"Daniel, of course. Your job is secure now that he is no longer among the living."

"Don't put that on me, Janet. You killed Daniel all on your own, and it doesn't matter what he was going to do, he did not deserve to be murdered."

"I did you a favor, bitch, don't forget that."

"Gee, does that mean we're not friends anymore?"

The line went dead.

"Was that smart making her angry like that?" asked Kirsten.

"Janet has been calling all the shots, she's completely in control and she knows it. Maybe she'll make some mistakes if she's rattled."

Jake nodded. "I agree. She wasn't in control of the conversation and that pissed her off."

"She sounds like an old coach of mine." Felix said, nodding. At everyone's surprised look, he grinned. "Minus the insane psychopath part of course. He always had to be in complete control, got pissed when he wasn't."

"I traced the call to a local number." Joe manipulated the controls on the console and a picture of a man displayed on the screen. "It's registered to a John Tamer, in Brooklyn. My guess is she's using some sort of spoofing software."

"What's that?" asked Mali.

"Spoofing allows the caller to display any number on the caller ID display that they want, so their own number is unknown and untraceable."

"So there's no way to trace it?"

He shook his head. "There are a lot of spoofing companies. We can contact them one-by-one with the information we know, date and time of this call, number displayed, etc., but it will be like searching for a needle in a haystack."

"Do it. Start with the most popular and reliable services when they open tomorrow," stated Jake. "Look everyone, this is going to be a long week. Go home, get some rest and plan on some long hours next week. Mali and I are heading to Frank's to finish preparing for the presser."

"I'm going to work a little longer," said Felix.

Jake nodded as everyone else shut down their computers and headed home.

* * *

Press Room, FBI Field Office, New York City
Sunday, September 6, 3:00 p.m.

The press room at the FBI Field Office was filled with reporters, standing-room only. Most were shifting from foot to foot, having been there for a long time waiting. The air flow from the air conditioning was minimal, the tepid air lending to the impatience rippling throughout the room. The chatter was non-stop as they waited.

When the door opened and two men walked in followed by two others, all talk stopped. One of the men stepped up to the podium.

"Good afternoon. My name is Ben Casey and I'm the Assistant Director in Charge of the FBI New York office. I will make a brief statement then our team will take a few questions." He looked down at his notes. "As you know, there is a woman identifying herself as Justitia who is kidnapping and killing individuals suspected of, and/or arrested for, pedophilia. She is using social media, including her own app, to broadcast these murders and encourage followers to support her cause. That woman has been identified as Janet Simpson." He held up a picture of Janet as well as Drake, taken when the ghost identified them. "This is the most recent picture we have of her and her accomplice, Drake Butcher. We are doing everything in our power to apprehend them both so they can stand trial for their alleged crimes. Vigilante justice is never the answer, and it is not condoned by the FBI or anyone in law enforcement. We are a lawful society with a justice system that works. Social media is exploding with videos and comments about each murder. We strongly encourage the public to refrain from accessing the LadyJustice app and from commenting on any social media venues that tag #JusticePrevails while we continue to investigate these crimes. If you have any information on the whereabouts of Ms. Simpson and/or Drake Butcher, or anything related to this case, please contact us at *justiceprevailstips.fbi.gov* or 1-800-fed-9999. As always, we are working diligently to solve this case. The safety of every citizen is our first concern. Thank you." He turned to Frank, who was standing next to Jake and Mali, and waved him to the podium. "Special Agent in Charge, Frank Grant, will answer some questions now."

Hands shot up and questions were shouted as each reporter vied for Frank's attention. He pointed to a reporter in the first row.

"John Spencer, Associated Press. Is this the same Janet Simpson who worked with Anthony Hunter at Hunted Inc and was behind the live Hunted Ones game a few months ago? And, if so, how do you know she's behind JusticePrevails? I thought she was dead."

"So did we, John. Yes, she's one and the same,

Anthony Hunter's sister and the true mastermind behind the Hunted Ones game. She has contacted our team and identified herself as the person behind these murders." Frank pointed to a woman two rows behind John Spencer.

"My name is Kim White, WABC. Why is she doing this? And why would she contact your team?"

"Janet Simpson was abused as a child by her brothers. She killed her oldest brother, Hank Hunter, a few days ago and her other two living brothers turned themselves in on Friday. We believe this is revenge against them and an opportunity to continue her killing, using other pedophiles as an excuse. As this is an on-going case, I am not at liberty to give details on why she may have contacted our team." He glanced at the reporters and pointed to an older man in the rear.

"Grayson Shepherd, *New York Times*. Can't you just remove that LadyJustice app like they did with Parler a while back? Have you identified who the next target is, and how can you protect those she is going after?"

"There's not an easy answer to removing the app. Suffice it to say we are working on the issue. As to your other questions, again, this is an on-going case and I will not discuss details at this time. One more question." He pointed to a woman standing to the side.

"Thank you. Liz Spector, *New York Daily News*. "Child abuse is a huge problem in this country and around the world. It's incomprehensible to me how anyone can harm a child. Speaking as the devil's advocate, the woman obviously needs help but she's doing everyone a favor by ridding the world of those disgusting perverts. Why arrest her?"

Frank reached for his bottle of water and took a few sips, observing the sea of reporters with their recorders, cameras, microphones, notepads. "We do not live in a country without laws, where vigilante justice is accepted. The days where everyone took the law into their own hands are gone. That only leads to chaos and loss of freedoms. If we allow this type of so-called justice to continue, what's next? If you are offended by what one group of people do or say, Liz, whether that group is political, religious, or anything else, will you take matters into your own hands and start killing them? That's why we have laws and a justice system. Not only that, but in this country, everyone is innocent until proven guilty. People have forgotten that. James Adams had not even been charged with a crime at the time he was murdered." His eyes narrowed as he studied everyone. "Janet Simpson has serious issues as a result of her childhood. One can feel sorry her but make no mistake, she is dangerous and should not be lauded. We urge the public not to compound what's going on by encouraging her. Don't respond to tweets, don't access the LadyJustice app, don't get involved. It's only a matter of time before we catch her and put her in jail where she belongs."

Frank turned and left the room with the Assistant Director, Mali and Jake right behind them.

"How did that go?" Frank asked as they headed back to Frank's office. "Good decision to call out Janet Simpson?"

Jake nodded. "I think so. Anything we can do to throw her off-balance can only help us. Your decision was a good one."

"Well, let's hope." He ushered them into his office. "Have a seat."

They rehashed the press conference and discussed next steps for thirty or so minutes when Frank wrapped up the meeting.

"Time to get home. Carol will have dinner on the table soon and it's movie night with the boys."

"How are they doing? School has started, right?" asked Mali.

"Yes, the week before they arrived home from Florida but they caught up quickly. I have to say it's nice to have them home."

Mali smiled. "You missed them as much as Carol did."

Frank laughed. "Don't tell her that. She won't let me live it down."

They all stood and walked out of his office.

"We'll have you two to the house for dinner soon. The boys have been asking when you'll be back. Josh said he's ready to whip you at chess, Hoop."

"And he can too," she chortled. "I look forward to that. Have a good night, Frank, and say hello to Carol and the boys."

"Keep me informed, Jake."

"Will do. Good night."

Jake insisted on taking Mali home. He pulled into the entrance, turned off the engine, and turned toward her.

"Thanks for this weekend," she said. "It seems like such a long time ago we were in Philly." She smiled.

"I know. The last few days have stretched out." He lifted his hand and played with her hair absently. "I enjoyed the weekend."

Mali's left eyebrow shot up.

Jake laughed. "Don't look at me like that. This visit was much better than the first one."

"I have to agree with you on that." She placed her hand on his cheek. "Thank you, for everything."

Staring into her eyes, he smiled. "You're welcome." He kissed her once, twice, three times. "Hmmmm...I wish I could stay but I need to get home." His mouth lingered on hers, rubbing back and forth.

Mali's breath caught in her throat.

Jake pulled back and gazed into her eyes before he looked at her mouth. When she licked her lips, he groaned and leaned down to capture her mouth in a searing kiss.

She wasn't sure if it lasted a minute or a lifetime but when he pulled her closer, she put her hands on his chest. With her lips a breath away from his, she whispered, "Go. I'm sure Heather wants to hear all about your weekend."

He closed his eyes and sighed.

They kissed one more time then Mali stepped out of the car. Opening the rear passenger door, she grabbed her weekend bag, said goodnight and walked to the door of her building, stopping with her hand on the handle. She gripped it tightly, wanting nothing more than to ask Jake to stay, knowing he would, also knowing it wasn't the right time. She took a deep breath and glanced behind her, before pulling the door open and stepping inside.

* * *

Mali's apartment
Monday, September 7, 4:10 a.m.

Roused out of sleep by the persistent ringing of her phone, Mali glanced at the time as she picked it up. Groaning, she mumbled, "Hello?"

"You bitch! How dare you make me out to be the bad guy in that press conference. And how the hell did you get those pictures?"

Fully awake now, Mali sat up and turned on the record feature of her phone. "I'm surprised you're calling me, Janet. I didn't think we were friends anymore. How did you get this phone number?"

"Apparently we both have secrets. And make no mistake, Agent Hooper, we are not friends." She clarified. "I gave considerable thought to our conversation yesterday and…"

"So you're going to stop these senseless murders and turn yourself in?" Mali interrupted.

"Oh, I don't think so. Quite the opposite, especially after the slander and lies your boss told today."

Mali shivered, despite the warm room.

Continuing, Janet said, "I am providing a service to

this country and I'm saving kids from future torment by ridding the world of the scourge of society."

"And Daniel? He wasn't a pedophile, he didn't hurt children."

"Daniel was a favor to you, when I thought we were friends."

"We've never been friends, Janet, and you didn't kill Daniel for me, you killed him for you." Mali stated coldly. "Maybe it's not just pedophiles that you abhor. Do you secretly enjoy what they do to you, like what your brothers did, and you hate yourself for it?"

Mali heard her gasp.

"You are not worthy of my talents," Janet hissed. "But before I get back to my true purpose, I've decided you, all of you, need to be punished for your lack of appreciation for all I've done for you and for the world. Do you understand me?" Mali held the phone away from her ear as Janet's normally controlled voice ratcheted up to a near-shriek.

"Are you threatening a federal officer?"

Janet cackled. "Oh I'm not threatening you, Agent Hooper, merely making a promise. You'll see." The click of the phone seemed to echo around Mali as her arm dropped to the bed with a muffled thud.

Mali raised a shaking hand and rubbed her eyes. Taking a few deep breaths, she dialed Jake's number.

He answered on the second ring, "Jacob Black, this better be good."

"I'm sorry to call you at this hour, Jake, but I just received a threatening call from Janet."

Mali listened to the rustle of covers being moved aside.

"Tell me exactly what she said."

"I recorded it, hang on." She pressed a few buttons and replayed the conversation.

"Jesus! I'm calling everyone in and will pick you up as soon as I can. Don't leave your apartment until I get there."

"She threatened everyone, not just me. I'm also concerned for your dad and Heather, not to mention everyone's families."

"You're the most likely target but I'll call Frank first so he can get the police and agency security ramped up for everyone on the team, including their families."

"I want the police at my parent's house too, Jake. She knows where they live."

CHAPTER FIFTEEN

Special Unit Warehouse
Monday, September 7, 6:30 a.m.

"WE'VE PASSED NUTCASE and have moved into scary," whispered Kirsten, as she sidled up to Mali. The team was all present and Frank had just walked in.

Calling everyone together, Jake said, "Thanks for coming in so quickly. Frank?"

"I can see everyone's concern. Rest assured, agents, and/or a police presence, are on their way to your homes or are already there. Your families are not to leave without an escort for the foreseeable future. And you will have protection at all times. Agents are on their way here and will secure the building and escort you wherever you go."

"Thank you, sir. That makes me feel so much better," said Susan.

"The police placed an APB on Simpson and Butcher as soon as the press conference concluded yesterday. I am confident they will make mistakes now that we've turned up the heat, and this increased security won't be needed for long. Stay focused and let's get the job done."

Jake added, "Meals will be brought in from the main office daily. Everyone is to stay on site during work hours and keep to your tasks. We almost caught them before, we can do it again. Hoop, Frank brought a burner phone for you to use for personal calls and outside this building. Leave your phone with Joe and he'll continue to pursue the ability to trace a spoofed call."

"What happens if she calls when I'm not here?"

"She'll either leave a voice message or hang up and try again later. Frank?"

"It may not seem like you're accomplishing much but you are. Stay vigilant." He looked at Jake, nodded toward the conference table, then left the group.

Jake continued. "Any updates on a possible property purchased by Hunter or Simpson in France?"

Jeff offered, "French intelligence have identified four high-priced properties in three towns, Cancale and two others, and are running them down now. They're supposed to contact us today."

"Any action with the ghosts and the targets they're watching?"

Joe shook his head. "Nothing out of the ordinary is happening with any of the targets. They're either remaining in their homes or going into work, entering and exiting from the same doors. We catch them when they enter and when they leave. No sign of Simpson or Butcher."

" Good. And the ghost on Hoop?

"Still operational whenever she leaves the building."

Jake nodded. "Okay, from this point forward, I

expect you to contact me when you're leaving here and when you get home. A text is fine. Let's get to it everyone." He turned and joined Frank at the conference table.

There was a buzz of activity as everyone buckled down to work.

4:40p.m.

BEEP, BEEP, BEEP, beep. The alarm sounded... #JusticePrevails was active again. Startled, Mali's eyes shot to the screens. They were currently off. Like the rest of the team, she stood and walked to the control center where Joe was opening Twitter. All nine screens blinked, becoming one large one, and Twitter displayed.

Navigating to #JusticePrevails, there was a simple message for all to see: Justice will always prevail, even in the face of adversity.

Below it was the top portion of an image. As Joe scrolled down to view the entire picture, there were gasps of shock and horror.

"Oh my God!" cried out Kirsten. Tears sprang to her eyes and slid down her face.

"No!" exclaimed Mali. She blinked rapidly, wrapping her arms around her waist, and shaking her head from side to side. *This is my fault.*

Susan choked back a sob and turned away.

Various expletives were barked out from the remaining team members as they stared.

Frank was propped up in a sitting position with his

back against a tree. His throat had been slit and blood covered his once-crisp white shirt, pooling on his pants. Five Shuriken protruded from various places on his chest. Behind him in the distance, the Statue of Liberty stood proud and tall.

In a deep voice, Jake commanded, "Get that picture off Twitter and anywhere else it may be. Send an agent to his house now!"

"Look at the comments," said Felix.

Joe scrolled down as Kirsten grabbed her phone with one hand to contact Twitter, using her other hand to wipe away her tears.

'Awesome! Look at those ninja stars, they're as big as my hand.'

'Love the visual with the Statue of Liberty behind him. Fitting.'

'Who's the guy?'

'Is this guy a pedophile too?'

'No, I think he's with the FBI.'

'I saw him in the news too. He didn't deserve that.'

'Hey, I feel ripped off. Why didn't we get to see the kill?'

'Pedophiles ok. Law enforcement no.'

'This ain't right.'

"That looks like Battery Park," Jeff noted. "I'll contact the police." He turned from the screen to make the call.

The comments continued, a few were excited about the latest murder but most believed it had gone too far.

"The tone is changing," stated Mali.

"I'm going to Carol's. I hope to God she and the kids haven't seen this. Hoop and Jeff, go to Battery Park. Call me when Frank's body has been recovered. Keep the ghost on Hoop," exclaimed Jake. "And get that picture off our screen!" He turned and stormed to the elevator as the image of Frank faded to black.

* * *

Parish of Most Holy Trinity in Williamsburg, Brooklyn
Sunday, September 13, 2:55 p.m.

THE WEEK HAD passed by in a blur for Mali. She had slept very little and accomplished even less at work. Her research had led nowhere and her mind was in a fog. After one task was complete, she couldn't focus on what was next unless someone, usually Kirsten, asked her for something. There were times she found herself staring at the computer and she had no clue what she was doing or how long she had been there. There had been no calls from Janet and #JusticePrevails had remained silent.

The day after Frank's murder, Mali had watched the team while Jake spoke. She noticed no one looked her in the eye or acknowledged her. Throughout the week, unless they needed information from her, she realized no one spoke to her unless she approached them first, even Kirsten. It finally hit home that everyone blamed her for Frank's death. Well, she blamed herself too, so they had that in common. Kirsten had said awhile back that Janet was making this personal with Mali, and she had denied it. If only she had acknowledged it and taken action. If only she had not provoked Janet during those phone calls. If only…

Mali had spoken very little with Jake outside of work. He had spent the early part of the week helping Carol with plans for the funeral and being there for the boys, until her family members arrived. He had called her once, that first evening, to ask how she was doing. The call had been brief, distant, and she had not spoken with him since, except at work. She figured he blamed her too.

Two days after Frank's murder, Mali had gone to Carol's to take her a casserole and pay her respects. Jake had answered the door and ushered her in. Someone had taken the casserole out of Mali's hands as Carol wrapped her in a bear hug. Carol was always more concerned of others than herself and had noticed Mali's peaked complexion, telling her to be sure to take care of herself. They had walked into the living room where the boys were sitting with an older woman, presumably their grandmother. Mali had given them hugs and told them how Frank had always spoken of how proud he was of his boys. She had left a short time later when a few more people had arrived to pay their condolences.

Now she was standing in front of this beautiful church, the same church she was briefly in a few short months ago for Ken Miller's funeral. Back then, Ken's wife had kicked her out before the service had even begun. That wouldn't happen today.

She walked up the steps and inside the building. As she approached the inner sanctum, she didn't admire the exquisite stained-glass windows that lined the upper tier of the church on both sides all the way back to the beautiful altar, nor did she appreciate the serenity. For her, there was no peace. The church was full. Some were whispering to each other, others were on the kneelers praying, and a few sat with their own thoughts and stared at the altar. She spotted Jake sitting next to Carol and the boys with her family. The team sat a few rows from the front. Mali walked down the center aisle, head held high, and looked at the team, eyebrows raised. Shuffling down, they made space for her and she sat next to Felix.

The service for Frank Grant was a beautiful tribute to a man who had given his life to service and to the country. Mali could feel the love for him, which gave her comfort. She hoped it comforted Carol and the boys as well. *Thank you, Frank, for all you've taught me, for your compassion, and for your friendship. I will miss you.*

* * *

Special Unit Warehouse
Monday, September 14, 7:30 a.m.

EVERYONE HAD ARRIVED and the buzz of activity was just ramping up when Jake walked out of the elevator with a woman. She looked Hispanic, was shorter than average, stocky but not overweight. She looked like she could take down a bull. When they arrived at the control center, she stood with feet apart and arms crossed. She was all business.

Jake hung his jacket on the back of a chair as he

called the team over. "First of all, I want to thank everyone for going to Frank's service yesterday. Carol was deeply appreciative. So was I. He was a good man and agent, and I have no doubt we'll all miss him." His eyes moved around the room, stopping briefly on Mali. His eyebrows drew together before he cleared his throat and continued. "But we have a job to do, one Frank would expect us to finish. With that mind, I want to introduce you to Rose Hernandez. She is the Interim Special Agent in Charge, recruited by the FBI right out of college. She…"

Agent Hernandez held up her hand. "We can get to know each other later." She studied each member before continuing. "Right now, you have a lot of work ahead of you. As I told Agent Black, while this taskforce has a certain anonymity and free rein, I will be more involved than Agent Grant. As such, until this case is resolved, I expect the team to work six days a week, ten-hour days. We can't let this continue and I will not have the FBI be the laughingstock to the public."

Jake's eyebrows shot up, which Agent Hernandez noticed.

"I realize we haven't had a chance to discuss this, Agent Black, but I decided to move forward just before we met upstairs. I am not pleased with how Janet Simpson and her team—yes, she has a team somewhere—appear to have expertise that far exceeds ours. This agency is the best in the world, as far as I'm concerned, so you can understand my confusion as to how this is even possible. I know you and your team have made great strides. Case in point is your ghost, and I look forward to seeing it in action. But the other technical aspects of this case have to be resolved quickly, and if that means longer hours, so be it. We can discuss adding more team members if you prefer."

Jake acknowledged what she said with a dip of his head.

"One final thing," she paused. "You're all grieving for Agent Grant. The best way to honor him is to catch Simpson and her cohorts quickly and put an end to this." She turned toward Jake. "Let's discuss some details in private before I leave."

Jake nodded and led her to the conference table. Returning to their tasks, most were mumbling amongst themselves as they did so.

"You're angry with me," Agent Hernandez said as soon as they sat.

"Respectfully, I would have appreciated discussing this with you in advance."

"Under normal circumstances, I would have. But these aren't normal times, and I don't have time to worry about hurt feelings."

"Can I speak freely?"

"I expect nothing less in our working relationship."

Jake pursed his lips. "Good. I'm glad to hear you want a working relationship. As do I. But if I'm going to lead this team, then I need to be the one leading them. I can't be undermined by anyone, including you. If you don't feel I can do the job, reassign me. Otherwise, I expect us to discuss changes you want to make or, at the very least, I expect you to inform me in advance of them so we can present a united front."

Agent Hernandez leaned back in her chair, eyes narrowed. She took a deep breath, releasing it slowly. "Understood. But I expect a call from you daily with a status update, sooner than that when JusticePrevails goes active or when you have sights on Simpson."

"Absolutely."

She nodded. "Good. And just to let you know, I will be stopping in regularly."

"We look forward to that."

"Now…Agent Hooper. Do you believe she still has the ability to do her job?"

They both searched the room and watched her working on her computer.

Jake turned his head back to Agent Hernandez. "Of course. Why wouldn't she?"

"Aside from the fact she's being targeted by Simpson, she looks like a puff of wind could knock her over. Does she blame herself for Grant's death?"

Jake opened his mouth, then frowned and glanced at Mali again. "I don't think she does. I haven't spoken with her much this week, nor the rest of the team for that matter. I was busy with Carol, the kids, the funeral, and our meetings together. She's not to blame for Grant's death."

"I know that, and you know that. Does she?" Pushing the chair back, Agent Hernandez stood. Jake followed suit. "I may have only minored in Psychology, but she looks haunted. Given her role in this case, I need you to ensure she's up to the task."

They turned toward the elevator. She stepped inside when the doors opened. "Next time I'm here, I want to see the ghost in action."

The elevator doors closed.

"Hoop," called out Jake as he returned to the conference table.

Mali looked up from the computer and nodded. Picking up a pad and pencil, she walked to the table, sitting in one of the chairs. Jake positioned the whiteboards for privacy, then sat next to her.

He looked at her, really looked at her.

Mali shifted in her seat, clasping her hands together on the table.

"Do I have a horn growing on my head or something?" she asked, somewhat waspishly.

"No, although now that I'm looking at you closely, I tend to agree with Agent Hernandez."

Mali's left eyebrow rose, and her lips parted.

"She said you looked haunted."

Snapping her lips closed, Mali argued, "We all just lost a great man. Of course, I'm upset."

"Do you blame yourself for Frank's death, Mali?"

Her eyes shot to his and her bottom lip quivered.

He placed his hand on both of hers.

"It's not your fault."

She looked at his hand resting on hers and swallowed.

"But it is," she whispered. "I was the one who riled her up on those phone calls."

"That's not why Frank was killed. It wasn't even because he spoke her name at the press conference." He squeezed her hands. "Look at me."

She raised her tear-filled eyes to his.

"Frank was killed because a sick, demented woman got her kicks out of doing so in the hopes of bringing you and all of us down. We can't let that happen."

"Everyone blames me, Jake. No one has spoken to me, not even you."

Jake leaned back with the force of her accusation. "I'm sorry I gave you that impression. I didn't call you this past week because when I wasn't helping Carol and the kids, I was meeting with Ben Casey, and then Rose Hernandez, at the main office. It was ten- to twelve-hour days, non-stop, then home to sleep. I didn't even see Heather or dad, and we live in the same house. I can't believe the team blames you, either. Everyone is grieving. But we have to set that aside if we're going to have any chance of catching Simpson. Can you do that?"

Mali swallowed and nodded.

"Good." He studied her. "You've lost some weight. When was the last time you ate?"

"Yesterday, I think."

"Hmmmm…" Jake stood, bringing Mali up with him.

"Can I have everyone's attention?" Jake walked to the main area with Mali beside him. When everyone was listening, Jake said, "It's only a matter of time before

Simpson contacts Hoop again. I want to be able to trace that call. Joe, figure it out. I want answers. Jeff, manage the ghost on Hoop as well as the ghosts on our targets. Susan, return to monitoring security here and at Hoop's apartment. Report any suspicious activity. And remember, no one leaves here alone and without notifying me as you leave and when you get home." He paused to study everyone. "One other thing I want to make clear. We are all grieving right now, and we all grieve in different ways. But we have to set that aside and focus on the job at hand, and we have to work together. There are a lot of moving parts and they're all interconnected. Work with each other and let's finish this!" He took a sip of Dr. Pepper. "Contact your families and inform them of our new work schedule. We'll be working from seven to seven, Monday through Saturday. "Questions?" he asked. When no one responded, "Good. Get to work."

Facing Mali, he reached into his jacket pocket, pulled out a strawberry pop tart, and handed it to her. She smiled, remembering the last time he gave her a pop tart.

"Heather put this in your jacket?"

Jake chuckled. "She told dad to make sure I wore this jacket to work today."

"Thanks Jake, for everything."

CHAPTER SIXTEEN

Special Unit Warehouse
Tuesday, September 15, 9:00 a.m.

MALI SLEPT THROUGH the night for the first time since Frank's death and arrived with a new sense of purpose. She had been studying past and present pedophilia cases since her arrival and was scrolling through national news when one in particular caught her eye.

"I'm concerned about an update on a pedophilia case involving a doctor in Miami," Mali said as she walked up to Jake, who was working at the conference table.

He looked up.

Sitting down, Mali continued. "Four years ago, Dr. Jessica Bradstone, a pediatrician, was arrested for abusing many of her patients. Her initial arrest involved six children. That count rose to eighty-two as authorities uncovered more evidence. The acts took place between two thousand and two thousand twelve with the victims ranging in age from ten months to twelve years. All were male except one." She turned her laptop toward Jake, showing him a picture of Jessica Bradstone.

"Jesus. I don't understand what possesses someone to do that. How the hell did she get away with it for so long?"

"Evidently there were warning signs including complaints of inappropriate behavior from parents back in two thousand seven, but the State of Florida didn't feel there was sufficient evidence to move forward."

"Unbelievable." He grimaced. "How was she caught?"

"A three-year-old complained to her mother that Bradstone had 'hurt her' when she took her to her office during an exam."

"My God."

"It gets worse. When police searched her property, they found more than twenty hours of video documenting her abuses, everything from rubbing infants and toddlers against her genitals to finger-raping them, and more. She was convicted of two hundred and ninety charges of crimes including rape, sexual assault, and sexual exploitation of a child. She was sentenced to life in jail with no possibility of parole and has been serving that sentence in the Homestead Women Correctional Institute outside of Florida City, Florida, for two years now. "

"So what is your concern?"

"A report this morning said the D.A. is reviewing her case. Evidently it may be overturned due to a technicality. Various local news outlets have reported this possibility the last few days, rehashing what she did, talking with the parents of her victims, that sort of thing."

"Christ. I'm assuming none of our ghosts are monitoring her."

"She wasn't even on our radar. There was no reason to since she was already in jail for life. This is a perfect target for Janet."

Jake jumped up and strode to the control center.

"I need everyone's attention."

All work stopped as the team's attention turned to Jake.

"Hoop just told me about a case that may be overturned due to a technicality. Hoop?"

"Joe, here's some info for the main screen." She swiped her laptop and moments later, the article and a picture of Bradstone were displayed. All eyes looked at her picture as Mali described the case.

"That is sick," stated Susan.

"I want to move one of the ghosts from a current target to the entrance of Homestead." Looking at Mali, Jake asked, "Which of the three targets we're tracking are the weakest in terms of being a potential victim of Simpson's?"

"Harvey Williams."

"I'm moving him now," said Jeff.

"Good. Kirsten, contact the local Miami field office. I want two agents placed at the Institute and assigned to protect Bradstone. Tell them we believe she is the next intended target of Justitia. Make sure they are aware of the ghost and how it works so the two agents can keep us informed via phone in tandem with the ghost. Do we have audio capability?"

Joe answered. "We believe we can link a mike to the ghost and hear whomever is wearing it as well as those close enough to it."

"Has that been tested?"

"Not yet."

Mali piped in. "Let's test it right now. Give me a mike."

"I'm calling Special Agent Hernandez while you test it. Felix, I want you and a member of the security team outside with Hoop," stated Jake. He turned away to make his call.

Mali was outfitted with a microphone and the three headed up to the street. Walking outside, she called Joe on her burner cell.

"Where's the ghost?"

"He's standing to the left of Felix. Hang up. I want to make sure we can hear you. Just speak in a normal voice."

Mali hung up the phone and made a face toward the other side of Felix.

"Joe said the ghost is right next to you, Felix."

"That's weird."

"Let's walk down the street. I want some distance from our building."

They had walked three blocks when Mali's phone rang.

"You really shouldn't be talking about me," said Joe.

"You heard us?"

"Every word. I'm going to move the ghost away from you a few feet at a time to measure the distance we can still hear what you're saying. Keep walking and talking. I'll call you in ten minutes or so."

They continued their walk, enjoying the sunshine

and occasionally making faces wherever they thought the ghost was standing. Laughing at their silliness, Mali mentioned she was thirsty. Seconds later her phone rang.

"Twenty feet, depending on the noise level around you. Since you mentioned you're thirsty, I want you to go inside the store at the end of the block to buy some water. I want to determine if audio is still available even if the ghost can't see you."

"Good idea." She hung up and explained what they were going to do. Walking inside, Mali bought a water, treating Felix to a Gatorade, before they walked outside again.

She had barely set foot outside when her phone rang again.

"You come across loud and clear, as long as you're within that twenty-foot range!" Joe enthused. "Jake says to head back."

Mali looked at Felix with a big smile. "We're in business."

Returning to the warehouse, they noticed Special Agent in Charge Hernandez speaking with Jake. There was a new energy in the air. Having the capability of hearing someone within a building was a huge step forward.

Jake was smiling. "The two agents are miked and will place a mike with GPS tracking on Bradstone as soon as they meet with her. We'll be able to hear any of them whenever the ghost is near, and we'll be able to track Bradstone at all times."

"I'm fascinated with what you've achieved," stated

Hernandez. "Congratulations to all. We have authority to access satellite imagery."

"Joe, give the top three screens to the satellite once it's up."

"The agents understand they have to be outside for the ghost to see them?" asked Mali.

"Yes," replied Jake, "and that the ghost only has a twenty-foot range. When they reach the entrance, one of them will drop their keys so the ghost can acquire them."

The Homestead Correctional Facility was a walled compound and contained four large cell blocks plus one maximum-security block, a health care building, a medium-security dorm, and a minimum-security building. The facility housed approximately six hundred and seventy inmates. Rebecca Bradstone was located in the medium security dorm.

As it was a non-visitation day, there was not a lot of traffic at the Institute. The only people entering or exiting were there on official business. Fifteen minutes after they started monitoring the entrance, a man and a woman, both in suits, walked toward the door. One dropped their keys.

"We've got them." The ghost was moved right next to the two of them.

"I don't understand how this ghost thing works but I'm assuming you can hear us. We're headed inside and will provide an update when we can."

Disappearing inside, they were heard talking to, and passing through, security before their voices faded away.

"Now we wait," said Jake.

As they waited, the ghost remained at the entrance monitoring all activity. An older man in uniform walked into the building as did a man and a woman, both wearing business suits. A woman wearing work clothes walked out. Nothing unusual was noted.

The satellite appeared on the top three screens as both agents stepped outside twenty minutes later. A woman, dressed in a navy pantsuit walked inside.

"We met with Bradstone. She said her lawyer was on the way to her with news. Bradstone was reluctant to wear the mike, initially, not understanding why she would be in any danger. She was unaware of the murders and Justitia. Once we explained it, she agreed. The mike is…" Both agents looked toward the building. "Hold on a sec." They rushed inside. Multiple people were speaking at one time, so the team could not understand what was being said.

One agent ran outside.

"Bradstone's lawyer just walked in, but the guards said two lawyers entered fifteen minutes ago and Bradstone was released to them for a court appointment. They were allowed to exit through a service entrance after expressing concern protesters were expected out front. John is still inside speaking with the lawyer."

"Christ!" exclaimed Jake. "What kind of car were they in? Jeff, raise the ghost above the buildings. Find the service entrance…"

Unknowing, the agent interrupted Jake. "There are two service entrances, by the way, one on the east side, the other on the south side."

The team watched the ghost rise above the buildings, slowly making a three-hundred-and-sixty degree turn. They spotted the two entrances.

John joined the other agent outside.

"They exited the south entrance and jumped into a silver Ford four-door sedan. They're pulling footage now."

Forgetting they couldn't hear him, Jake said, "Get a plate number if you can."

"I'm going to see if they got the license number of the sedan." John stated simultaneously and rushed back inside.

"Tell me we're tracking Bradstone," said Jake.

"Working on it," replied Jeff.

Jeff had already moved the ghost to the south service entrance. Two guards were milling about outside. He set the ghost at the end of the road that led outside the facility and looked both ways. The only vehicle on the road was a black truck heading east.

"Damn it!" Jake's nostrils flared. "Move the ghost back to the agents."

"…and an APB was issued on the vehicle." John was saying.

"Get John on the phone," Jake instructed Joe.

They spoke with the two agents for a few minutes before the agents went back inside to view the footage.

While they waited, Mali said, "Jake, can we look at the recording from the ghost? People were entering the facility while we were waiting."

"Good idea. Joe?"

The recording was replayed, and the team agreed the man and woman who entered the building a few minutes after the agents were probably the imposters.

"Is that Simpson and Butcher?" asked Kirsten.

Mali squinted her eyes and took a few steps closer to the large screen. "Hard to tell from this angle. Any way to zoom in?"

"Not without distorting the image," replied Jeff.

Both agents returned outside.

John said, "The vehicle headed west when it exited the facility. The police are narrowing their search to an area of about twenty square miles from the south service entrance."

"We've got a picture of the two who claimed to be Bradstone's lawyers," stated the other agent as he held up a picture.

While neither individual in the picture was looking up at the camera, Janet and Drake were clearly identified.

*　*　*

Agent Hernandez groused, "That was one of the most brazen acts I've ever seen."

"GPS tracking is up, and they're headed west," said Jeff.

"Get the two agents on the road. We'll instruct them where to go. We need a chopper in the air. I want Simpson and Drake to feel the heat," instructed Jake.

Joe increased the satellite imagery to the top six screens, leaving the bottom three with the ghost and two agents.

Jeff manipulated the controls for the satellite. "This is nine minutes ago." They watched three people get into a car just outside of the building at the south service entrance.

"Zoom in," said Jake.

Upon zooming in, even though the image was blurry, they could identify Janet and Drake with Dr. Bradstone. She was cuffed and Janet helped her into the back seat then climbed in beside her. Drake was driving. The car exited the south entrance and turned west.

The agents zoomed to the south service entrance leading out of the facility and made a hard left onto the road heading west. Three police cars soon joined the agents in the pursuit.

Jeff said, "We're going to lose satellite in sixty seconds. GPS tracking is still strong however."

"Can the ghost go to Bradstone based on the tracking?"

Jeff's eyes lit up. "Yes, on it."

"Call John since we're moving the ghost."

Jeff moved the ghost forward based on the coordinates provided by Joe, as the car with the agents sped down the road in an attempt to catch up. Despite the gravity of the situation, Mali was flabbergasted by the ghost and its capabilities.

After a couple of minutes, John asked, "Did you say they turned onto state road ninety-three-thirty-six?"

"Yes. They turned west. That was four minutes ago," said Jeff.

The team watched as the ghost approached the rear of the sedan.

"They're headed to the Everglades," he informed them.

"Yes, the sedan is in the Everglades. Transmit the location to the chopper."

"Since Bradstone is wearing the mike, shouldn't we hear something via the ghost?" asked Kirsten.

Before anyone answered, Mali asked, "Isn't ninety-three-thirty-six the main road going through that part of the Everglades?" She was looking at a map online.

"Yes, it is. The road is forty-five miles long and fairly open," stated John from the car.

"Block the other end of the road. Have additional cars move in from that end and let's close the gap," said Jake.

"Why would they go on a road that could trap them?" asked Mali.

Joe asked, "Why isn't anyone talking in the sedan? Surely they hear the chopper? Is audio still working on the ghost?"

"Audio seems to be working," said Jeff.

The occasional whop-whop of the chopper and police sirens, via Bradstone's mike, were the only sounds as the ghost continued to follow the sedan. Jeff turned the ghost around and they saw the police cars, now in front of the agents. The helicopter could be seen in the distance as well. Facing the ghost forward again, the team watched the sedan pass sabal palm trees that lined the road here and there and fields of evergreen grasses, which were sprinkled throughout on both sides of the road. They flew by in a blur as the sedan raced down the state road.

Two minutes later, the sound of the helicopter grew louder as it moved in front of the sedan and bobbed up and down to slow it down. The sedan screeched to a near halt, spinning around to face the police cars, and coming to a stop in the middle of the road. The ghost watched the chopper set down behind the sedan before Jeff turned it to face the police cars.

What happened next was a blur of activity as the officers jumped out of their vehicles, guns drawn, and approached the vehicle. The front door on the driver's side was thrust open and a man was pulled out and shoved to the ground. The ghost was in the perfect position above the sedan for the team to observe everything. The passenger door was then thrown open. Shouting was heard before one of the officers shook his head.

"All secure," shouted another officer.

Only one person was lying face down on the ground. No one else was in the sedan.

An officer handed something to John's partner. He held it up…the mike/GPS tracking device.

The team was silent as the implications were apparent.

"Shit!" exclaimed Jake. "A bait and switch."

"When did they do it?" asked Felix.

"Damn it! More than likely, right after they headed west out of the facility."

Agent Hernandez said, "Place all bus and train stations, area ports, as well as the Miami airport and smaller airstrips on alert."

Jake nodded. "A good precaution although with her

resources, and considering they have Dr. Bradstone in tow, I doubt she'll use any of them."

"Dr. Bradstone is her next victim and there's nothing we can do to stop it," forewarned Mali.

CHAPTER SEVENTEEN

Special Unit Warehouse

Everyone jumped into action, placing calls to lock down public transportation, ports and airports, and reviewing the satellite and ghost recordings.

"Talk to me, people," urged Jake.

Joe jumped in. "We believe they switched vehicles moments after turning west out of the south gate. If you'll recall, the only vehicle on the road was a black truck. We believe they were in that truck." The ghost recording was put on the screen. They watched the ghost look both ways on the road at the south entrance. The black truck could be seen approaching from the west, heading east.

"Can you zoom in and read the plate?"

Jeff zoomed in. The license plate was blurry.

"Is that HKJ 3B9?" asked Jake.

"I think the B is an 8," offered Mali.

"Run the plates for both."

Two minutes later, Kirsten said, "I have a black Chevrolet Z seventy-one, license plate HKJ 889, that was reported stolen three hours ago. I've sent the info to the police. They're searching for it now."

"Jake, I've been researching Dr. Bradstone—where she lived and worked, places she frequented. My thought is that since Janet killed her brother in the house where they grew up, maybe she'll do the same and take Bradstone to a place familiar to her."

"Good idea, Hoop. Out of an abundance of caution, let's get a team to her house and to her business."

"Already done."

Jake nodded.

Two hours later, Kirsten raised her voice over the chatter of activity. "Jake?" When he looked up, she continued. "The truck has been found." She sent a picture to Joe, who displayed it on the large screen. "It was parked on the outer edges of a grocery store parking lot. No cameras in that area."

"Damn it." He grimaced, shaking his head. "Unbelievable that they can stay one step ahead of us despite the technology we now have to ID and track them. It's almost as if…" His eyes roamed the room until they locked on Mali's.

Her jaw had dropped open. "She can't possibly know about the ghost," exclaimed Mali. "Can she?"

The sound of the alarm signaling #JusticePrevails going active, interrupted that revelation. The team rallied around the control center as Joe brought up Twitter and navigated to #JusticePrevails.

"Click to participate in our next poll. If you haven't

signed up yet, you'd better hurry. You have twelve minutes…go!"

Joe clicked the link and LadyJustice opened. Placed to the right of the Join Now button was a new one labelled Sign In. He clicked the button to sign in and logged in with Gonnafly and the burner phone number that had already been established.

The same welcome message displayed, as before, instructing the user to scroll down the page to cast their vote.

When Joe scrolled down, a picture of Rebecca Bradstone appeared. She was wearing a doctor's white lab coat and the same prison pants as before. A stethoscope was draped around her neck, hanging down in front. She was gagged and tied at the waist to a metal table positioned vertically. Her bare feet were secured in stirrups and her arms were shackled to her sides.

She was surrounded by four identical pieces of equipment. Each had a square base that supported a hinged mechanical arm holding some sort of tool. To the side of each one was a cart containing a computer console and other equipment.

"What the hell is all that?" asked Kirsten.

Ignoring Kirsten's question, Jake asked, "Can we identify where she is?"

"There's nothing to go on from that picture," Jeff said. "We can't even tell if she's in an office building, a house, or outside for that matter. It's too dark."

"Scroll down, Joe."

The message read: "This is Dr. Rebecca Blackstone,

a pediatrician. She was convicted of more than eighty counts of rape and sexual assault on children, ages ten months to twelve years. She has been in jail for a couple of years but was about to be released on a technicality. She does not deserve to live. You have a choice: watch her execution after she confesses her sins or do not watch and be satisfied justice will prevail in the end. Her confession and execution start immediately after this poll ends. Majority rules. Vote now to participate."

"That is really sick," stated Felix.

Joe said, "The countdown clock shows one minute and thirty seconds until the poll closes."

"There's nothing we can do?" asked Agent Hernandez.

"I think I know where she is!" Mali's voice rose in her excitement. "She used to be a guest speaker at the Miami University Miller School of Medicine. It's located right next to the Jackson Memorial Hospital." She looked up from her screen. "The entire pediatrics wing at the hospital is empty and closed for renovations."

"Get the police there now! And place all ghosts at each entrance with one on the roof. If we can't save Bradstone, I want to at least catch the bitch." Jake looked at Joe. "Select Do not watch."

Joe made the selection with fifteen seconds to spare.

"Wow! More than sixty thousand votes, looks like most people want to watch." Felix was still looking at the screen.

The team watched as time ran out and the screen turned black. A slow trickle of red appeared and dripped from the top of the screen downward, as before.

In bold red letters, the screen flashed Majority rules. Watch justice prevail.

The screen flashed again, and a livestream appeared.

* * *

One. Two. Three. Floodlights positioned behind the camera, at the foot of the metal table, flashed on one at a time. Four large machines were positioned around her upper body. A dirty wall, partially torn down, was the only thing visible beyond Dr. Bradstone and the machinery.

Dr. Bradstone turned her face away from the lights. An instant later, her head whipped back toward the camera, eyes wide. She struggled and moaned as tears formed and rolled down her neck.

"Ah, you noticed the machinery," said Justitia from her position behind the camera, her distorted voice laced with humor. Taking a step forward, her backside from the waist up appeared. She was wearing a white jacket and her hair was in a tight bun at the nape of her neck. She was holding a cigarette in her hand. "I have to say that robotically-assisted surgical devices are quite impressive up close."

Dr. Bradstone continued to struggle, shaking her head from side to side.

"I was going to allow you time to confess your sins so you have an opportunity to redeem yourself before God, our creator, but you're not sorry at all, are you? If I recall correctly, you pled guilty to reduce your sentence. They cut it in half, I believe. And now a technicality will get you out of jail? That is not justice." She paused, flicking the ashes from her cigarette.

A wrist appeared in the camera view. She looked at the watch and nodded.

"Apparently, we don't have much time before the police arrive. Hospital staff are almost upon us. They aren't so inept that they won't find us. However, they won't succeed in breaking into this room. The police, on the other hand, will come prepared. So no time to dawdle."

A large man, dressed all in black including a hood covering his face, moved quickly into view and to the first machine. He moved it closer to the table, lowered the arm horizontally, and positioned the tool below and to the side of her belly button. It rested five inches above her body. The other three machines were positioned similarly so all four tools formed a square around her belly button.

Justitia continued to talk as this was being completed. "Sexually deviant behavior has an interesting past. Long ago, a man would be castrated for such behavior. Cutting off testicles was very painful, but the belief was those temptations would subside without ones' balls." She laughed. "Over time, they moved to chemical castration where regular injections of anti-androgens were given to the pedophile. Sadly, now one only needs to see a therapist and take some pills to be considered able to control those urges. Personally, I don't believe that." She paused, taking a deep drag of her cigarette before dropping it onto the ground. "But what about women who are sexual deviants?

There's nothing hanging to castrate. I suppose chemicals can be given to reduce or eliminate those urges but, again, I don't believe those work. So what to do with you?" A short pause. "After giving it considerable thought, I've decided to perform a surgical procedure, of sorts. These four machines and the tools that are usually attached are specifically designed for hysterectomies. We've modified it, of course, but I figured you'd enjoy the irony. A pity we won't be able to watch until the end."

As soon as the man finished positioning the robotic arms, a soft hum sounded, becoming louder as each machine was turned on. He moved out of the screen shot and, moments later, the video camera was repositioned so Dr. Bradstone's mid-section could be easily seen.

"I can't watch this," said Kirsten, turning away.

Dr. Bradstone screamed behind her gag, shaking her head, pulling on her arms and legs in a vain attempt to escape. The camera zoomed in on the tools, now clearly seen to be scalpels. They were moving in an up and down motion. The team watched in horror as they inched toward her mid-section.

"Oh God," exclaimed Mali. Her stomach clenched as the blades moved closer and closer.

Susan choked out, "Look at the comments. How can they be so uncaring?"

Below the livestream, comments were flying in faster than the scalpels moved.

"Totally rad, man!"

"The bitch is getting what she deserves…ten-month-old babies!?!"

"Justitia is right, she doesn't deserve to live."

"Cool!"

"The parents of those children are getting justice."

"Wish I was there in person."

The comments continued.

Dr. Bradstone froze an instant before the first blade hit its mark. When it did, her body jerked and bucked. Sweat poured off her face, from the lights and the pain as the scalpels moved up and down, up and down. The robotic arms continued their downward descent and soon half the scalpels were inside her body. Blood squirted out and ran down her body, dripping onto the yellow-ish floor. Dr. Bradstone lost consciousness but the robotic arms did not stop.

Muted pounding in the distance could be discerned but the only immediate sounds were the hum of the machines and the sucking of the scalpels as they moved through Dr. Bradstone's body.

"Jesus!" Jake shook his head. He cleared his throat. "What's the ETA on the cops? It also sounded like Simpson was going to split. Are the ghosts picking up anything?"

Jeff responded. "Nothing at the entrances or on the roof."

The sound of pounding outside the room intensified. The team heard wood splintering seconds before four officers raced into the room and into camera view. They stopped short at the grisly sight that greeted them. One officer turned to the side and vomited. Another officer turned back toward the door, presumably to secure the room.

The remaining two officers were trying to find a way to turn off the machines. When they saw the video camera and realized it was still running, a grim-looking officer rushed over and, blocking the view, reached up and pressed something. The screen went black.

There was a brief silence in the room.

Mali said, "I'm on the phone with the authorities. The murder occurred in a secure area on the second floor of the six-floor building. Other officers have begun to search the remaining floors. The rest of the hospital is being secured. Helicopters are in the air and they're setting up a perimeter. Local agents are on their way."

"There's activity on the roof," said Jeff. "A police chopper has landed. Three officers exited and are talking with two officers already on the roof." Everyone looked at the lower middle screen on the wall that showed the ghost on the roof. As they watched, all five officers turned and walked toward the door.

Mali took a deep breath. "They could be anywhere, Jake. They would have planned an exit strategy and there are too many exit points for our ghosts."

Jake frowned. "Wait a minute. How did two officers get up to the roof so quickly when they have just begun to search the rest of the pediatrics wing?"

"Shit. They're dressed as cops," exclaimed Agent Hernandez.

The team moved into action with the four ghosts and in coordination with agents on the ground and the police. But they were too late. Simpson was gone.

CHAPTER EIGHTEEN

Special Unit Warehouse
Friday, September 18, 8:20 p.m.

THE DAYS THAT followed Dr. Bradstone's murder had been tough ones for the team. Social media was still lauding the work of Justitia even as most media outlets and late-night television hosts were mocking the inability of the FBI to put an end to the murders.

There had been no word from Simpson.

French authorities had finally confirmed a property in Cancale was purchased five months ago by Anthony Hunter. It was a compound, just under an acre in size, with a house, pool, and a smaller outbuilding. Palm trees were scattered here and there, and grass covered every surface except the driveway. The compound was encircled by a ten-foot-high white cement wall, and security cameras were seen at strategic points on top of the wall as well as around the house. Two guards were posted at the front entrance gate, and one was positioned near a walk-through gate at the back of the property. All were armed. It was a veritable fortress.

A local team was in place and had been surveilling the property for forty-eight hours. They had confirmed there were six individuals working inside who never left the house. Three additional guards were located inside the smaller outbuilding, who rotated every four hours with those stationed at the gates. Three were on and three were off at all times. Food and supplies were delivered twice a day. No other people were allowed inside the gates.

They had also determined the best time to infiltrate the property was between one and three a.m. when the six people inside were asleep and the guards were most vulnerable. They were planning to breach in ten minutes, at two-thirty a.m. local time. Jake and the rest of the team were watching. The top six screens on the back wall were a view from a bodycam on the team leader. The bottom three displayed the live satellite.

All ghosts were positioned around the compound. Two were manned by Jeff, one of which was on the top of the wall at the main entrance and the other was posted at the rear entrance. The other two ghosts were manned by Susan, one stationed outside the smaller outbuilding where the other three guards were located, with the 4th roaming the grounds. The ghosts would act as additional eyes for the team on the ground.

"We have three teams of two men, one at each entrance and one at the wall by the outbuilding, all ready to breach," said the team leader. "I want confirmation of the location of everyone in the compound."

"Copy that." Jake looked at the satellite. "The guards on duty are in their designated places, the two in front are standing next to each other in the center of the driveway, just inside the gate. You should have a visual. The guard in back is approximately three feet to the left of the gate, leaning against the wall. All guards in the outbuilding are in the main room, two are horizontal, one is vertical but stationary. The six inside the main house are in three rooms to the right once you enter the front door. All are horizontal, probably sleeping. No other movement. Will keep you apprised of any changes."

"Who has eyes on the security cameras?"

"Unknown, possibly the third guard in the outbuilding."

"We'll take them out first then, before proceeding with a full breach. Team Delta, a technical crew, is on standby once all is secure. Do we have the green light?"

"Yes."

"Roger. Let's roll." The team lead gave final instructions to his men, and they began to execute their plan.

"Hold," said Jake. "One of the guards in the outbuilding is walking to the door."

"Which one?" asked the team lead.

"The guard who was already standing. Susan, you should see him now. Satellite is moving out of range. Follow him and tell me where he goes."

Susan nodded.

"If that was the guy watching the cameras, our job just got easier," responded the team lead. Speaking to his ground team, "Alpha, take out the guard once he's outside the building, then the others. Bravo and Charlie, we go in immediately after."

"He stopped just outside the front door. Looks like he's going to take a whiz," stated Susan.

"Joe, put that ghost's view on the bottom middle screen." The view appeared and the team observed the guard as he glanced around while unzipping his pants. Before he could reach inside with his hand, they watched him jerk then drop to the ground.

"Move," said the team lead. There was controlled chaos as Alpha team took out the guards in the outbuilding then the other two teams neutralized the guards at the entrances, before all three teams moved as one unit toward the house. Capturing the six inside was rather uneventful. None were armed and they immediately surrendered when faced with multiple guns pointed in their direction.

"We're all secure and the technical team is inside. The six who have been captured are cuffed and sitting in the living room. We will interrogate each as the technical team reviews the equipment and data. This will take some time."

Jake said, "Set up an interrogation area in another part of the house. I want to be present when you speak with each one. And I want one of my team members looking over the shoulder of each person assessing the equipment. My people are more familiar with this case and may be able to identify what they're doing, or who their next target is, faster than you could."

"Roger. We'll get the necessary feeds set up."

"Good." Jake looked at his watch. "Let's meet in one hour." When the team lead nodded, they signed off.

Jake rubbed his face. "Call your families and tell them you won't be home tonight. Remind them they should remain at home for the foreseeable future. If they have to leave, an agent must accompany them." He reached into his pocket and pulled out sixty dollars. "Susan and Felix, grab some pizzas from that joint a few blocks down the street, plus some water and sodas. I want a brief meeting in forty minutes before we join the team in France."

Mali dialed her mother's phone number as she navigated around the tables to her work area.

"I was wondering when you were going to call, Jasmine. Your short and cryptic message last week provided no explanation as to why there are two officers sitting in our foyer." Willow was not pleased. "You're on speaker phone, by the way. Your father is sitting next to me."

"I'm sorry, Mother, sorry I haven't called sooner to explain and sorry this is even happening. The case we're working on has taken a personal turn and the security is just a precaution."

"Personal against you?" asked Charles, concern in his voice.

"Against the entire team. Everyone has security."

"Even the parents of all team members?" Charles was a shrewd man. He wouldn't have achieved his success in business otherwise.

Mali hesitated. "No."

"So this has something to do with why you looked so exhausted at your father's dinner last week?"

Mali didn't answer directly. "I really am sorry if your work and social calendars have been affected."

"Your Father is still going to work every day with the security you've provided. I have opted to remain home. While my friends are wondering why I didn't participate this past Monday evening in our monthly book club meeting or my weekly tennis match on Wednesday, the time home has given me an opportunity to catch up on my correspondence. It was a little more difficult explaining why we did not attend the symphony last night." As major donors of the Philharmonic Symphony, Mali's parents attended every event. It was a given and would be noticed if they were absent.

When Mali's mother sniffed, she felt guilt creep up her tensing shoulders and sighed. "There's nothing I can do about it. I'd much rather have you miss a few events and be safe at home than go on as usual and have something happen to you."

"Well, when you put it like that…"

Charles chuckled. "We are just fine, Jasmine. Take care of yourself and call again when you can."

* * *

"Everything okay?" asked Jake when Mali returned to the control center.

Mali nodded. "Just the usual dramatics from my mother. But they've curtailed all their social activities and my father leaves just to go to and from work. Mother is staying home."

"Good."

"How about your dad?"

"He's fine, understands the nature of our business. He said Heather has been taking so many cookies and milk to the security team that they have all complained of gaining weight. But there's no way they'll say no to a cute six-year-old."

Mali laughed with Jake at the image. "An adorable six-year-old, you mean."

They were all was sitting at the conference table munching on pizza and providing updates to Jake.

"Joe, where are we with tracking Simpson from Hoop's phone?"

"After contacting three of the best spoofing companies and giving them the latest date, one has confirmed their company is being used by Simpson. They're located in New Jersey, just west of Staten Island. While they indicate they will cooperate with us, they won't provide any more information without a subpoena. We…"

Jake interrupted. "I'll contact Agent Hernandez for that."

"They normally delete all call information twenty-four hours after a call is completed. We asked them to save all data until we can obtain the subpoena, in case Janet calls and we don't get the subpoena quickly. They were willing to do that."

"Good. We're making progress. Let me make that call." He stepped away from the table.

Mali looked at Kirsten. "Jen doing alright?"

Kirsten scrunched her nose. "Yes and no. She's

fortunate to be able to work from home most of the time, although there's an event coming up next weekend she says she has to attend. And come Monday, she'll have to handle the final details in person. She's not happy she has to have an escort, says it curbs her freedom." Kirsten smiled. "But she understands and wants to be safe. She's also concerned about my safety, and yours especially."

"Well, with luck, we'll be done with this case soon."

Jake walked up to the table saying, "Agent Hernandez is working on the subpoena. Where were we? Ah, any noise from social media?"

Kirsten shook her head. "Twitter and other venues voluntarily deleted all data from Bradstone's murder. Chatter on #JusticePrevails is minimal, most are wondering who the next target is. Some are making suggestions."

Mali frowned and took a bite of pizza, chewing as she considered all that was being said.

"And the ghosts?"

Jeff spoke up. "The only movement at the compound are from our people."

"Good. What about the…" Jake's phones rang. It was a short call. "We've got the subpoena. Kirsten, get on the horn with the spoofing company and let's get Simpson's number. Jeff, I want Hoop's phone set up for tracing quickly. Keep the forward momentum going, people."

10:50 p.m.

THEY WERE READY when the call came in from France, spending the next four hours assessing the equipment and interviewing Simpson's technical staff. Her people had three areas of focus— research, the LadyJustice app and the blockchain, and an event coordinator, for lack of a better term. They had been working for Janet for more than a year, starting in Switzerland and moving to France when the property was purchased.

The two-member research team had identified and compiled a list more than three hundred wealthy and powerful suspected pedophiles and child traffickers in the United States alone. The list included Hollywood elites, politicians, and corporate CEOs. Number one on the list, however, was Simpson's brother, Hank Hunter, who was neither wealthy nor powerful. Thomas Martin was number five, James Adam was seventh, and Rebecca Bradstone was fortieth. They were instructed to pursue the top twenty first, not in any particular order, before moving down the list. They only bumped Bradstone up because of her pending release.

The second area of focus, the app and the blockchain, was developed by three staff who were identified by Jake and the team as being the top three hacker/developers in the industry and high on the FBI's most wanted list for various cybercrimes. While they developed the tool per Janet's specifications, Janet and Drake operated it.

Event coordination was the last area of focus and run by the remaining member of Simpson's staff with the others assisting, as needed, once they went operational with a target. Her purpose was to seek out and coordinate all stages for the events Janet hosted. They worked with a network of operatives across the states to plan and set up everything from transportation to drone operation at each event, to assisting with the capture of each target. All preparations were handled from the event coordinator and passed on to Janet at the appropriate time.

"How does Janet determine who to go after next?" asked Kirsten.

The team lead responded. "The researchers track everyone on the list. Janet also has the list but allows the researchers to recommend two or three at a time. She decides from that short list who is next. The event coordinator starts the planning for all profiles given to Janet, so they are ready to move with whomever she chooses. It was different with Bradstone."

Jake added, "Janet informs her team, via text, when she's ready for the next target. There is evidently no set timeframe."

Felix jumped into the conversation. "Not to change the subject or anything, but we've learned a lot about the blockchain network. For example, it's a public-permissioned system allowing anyone to join the network."

Mali mumbled, "Whatever that means."

Jake asked, "So can you break the chain, delete all users, remove the app…anything that could help us?"

"We can effectively just turn it off. But we can take things even further."

"What do you mean?"

Jeff was nodding his head. "He means we have control of their entire operation. This is Simpson's operational center. Per the event coordinator, Janet has the list. But we can select two or three profiles to send her, set up an event at a locale of our choosing, and lead her right to us."

The excitement in the room grew as realization hit the team.

"We have just one problem." When Kirsten had everyone's attention, she continued. "It looks like three profiles were provided to Janet over eleven hours ago."

CHAPTER NINETEEN

"WHAT!" EXCLAIMED JAKE. "None of those interviewed mentioned that. Put their profiles on the screen."

The team lead at the compound excused himself to have another conversation with the event coordinator.

Kirsten passed the information to Joe who moved them to the three upper screens.

"The man on the left is number fifteen on the list, Jaime Garcia, CEO of Bank of the West in Eagle, Idaho. He was arrested yesterday on forty-three counts of child pornography, indecent exposure to a minor, and a couple other charges. The minor was an eleven-year-old girl he was having an online relationship with. Her parents found out and called the police. He is currently out on bail. The man in the middle, David White, a junior representative of the House and number four on the list, is suspected of child trafficking in Las Vegas. Three days ago, an eight-year-old boy escaped from a house owned by White and was taken to the authorities. He said there were about fifteen other children there. All were told they were going to a beautiful land with lots of beaches. White has denied all charges saying he hasn't lived in that house since he was elected, spending all his time in DC. He currently resides at an apartment in Alexandria, Virginia. And you may recognize the man on the right. That's George Watson, one-time child actor and now director of blockbusters like *The Long Road Home* and *Making Twenty-One*. He's number eight and lives in Malibu."

"Thanks Kirsten," said Jake. "Has she targeted the next person yet?"

"No target has been identified by Janet yet." The team lead stepped into the camera's view. "We convinced the coordinator it was in his best interest to provide all information. As your agent said, the profiles were provided to Janet at approximately nine-thirty last night, local time. She usually responds within twenty to twenty-four hours. The event coordinator was in the initial stages of researching possible locales for all three so they could move quickly once she decides."

"Have we confirmed the location of where the three are right now?" asked Jake.

"No. I'm researching that, starting with information on the profile. Kirsten is helping with some phone calls," said Mali.

"How long from the time she identifies the target to the time of execution?"

The team lead replied, "Anywhere from twenty-four to seventy-two hours, depending on the case and how elaborate Janet wants to make it."

"So we've got a little time. Jeff, as soon as Hoop identifies the locations of the three targets, send the ghosts to them for tracking."

Mali returned a few minutes later. "We can only place George Watson at his residence in Malibu. The location of the other two are unknown at this time."

Jeff said, "I've placed all ghosts at the residence of each, assuming for now the other two are home as well."

"Good. Okay, it doesn't look like anything is going to happen for a few hours. Continue to monitor Hoop as well as the three targets. You'll stay?"

Jeff nodded.

"Everyone else, go home and get some shut-eye." He looked at his watch. "It's after three, be back at o-nine-thirty."

Kirsten had returned to the group as Jake finished talking. "Jake, I've contacted the field offices located nearest to Garcia and White and requested their assistance in determining if they are home. They'll contact Jeff as soon as they get that confirmation."

Everyone gathered their things and left. Mali recognized Jake speaking with the team lead in France as the elevator door closed.

* * *

Special Unit Warehouse
Saturday, September 19, 11:00 a.m.

THE ENERGY IN the room was palpable. While there was no activity with the ghosts or on social media, the local agents had confirmed all three were in their respective homes. Agents and ghosts had them under surveillance.

Kirsten and Jeff were working with the team in France studying the event coordinator assessments of locales and trying to determine the best place to set a trap for Simpson. Now that they had access to the blockchain network, Felix and two team members at the compound were analyzing the code with plans to turn off the network so Janet couldn't use the app or anything else associated with it. Joe had obtained Simpson's phone number and had set up tracing capabilities on Mali's cell phone as well as their landline, in case she called through the office as she had before. The hope was she would use the same phone.

Now it was a waiting game.

Jake and Mali were sitting at the conference table and had been talking non-stop for the past thirty minutes. Despite the circumstances around them, Mali felt a warmth in her heart because of him. She had never met a more caring or dedicated man. He made her laugh and comforted her when she needed it. It was a little unsettling to be with someone who truly knew her better than anyone else. She realized she trusted him, and that was saying a lot.

"I'd like to plan a weekend with Jerry and Heather at my parent's house," Mali mentioned during a lull in the conversation.

Jake squeezed her hand, which was resting on the table.

"I'd like that. So would dad and Heather. Were you thinking of a specific weekend?"

"Well, how about next weekend or the first weekend

in October? The fall colors are beautiful. Given their lack of social life right now, it could be fun. I'll need to confirm with my mother first."

"Just give me the date and we'll be there. Heather will be very excited to go on a road trip. And she'll probably flip when she sees the house you grew up in."

"It should still be warm enough to swim in the pool, and it will be fun to explore the gardens with her."

When the phone line on the table rang, Mali and Jake came to attention. Jake whistled to Joe, silencing everyone in the process. Mali picked up the phone.

"Phone call for you, Agent Hooper," said Becky from upstairs.

"Thanks Becky. I'll take it here."

Mali answered the line when Joe indicated he was ready to trace the call. She put it on speaker phone.

"Good morning, Agent Hooper speaking."

"My, my, my. You have been a very busy bee, Agent Hooper."

"So have you, Janet. Your murder of Rebecca Bradstone was brutal and horrendous."

"That bitch deserved to die. Aren't you concerned about the children she molested?" Mali listened to her inhale then blow smoke out of her mouth. "But that's not why I've called."

"So you didn't call to gloat?"

Ignoring that, Janet continued. "I am surprised and impressed at the ingenuity of the FBI. You figured out what my brother couldn't."

"I have no idea what you're talking about."

"Oh, I think you do. You've figured out how to place watchers on the street, real time. I thought that was the case when you displayed those pictures of us at the news conference. There was no one around, and no way anyone could have taken a picture from that angle. By the way, were you the one who figured out Bradstone was next on our list?"

"Not hard to do, Janet, you've become predictable."

"The mistake you made, Agent Hooper, was in revealing you have watcher capability. I knew when we were going to grab Bradstone that a diversion was in order, an alternate plan as it were, just in case you were around with it."

"Better watch out, Janet. We almost caught you. We'll do so in a very short time. You are becoming lazy and sloppy, like a fat cat."

Janet gasped. "You stupid bitch. Killing Agent Grant wasn't proof enough to you that you can't mess with me? His blood is on your hands because you didn't take me seriously nor did you appreciate all I've done for you."

Mali's lips thinned in anger. Jake tapped her hand. When she looked at him, he shook his head. Taking a deep breath, Mali replied, "The only killer here is you, Janet. You are a sick, demented person because of the abuse you suffered when you were a child, and by your own brothers no less. No one to help, not even your parents."

"Enough!" shouted Janet. "I won't listen to this! How dare you try to analyze me!"

"You're the one who called. There must be a part of you inside crying out for help."

"You think you know it all?"

"We're learning more every day. Now, why are you calling? You're wasting my time and I'm getting bored."

Janet sputtered. "I'm calling to tell you the justice meted out to Rebecca Bradstone is nothing compared to what's next."

"Blah, blah, blah. You really are quite droll, Janet. I'm done with this conversation." Mali hung up the phone.

"That was brilliant," said Jake. "You got to her."

Mali smiled.

"She's in Las Vegas," exclaimed Joe.

CHAPTER TWENTY

JOE PLACED A map of Vegas on the screens. "Her phone pinged a tower in North Las Vegas." He set a marker at that point. "If she makes additional calls, we may be able to pinpoint her location.

"Good," stated Jake. "Jeff, move the ghosts to Vegas. Place one at either end of the strip and one in the middle, for now, until we have a better idea of her location. Kirsten, contact the local FBI office. I want as many agents as they can spare on the streets. Get the police involved too. Joe, get access to city cameras. Start in the Strip and work outward. Put them on Susan's security monitors and I want both of you to monitor them as they come online. I'll call Agent Hernandez for satellite access. Let's move people. We need to put an end to this."

The team worked as one in their unified purpose to catch Simpson. The movement in the room was poetic as phone calls were made, agents moved from their monitors to those of other team members, the screens at the front of the room were flashing and images displayed as elements of their plan came together.

"The team lead in France is contacting us, Jake," said Joe.

"Put him on speaker."

"Simpson just texted the event coordinator," he stated without preamble.

"So soon?" asked Mali. "I thought she didn't respond for twenty hours or more."

"The coordinator said she bumped up her plan and wants to execute within twelve hours."

"So who is her target?" asked Jake.

"Jaime Garcia."

"In Idaho? Then what's she doing in Vegas?" wondered Kirsten.

"Does Garcia have ties there?" asked Jake. His eyes found Mali.

"On it," she said.

"Kirsten, contact the agent at Garcia's home. I want him in custody, for his own safety."

Mali cleared her throat. "Jake, Garcia has no ties to Vegas other than an occasional stay at The Bellagio. He gambles minimally and attends a few shows."

"Hmmm…"

Kirsten rushed over. "Garcia's in custody. They're taking him to a safe house."

Jake's frowned, then his eyes widened. "She played us. She's in Vegas for David White."

"I'm confused. White lives in Virginia," said Susan.

Mali glanced at Jake, shaking her head in disbelief. "But his trafficking accusations are based in Vegas. Jaime

Garcia was a test…" She paused. "…and we failed. She now knows we're in control of her operation in France."

"Jesus, she's making us look like fools!" exploded Jake. His face was red, and it looked like he was going to explode. He looked at Jeff. "Any activity at White's home?"

Jeff shook his head.

Jake fired off his instructions and questions. "Kirsten, contact the agent outside his house. I want visual confirmation he's inside. In fact, contact agents at both houses. I want White and Watson taken into protective custody. And I want a ghost in front of White's place in Vegas. Felix, were you able to shut down the app?"

Felix shook his head. "Working on it."

The control center beeped and flashed red. All nine screens at the front were blinking. #JusticePrevails was active again.

As Joe opened Twitter and navigated to #JusticePrevails, Kirsten returned to the group. "Watson is in custody. David White is not in his house. A man inside said he was paid to stay there. He's been taken into custody for further questioning."

"How the hell did they get past us?"

Everyone looked at the screen and read: "The FBI actually thinks they can catch Justitia. No one can stop justice from prevailing. Go to LadyJustice now, prove them wrong."

"Open the app."

After Joe signed in, he scrolled down the page. A picture of David White appeared. He was sitting down, hands tied behind his back. Shirtless, a capital C and T had been carved into his chest. Trails of red were visible from the letters down to his pants. The message below read: "The new scarlet letters for child traffickers. Below is just one example of the lies he has spewed."

Joe scrolled down and there was another picture of White in a house. A little girl was perched on his lap as he spoke with a man sitting next to him. They were in loungers next to a pool. Four other girls were sitting on the edge of the pool with their feet dangling in the water. All appeared to be eight-to-ten years in age, all wore only underwear.

The message continued beneath this picture: "This is a picture of White at his pool in the backyard of his house in Las Vegas. The picture was taken six months ago. The man sitting next to him is Aleksei Stropov. He is the leader of the largest human trafficking organization in the United States."

"Can we verify this?" asked Jake.

Jeff responded. "Moving the ghost to the back right now."

The team looked at the back of the house and compared it to the picture. It was a match.

They continued to read. "While Justitia is throwing a wrench in Stropov's organization by removing White, the trafficking continues. Justitia needs your help. We must send a message to Stropov and all who work for him that we aren't going to take it anymore. At two p.m. this afternoon, PST, you have an opportunity to end the life of this devil together. Wear a face covering and come to one of the addresses listed below. Do not bring any weapons, they will be provided. Don't let the authorities stop you from what must be done in the name of justice. The more, the merrier."

Listed below were three addresses in the Vegas area.

"Am I reading that right?" asked Susan. "Is she encouraging a mob to kill David White?"

"Yes, she is."

Susan glanced at the clock. "That's less than two hours from now."

Mali looked up from her laptop. "The man sitting next to White in the picture *is* Aleksei Stropov." She sent a picture to Joe who moved it to one of the screens. "He is number thirty-two on our most wanted list, with a network of traffickers across the United States. It is estimated that more than eight thousand four hundred children are being sent to Russia, Egypt, Turkey, Israel, and across Asia every year."

She rubbed her arms as chills ran down them. *It was beyond her comprehension to think that all those young children could be taken and sold into sexual slavery. A part of her wondered why they were trying to stop Janet. She was ridding the world of the worst-of-the-worst in society. Who cared how they died as long as they were stopped?* She sighed and refocused.

* * *

By one forty-five p.m., the crowds at each of the locations swelled to more than one thousand people each. Jake and the team had coordinated with the local FBI and police, who were trying to control the crowds. Fire trucks were positioned at strategic points to help with crowd control, spraying water to slow people down when needed. The President had gone on-air imploring people to stay home and not partake in the brutal murder of a sitting representative. Mali didn't believe it was going to be enough.

People were pushing past barriers, setting fire to police cars, breaking glass windows of local shops. There was chaos everywhere. Mali marveled at how quickly people could congregate and was saddened and shocked at how many were so eager to kill a man.

At ten minutes past two, there was still no sign of Simpson or David White. The crowds at each location were getting increasingly unruly, with the authorities barely able to maintain control.

"What the hell is going on?" asked Agent Hernandez, who had arrived at the warehouse to observe and assist.

Before anyone could answer, Susan said, "Look! There's another tweet on #JusticePrevails."

The team looked up at the screen, where Twitter was still displaying.

"How gratifying to know so many are as outraged by the trafficking/sex trade of children that exists in this country as I am." Immediately following that tweet, "Watch together and rejoice!" with a link to a YouTube video.

Joe clicked the link and Daniel White appeared in what looked like an empty warehouse. He was standing with his back to a metal beam that ran from floor to ceiling. His arms were chained together to the same metal beam and his bare feet were bound and secured as well. His breathing looked erratic, and his face was pinched in pain. Wearing jeans and no shirt, the carved letters C and T were clearly visible on his chest. Lights from the high windows provided minimal light but the team could make out empty boxes, metal beams, papers, and other trash scattered on the ground behind him.

The back of Janet appeared in camera view.

"David White, you are charged with multiple counts of child kidnapping and trafficking, selling more than five hundred and sixty children for sex over the past ten years. We have shown one picture of you with Aleksei Stropov and have more proof of your crimes on the table behind me. What say you before we proceed with this event?"

"Go to hell, bitch!"

Janet sighed. "Tsk, tsk. You're not representing your constituents very well Davey. But no matter." She stopped to look to her left then to her right.

"So are you going to kill me now? Does that make you feel empowered or whatever you broads want these days?" he asked, sarcasm dripping from his mouth along with the sweat that was running down his face.

"Oh, I'm not going to kill you, Davey…they are."

Out of the shadows wearing black robes and hoods that covered their entire bodies, they shuffled toward White. There were too many to count and each person was holding a weapon. As they drew nearer to White, Janet stepped backward out of the camera's view.

"There are knives of various lengths, hammers, a meat tenderizer, an ax. Oh my God!" exclaimed Susan.

"Is anyone identifiable?" asked Jake.

"No. They're completely covered from head-to-toe," said Joe.

Mali said, "The comments from those who are at the three locations are disgusting. Most were angry at first, wanting to participate in the killing. They've shifted now and are cheering them on."

"The news outlets have been reporting live at the three locations. Even they seem disappointed it didn't happen at one of those locales," noted Kirsten.

David White struggled, attempting to shift away from them. But they encircled him, not saying a word as they stepped closer and closer. One by one they stepped up to him to exact punishment. The first person to reach him, hit him in his mouth with a hammer. White howled in pain as his teethed crunched from the blow. He spit out two teeth and some blood. The next person smacked the side of his head with a meat tenderizer. White cried out then twisted in agony as a third person plunged a knife into his side. White screamed and begged for mercy. They showed none. The attackers then swarmed around him like bees. In moments, White couldn't be seen through all the bodies and black robes. The attack continued for approximately seven minutes, long after the screams stopped. Eventually, they stepped away, fading back into the room until one couldn't distinguish a body from the interior. White hung limply, held up only by the bonds tying him to the pole, his body covered in blood.

The screen faded to black, and a red drop of blood rolled down the screen. Justice Prevails displayed as well as an address below it before everything faded to black.

There was silence as everyone tried to process what they had just witnessed.

Jake spoke first. "Send a ghost to that address and get the authorities out there. I'm assuming that's where White's body is located. I want the area secured. And I want to know when this happened."

Mali's cell phone rang, the sound echoing around them.

With a shaking hand, Mali picked it up when Joe nodded he was ready to trace.

"Bored with me now, Agent Hooper?" The phone line went dead.

CHAPTER TWENTY-ONE

Special Unit Warehouse
Saturday, September 19, 4:20 p.m.

WHEN THE GHOST appeared at the address provided on the LadyJustice app, it confirmed what they already suspected. David White's murder was pre-recorded. The warehouse looked deserted, the door leading inside was wide open and there were no cars in the parking lot or anywhere nearby. As the ghost moved closer, they noticed groups of people were arriving at the scene.

"Curious-seekers," said Mali. "The address displayed for all to see."

Jake shook his head as a man walked inside. "Jesus, I hope they don't contaminate the scene, if that's where the murder actually took place."

Just as the man ran outside, two police cars drove up, lights flashing. They immediately pushed the gathering crowd back to establish a police crime scene barrier, and they detained the man who had exited the property. Two cops walked inside as an FBI vehicle pulled up. Both agents hurried to join them.

The wait felt much longer than the three-minutes it took for the initial assessment by the agents. Jake was patched through to them as soon as they stepped outside the building. One man was carrying a manila envelope.

"White is inside. According to the police, it appears as though he was killed early this morning. The coroner will confirm time of death when he arrives."

"No one else is there?" asked Jake

"No. A file of information detailing White's personal propensity of having sex with children as well as his involvement in human trafficking was left behind. We'll analyze it." He held up his hand to pause the conversation as someone spoke in his ear. "The police will run fingerprints, if they find any."

"I doubt they will. What about outside? Are there cameras? Any witnesses to cars arriving and departing?

"No. This warehouse is slated to be demolished next week and hasn't been in use for more than a year. Given the tire marks inside, we believe all vehicles were parked in the warehouse to minimize suspicion in case anyone passed by. It's fairly secluded where we are. We're bringing more agents onsite and will canvas the area with the police for possible witnesses."

Jake rubbed the stubble on his chin. "Were the robes left behind?"

"Excuse me?"

"The robes the participants wore?"

"Oh. No. Nor are there any weapons."

"Simpson took them with her to dispose elsewhere," suggested Mali.

Jake nodded.

"I want all accusers in the Las Vegas area located and interviewed as to their whereabouts yesterday and today. We'll look into all their business and personal dealings on our end."

"Roger."

"Keep me informed."

Mail said, "I'll research each accuser, check their bank records and phone calls, texts, that sort of thing. Kirsten, can you help me with that?"

Kirsten nodded.

"Good," said Jake. "My guess is you won't find anything. If any of them are involved, I have no doubt alibis would have been supplied."

Over the next few days, long hours were spent on research and interviews, as well as disabling the blockchain network so Simpson couldn't use her app. There was no action on #JusticePrevails, much to Mali's relief, and there was no action at the compound in France. No one was surprised about that. While they did not have significant forward motion in terms of catching Simpson, progress had been made.

Now Friday, Jake called the team together at noon.

"We've had a brutal week so I'm releasing everyone for the weekend. You're all on-call so be prepared to come in at a moment's notice. Keep your security detail with you at all times. Jeff, monitor the ghost on Hoop as well as the three new potential targets we've decided to track."

"You got it."

Kirsten piped in. "Why track anymore targets? We've got her team in France. There's no staff to help her…"

"…that we know about," interrupted Jake. "She has made it clear she will continue. She has the list and an unknown number of operatives across the states. We may have slowed her down, that's all."

"Jake?"

Jake looked at Mali.

"I've been thinking. Janet always seems to be one step ahead of us. We get close and she evades. Or we think we're close only to realize she's gaming us. We've slowed her down, true, and she's going to need time to regroup."

"Your point?"

"Let's not give her that time. We've proven we can rattle her, so let's rattle her."

"How? We have no way of reaching her."

"Not directly, no. But let's have another press conference, draw her out so she contacts us again. We need to provoke her into taking a new target sooner rather than later."

"How does that help us?" asked Felix. "We still won't know who she's going to target."

Jake frowned. "Hoop…" He dragged out her name.

Mali held up her hand to stop him. "Jake, Kirsten was right when she said this was personal. It is, which is why we need to make sure the next target Janet takes is me."

Everyone voiced objections.

"Whoa, we don't need to go that far, Hoop," stated Felix.

"Are you nuts?" exclaimed Kirsten.

Susan murmured, "There has to be another way."

"Absolutely not!" Although spoken softly, Mali heard Jake.

* * *

Mali's apartment
Friday, September 25, 2:00 p.m.

JAKE ONLY AGREED to a press conference and had contacted Agent Hernandez to set it up for Sunday. Weekend plans for everyone was altered to being on-call Friday and Saturday, returning to work on Sunday. After everyone was released, Jake took Mali home. Mali wisely kept quiet during the car ride. Jake's knuckles were gripping the steering wheel with so much force, she thought he was going to rip it off. At one point, she was going to make a joke about it to try and lighten the mood, but one look at his rigid jawline and accompanying scowl and she decided otherwise.

When they walked into her apartment, Jake shut the door and turned her to face him.

"What the hell are you thinking?"

"My suggestion is a good one. In fact, it's the only way we can draw her out."

Jake looked up at the security camera, his scowl turning darker.

"On the balcony."

Taking her arm, he led her to the sliding door, opened it, and ushered her outside.

Jake was breathing heavily through his nose. He

turned toward the Hudson, gripping the rail, his knuckles white.

Mali leaned against the rail, studying Jake. When she put her hand on top of his left hand, he looked first at her hand then he turned his head to stare into her eyes. The intensity of that stare took her breath away. He looked out at the Hudson again, taking deep breaths. The sounds of boats passing by on the Hudson, birds chirping in the trees, and a bee buzzing around by her flowerpot, all registered in her brain as she waited for him to continue.

"When I lost Christa, I thought that part of me was done. I turned all my energy to Heather and to my job. I figured that was enough. And it was…" He looked back at Mali. "…until I met you."

Mali's breath caught in her throat.

"I'm in love with you, Mali, have been almost since we first met."

Her left eyebrow quirked up and an impish smile curled her lips. "Almost?"

Jake chuckled. "Well, probably from the first time we were introduced during that video conference call when I went to get Ken. But I couldn't allow myself to think like that."

"You were grieving for your friend. Not to mention the fact you believed my analysis caused his death." Mali smiled back.

Jake grimaced. "I'm sorry. That was grief talking. I was looking for someone to blame."

"I know. And you already apologized. No need to do so again."

"I won't put you in danger, Mali. I nearly lost you once, I won't again." He turned to face her, cupping the side of her face with his hand.

Mali stood on tiptoe to feather kiss his cheeks then lips. She looked deep into his eyes. "I love you too, Jake. But you can't keep me in a bubble, and you can't treat me like a girlfriend when we're at work." She dropped back down so she wasn't standing on her tiptoes. Removing her hands from his shoulders, she stepped back until they were no longer touching.

"Where do we go from here?"

"Well…" This time, the buzzing sound distracted her enough that she looked around. "Damn bee."

Jake laughed.

When she spotted the offending critter. She walked over to the flowerpot where it was hovering and took a swipe at it.

"Ouch."

Jake laughed again.

Mali frowned.

"I'm sorry. I always tell Heather not to swipe at bees but to come and get me instead. Did you get stung?"

She shook her head. "Next time I'll do that. It didn't feel like a bee."

They both tried to find it, to no avail. He picked her hand up and kissed the small red spot where she had connected with it.

"Better?"

She opened her mouth to answer but her phone rang.

"That will be my mother. She said she'd call when they arrived at the hotel. I left my phone inside." She stepped inside the apartment to answer her phone. Instead of Jake's family meeting Mali's at her parents' home, they had decided to meet in the city. Mali felt it was too soon for Heather and Jerry to meet her entire family and preferred they meet her parents first. They planned to get together tomorrow. Tonight, it was just the four of them.

"Hello Mother."

"I will never understand why you enjoy this city so much," she began without preamble. "There is entirely too much traffic and noise."

"So you and Father made it to the hotel?"

"Yes, but barely. A delivery truck of some sort nearly ran us down when he crossed lanes. I'm amazed the driver was able to avoid it, although he drove entirely too fast overall for my comfort. I'm surprised we made it here in one piece."

Mali laughed.

"It's rude to laugh at someone."

"You're just not usually so…ummmm…"

"Scared?"

"I was going to say dramatic."

"Jasmine Suzanne!"

Mali laughed again. "What time and where would you like to meet for dinner?"

"I have no energy to traipse around this city with a security team in tow. Why don't you and Jake come here? We're in the Royal Suite this time. Plan to arrive at seven. I want to rest and then clean up before you join us, and your father has to make some business calls. We'll order our dinner when you arrive and eat in."

"That sounds lovely Mother."

An historical Manhattan icon, the Ritz-Carlton in Central Park was the perfect blend of classic and contemporary, effortlessly combining twenty-first century elegance with an artsy vibe of an era long gone. The result was a tranquil setting that encouraged its guests to relax and be pampered.

"I've never been inside this building," commented Jake as he studied the lobby with interest. "It's stately, elegant."

"I've only been inside a couple of times. My parents have never spent much time in the city. They only brought us here once or twice when we were growing up." She glanced at him. "You look very handsome, by the way."

Jake had returned home to shower and change, before picking Mali up at the entrance to her building. He now wore black slacks, a black shirt opened at the collar, and a gray tweed sports coat over his shirt.

He squeezed the hand he was holding. "Thanks. Have I told you how gorgeous you look tonight?"

"Only about five times since you picked me up." Mali laughed, delighted.

They arrived at the Royal Suite promptly at seven, tardiness being frowned upon by her parents. An agent opened the door, nodded at Jake and Mali, and stepped aside so they could enter. They walked through the foyer, passing through the study and into the main living room.

"Jasmine, Jacob," boomed Charles, turning from the window to greet them.

"Hello Father," Mali said as she hugged him.

Jake and Charles shook hands. "Good to see you again, Charles."

"Your mother will be out in a moment. What can I get you to drink in the meantime?"

By the time drinks were served, Willow had stepped out of the bedroom.

After greeting them, she said, "I've taken the liberty of ordering filet mignon, French gratin dauphinois, and a truffle-infused salad. And for dessert, I thought we'd go all-out with flambéed strawberry crepes. It should arrive shortly. I hope you don't mind."

"You're a woman after my heart, Willow. Steak and potatoes are my kind of meal."

Willow blushed. Mali rolled her eyes.

Dinner was a relaxed and enjoyable affair, which surprised Mali. She had never really spent one-on-one time with her parents, and she realized they were funny.

After their sumptuous meal, the men excused themselves to get a drink at the bar. Willow and Mali lagged behind, sipping tea at the dining table.

"How is the case going?"

"We're getting closer to solving it."

"That's a relief. While I appreciate the security, I'm tired of the curtailment of my social schedule."

Mali made a face.

"Oh, don't worry, Jasmine. I'll survive, and I do appreciate your concern."

They finished their tea and joined the men in the living room.

"We need to leave soon, Mother."

"What's the plan for tomorrow? I'm looking forward to meeting your father and daughter, Jacob."

"Heather is very excited to meet you. She told me you must be very beautiful to have such a pretty daughter."

Mali's jaw dropped when Willow blushed for the second time.

"Heather loves Central Park and since you're right here, I thought we'd take a walk in the park then have lunch."

"That sounds wonderful. I'll order a picnic lunch for us, and we can enjoy the afternoon together. Let's meet in the lobby at noon, if that's alright."

"Noon it is. Thank you for an incredible meal and, more importantly, a wonderful evening." Jake shook hands with Charles and leaned down to kiss Willow on the cheek.

For the third time, Willow blushed. Mali walked out of the suite in a daze, her mouth still hanging open as the door closed behind them. When Jake winked at her, she snapped her mouth shut and glared at him.

CHAPTER TWENTY-TWO

Central Park South
Saturday, September 26, 12:00 p.m.

"How DO YOU do? My name is Heather, and you are much prettier than I imagined. Miss Mali is so pretty so I figured you would be too, being her mother and all. My mama went to heaven a long time ago." Her eyes widened when she looked up at Charles. "Wow, you have hair on your face. Oooh, this hotel room is so big and pretty. Can I look around?"

To say Heather Black made an impression on Mali's parents was an understatement. No sooner had they been ushered into the suite and living room had she rattled off her sentences so fast, they rolled together. And just like that, without waiting for a response, she was skipping around the room looking at everything.

"Keep your hands to yourself, young lady," called out Jake, as he looked at his daughter over Willow's shoulder. "She's a pistol." He shrugged and smiled, leaning down to, once more, kiss Willow on the cheek. Standing up, he said, "Hello Charles."

Charles laughed. "I'll say. Hello Jacob."

After shaking hands, Jake made the introductions.

"We'd offer drinks for everyone, but we don't have time," stated Willow. "Our entourage should be waiting for us downstairs. I'll collect Heather." She left to find Heather, following the non-stop chatter coming from the bedroom. Charles excused himself to answer a call, saying he'd only be a minute.

Jake whispered to Mali, "Entourage?"

Mali smiled. "We're having a picnic, Willow style."

When the group arrived downstairs, the concierge was there to greet them. He told Willow the others had gone ahead to set everything up, then escorted them out the doors where two horse-drawn carriages awaited them. Heather squealed when the horses came into view, jumping up and down in her excitement. Charles, Willow, and Jerry stepped into the first carriage with Jake, Mali and Heather in the second.

Jake pulled Mali close to his side as Heather bounced up and down on the seat across from them, pointing at the birds, cars, trees, everything they passed, talking to no one in particular. Her eyes sparkled in her excitement drawing an appreciative smile from Jake.

"This is amazing and very special. She's never ridden in one of these."

"I'm so glad she's having fun. My mother never does anything halfway."

They leaned back in their seats, enjoying the ride as much as Heather. As they turned into the park, the honking horns faded, and the clip-clop of the horses lulled Mali into a sense of peace. She looked up at the trees, admiring the changing colors. The leaves were in various shades of yellow and orange, with some leaves still green. They littered the street and Mali watched some float to the ground as they passed by. The sun filtered through, shooting rays to the ground below. Despite all the people she could see, and the occasional car passing by, Mali felt the serenity of the park draw her in.

The carriages slowed to a stop, and everyone exited. Heather was vocal in her disappointment until she saw the pond in the distance.

"Wow!" Jerry exclaimed. Sitting on the grass was a table covered in a white tablecloth with six chairs around it. The table was perfectly set with a gold charger plate and a full complement of silverware. The navy blue napkins were laid across each plate and crystal water glasses were situated in their proper place above and to the right of each plate. Two waiters stood to the side next to a table that held covered dishes, water and various drinks.

"I can honestly say I've never had a picnic like this before," Jake murmured to Mali.

Mali chuckled. "Like I said, this is a picnic, Willow style."

"Where's the blanket to sit down on?" asked Heather.

"We're having a different kind of picnic," responded Jerry.

"Sit down everyone," boomed Charles. "Sit down."

The security team surrounded the entourage at

a discreet distance as everyone took their seats. One waiter poured water and took orders for drinks, as the other served the meal, one plate at a time. Approaching Heather, the waiter made a show of uncovering the dish for her. Inside, sitting on delicate china, was a hamburger and french fries.

"Yum!" Heather exclaimed, clapping her hands.

Willow leaned over, whispering to Jake, "I figured she'd prefer that to what we're having,"

"You knocked it out of the park, Willow. Thank you."

The rest of the group was served Caesar salad followed by seared salmon with asparagus, in a garlic puree and romesco sauce. Complementing the meal was a 2014 Cabernet Caymus from Napa Valley.

The conversation was lively as everyone enjoyed the day and each other's company.

Jerry was the first to finish eating. He leaned back and patted his belly. "That was the best meal I've ever had! The salmon was perfectly prepared. Thank you so much."

Willow smiled. "I hope you saved room for dessert."

"I don't know…"

"It's the Ritz's famous chocolate cake with a Grand Marnier ganache and—"

"Say no more, I'll make room."

The adults laughed.

Heather, who had perked up when she heard chocolate cake, exclaimed "Papa, you always have room for dessert," which sent the adults into another round of laughter.

As the cake was being served, Mali swatted at the buzzing around her head. "I don't believe it. Another bee." She covered her piece of cake with her hands to protect it.

"Where is it?" asked Jake. He, too, looked around. "I'd better kill it before Heather realizes one is around. She's afraid of them."

He stood as he spotted it. Moving quickly, he swung his arm, hitting it as it tried to fly away. "What the…?" He bent down to pick it up and shook his head, his eyes shooting to Mali.

Frowning, she joined him on the grass.

"It's not a bee." He opened his hand.

"What is it?"

"Some sort of technical device." He closed his hand around it again. "Jesus. We need to analyze this now. I'm calling the team in."

As Jake walked away to make some calls, Mali went back to the table to explain what was going on.

"I'm so sorry we have to leave."

"No need to apologize," Charles said. "We understand."

"Sort of," added Willow.

"I'll take Heather home. Do what you need to do," added Jerry.

When Jake returned to get Mali, they both thanked Charles and Willow for the meal, hugged Heather, then took their leave. Mali promised to call her parents as soon as she could.

* * *

Special Unit Warehouse
Saturday, September 26, 3:30 p.m.

JAKE LAID THE device down on the conference table. Everyone leaned in to look at it. Jeff picked it up.

"Is it on?" asked Jake.

"No. You broke it when you hit it."

"What is it?"

Joe responded, "It's a nano-drone."

"A what?" asked Mali.

"It's a spy tool, and an effective one because the sound the motor makes is similar to a bee," said Jeff.

"That's exactly what it sounded like." Mali's eyes widened. "I've noticed a buzzing off and on for weeks now. Remember, Jake, just yesterday I tried to take out a bee on my balcony. It was by the flowerpot."

Jake nodded.

Everyone looked at Mali as the implications became clear.

"She's been watching me, listening to me?" Her voice rose as her ire grew.

Jeff was studying the device. "Not listening. Only watching. There's a camera but no mic." He handed it to Joe, who nodded in agreement.

"I've never seen a drone so small," commented Kirsten. "What's it's range? And how far away does the operator have to be?"

Joe shook his head. "Not sure. We need to study it." He looked at Jake with his eyebrows raised.

"Go. That's why we came in today. We need answers fast."

Everyone left the conference table except Mali and Jake.

"Mali, when and where did you notice the buzzing? And what was going on in those moments?"

"I'm not sure. Yesterday of course. I also heard it…I don't know." She shook her head.

Jake placed his hand on top of hers. "Take a few deep breaths and think."

Mali looked down as she tried to retrace her movements of the last few weeks. "I need to write things down." She grabbed a whiteboard. "Not one word." She looked back at Jake, who smiled.

Her first bullet listed "September 25, on my balcony, talking about feelings." She blushed as she looked at Jake. "We also talked about making me her next target."

Jake narrowed his eyes. "We didn't hear it until after that part of our discussion. Regardless, she can only watch not listen. We'll have to assume she doesn't know what is being said."

Mali nodded.

"What else?"

"I remember hearing that buzzing when we were testing the ghost and Daniel approached me on the street. I ignored it." Her next bullet read "August 19, on the street with Daniel, he was reminding me about the money."

"That's probably how she learned about him. It would have been easy to tail him, strike up a conversation at a bar or somewhere, and learn about your relationship. We need to try to retrace his steps. Perhaps he went to that strip joint more than one night. After a few drinks, people talk."

"That wouldn't surprise me. He was pretty sure he'd get the money from me."

"What else?"

"A thought just occurred to me. What if she had a lip-reader with her and learned of my relationship with Daniel that way?"

Jake shook his head. "Since there was only a camera on the drone, it would have to be facing you or Daniel almost directly to be able to read lips. It would be too obvious if a bee was flying back and forth between you."

"Good point. So we'll assume she had no idea of the nature of any conversation." She paused, tapping the pen on the whiteboard. "Um, I think that's all. No, wait. I remember hearing it at my father's business anniversary dinner." She wrote another bullet as she talked. "I was at the pool waiting for you to bring us drinks. I moved away from the light, assuming the bug was attracted to it, when Richard approached…" Her eyes shot to Jake. "You don't think she'd go after him, do you?"

CHAPTER TWENTY-THREE

Press Room, FBI Field Office, New York City
Sunday, September 27, 9:02 a.m.

"GOOD MORNING, EVERYONE. My name is Special Agent in Charge, Rose Hernandez. Just more than one week ago, Representative David White was the latest victim of a brutal series of murders orchestrated by Janet Simpson." She shook her head, lips thinning as she looked at the press. "While the murder itself was horrendous, what was most appalling were the willing participants who executed him and the thousands who cheered them on. While we can't arrest those who were rooting for Representative White's death, we can and have arrested more than one hundred and sixty people for rioting, destruction of property, and resisting arrest. And make no mistake, we will find all of those involved in the murder itself and they will be prosecuted to the fullest extent of the law. Agents in Las Vegas are combing the murder site for evidence, and we have identified multiple people of interest."

Jake and Mali stood to the left of Agent Hernandez.

Mali surreptitiously studied the reporters. Despite the room being full of reporters, all were silent as they listened.

"To update you on our progress…we discovered and dismantled her operational center, for lack of a better term, in France. This center researched and identified pedophiles and human traffickers, presented target options for Simpson, then coordinated all aspects of each kill. This center was located inside a one-acre compound, located in Cancale, a coastal town on the west side of France. It was fortified with ten-foot cement walls around it, and had heavily armed guards. Inside the compound was a large house and a small outbuilding used for their security team, which our team easily neutralized. The six-member team inside the house were unarmed and quickly gave up. They have provided us with valuable information regarding Simpson's operation. I want to thank the French authorities for their assistance in finding and closing this center. We have made a significant dent in her ability to continue."

She paused to take a sip of water, glancing at Jake and Mali before continuing.

"Simpson's brothers have provided us with more insight into the horrors she faced as a child. Janet Simpson was adopted at the age of six into a family with four boys. Within one year, they were going into her room every few days to gang rape her, abusing her in every conceivable way. They threatened her with death if she told anyone. This continued for more than two years. Can you imagine how that would forever change a person? She can be pitied, and we can feel sorry, for the child she was. But Janet Simpson is a brutal killer, she became one out of the ashes of that childhood. The adult she is now is twisted and sick and must be apprehended to face true justice." She took another sip of water. "We learn more about her and her operation every day and we are closing in. It's only a matter of time before we put an end to this. I'll take a few questions at this time."

Noise erupted as each reporter raised their hand and called out, vying for a chance to ask a question. Agent Hernandez chose a man in the second row.

"Thank you. Grayson Shepherd, *New York Times*. How could people in France execute those murders? Some were elaborate. And where is Drake Butcher in all of this?"

"Her team in France coordinated with operatives in the U.S., planning each event, as Simpson calls them, to the minutest detail. Drake Butcher helps Simpson execute each murder. We believe he actually kills some of the victims. For example, we believe the bolt that killed James Adams was shot by Butcher." He pointed to a man in the back.

"Bob Smithson, *New York Daily News*. Operatives? That sounds like a military operation. How many are there?"

"You're right. Each murder has been calculated and executed with military-like precision. We have no idea how many operatives there are or how they are contacted and mobilized. We are still working on that with our team in France. Next?" He pointed to a woman.

"Chrissy Sampson, WABC. So if you now control this operational center, why not just shut everything down?"

"We did not have enough time to shut down the LadyJustice app before White's murder, but I've been told it is no longer operational. Last question." He chose a woman sitting in a wheelchair.

"Thank you. Elma Rodriguez, Fox News. You mentioned this center researched pedophiles. Is there a list of them? It was also reported a file was left at White's murder scene. Simpson showed a picture on her app of White with another man and children sitting nearby. Did that file have proof White was a pedophile? And was that picture in the file?"

Agent Hernandez took a deep breath. "There is a list of people that were researched. And before you ask, that list will not be released to the public. As to your second question, yes, there was a file regarding White. We are verifying the information now." She paused. "This is still an on-going investigation, one we hope to conclude soon with the arrest of Simpson and Butcher. If members of the press really wanted to help, they would stop exacerbating the situation by elevating Simpson to near-celebrity status. You have reported every murder practically with a gleeful attitude. You were disappointed White's murder did not occur in one of those three public places. The media, news outlets and social media alike, are complicit." She held up her hands when complaints were shouted at her. "Don't throw freedoms of the press and speech at me. I am simply saying it would be refreshing if news outlets and social media willingly exercised restraint without having to be asked. But I'm asking now. Please stop reporting anything or allowing anything on social media that would encourage this sick soul to continue. Thank you."

The three exited the room to a cacophony of shouted questions from the reporters.

* * *

Special Unit Warehouse

Immediately following the press conference, the team returned to work. They were pleased with how things went and fully expected Janet to call at some point. They didn't have to wait long.

Joe and Jeff were at the control center studying the nano-drone. Kirsten was working with the team in France trying to locate a list of operatives, if one existed. Felix was monitoring the ghosts and Susan was monitoring security of the building. Jake and Mali were working at the conference table.

"Father confirmed two agents are providing security for Richard. He doesn't understand why, neither does my father. I didn't go into details."

"That was probably wise. It's a good precaution."

When the phone rang, everyone stopped what they were doing and looked at Susan.

"Call for you, Hoop. I'm patching it through."

As they gathered around the conference table to

listen, Joe shook his head. A different number was being used, no trace was possible.

Mali picked up the receiver.

"Agent Hooper speaking."

"How dare you tell the world about my past?"

"It was relevant, Janet. People need to know how and why you are who you are."

"That's bullshit. Maybe the world should be told about you and your quickie marriage and quicker divorce. Or…"

Mali cut her off, laughing. "You're joking, right? No one is interested in the love life of an FBI agent. They're much more interested in the inner workings of a brutal and manipulative killer." There was heavy breathing on the other end of the line. Mali was getting to Janet. Smiling, she continued. "I guess you figured out we were tracing you."

"You think you're so smart. Well, you're not. I am Justitia and I will continue my efforts to rid the world of pedophiles." Her voice rose with each word spoken.

Mali laughed again. "Are you stamping your foot right now? Because you sound like a six-year-old who's not getting her way and is about to throw a temper tantrum."

"Damn you! And damn you for disabling my app."

"Don't forget how we've dismantled your entire operational center. No one to help research or coordinate."

"I have the list and I don't need them."

"Oh, I believe you do need them. You also need those

operatives, and we are about to locate that list. Once we do, all of them will be arrested. Oh, don't forget about the little nano-drone we found." Her lip curled as she continued, her words dripping with scorn. "You are a coward, Janet. You expect everyone to do the work and you just show up at the appointed time for your theatrics. Well, the gig is up."

Janet shrieked and let loose a string of profanity. Mali's eyes widened and others smiled.

"Yep, temper tantrum. I haven't heard of half of those colorful words you used. You're not being very lady-like."

"Go to hell!"

"Do you need time to light up? I can wait."

"You think you're so funny. You won't be laughing for long."

"Oooh, is that a threat?"

"Oh, it's a promise. Justice will prevail. I'll make sure of it. And then I'll be the last one laughing." The line was disconnected.

Felix whooped, throwing his pumped fist in the air. "Great job, Hoop. She's really pissed now."

"That's what worries me," stated Kirsten.

"If you wanted to be the target, you surely are now. No doubt she's planning how she can grab you." said Jeff.

Jake looked at everyone before his eyes returned to Mali. "We have work to do before that happens."

Joe said, "I have an idea."

Everyone looked his way.

"Simpson knows about the ghost and will be able to evade it. We can modify the implant from the HuntedLives game to track Hoop. We might even be able to use the console from the game to do it."

Mali shivered. "Let me get this right. You want to put that implant *with the cyanide* back inside me?"

CHAPTER TWENTY-FOUR

"We'd take the cyanide out, of course. But yeah. It already has GPS tracking built into it. And it has a receiver, too, so we'd be able to monitor your communications."

Mali did a double-take when she glanced at Jake. "You're actually considering this?"

"Joe's right. We need a way to track you, and the ghost will be useless. A wire would be found, so would our contact lenses technology. But an implant? I doubt it would occur to Simpson that we'd use it."

Mali put an elbow on the table, resting her chin on her hand. Everyone was quiet as they waited. The decision was ultimately hers.

"We need to know where you are. This is the best way." Jake spoke in a low voice, but she nodded, acknowledging his words.

Mali looked at each team member. Kirsten was biting her lip but gave her a thumbs up. Joe and Jeff smiled their support. Susan flashed her a smile that didn't quite reach her eyes. Mali could tell she was nervous. Felix was nodding slightly with a silly grin on his face. He gave her two thumbs up. And Jake, well he was staring at her with love in his eyes. These people were not only her co-workers, but they had also become her friends and they'd look out for her.

"Is there any way to add the capability for me to hear you?"

Jeff shook his head. "I doubt we'd have time to figure that out."

She let out the breath she didn't realize she was holding. "Okay. I wanted to be her target. Let's do this."

Jake nodded. "That a girl." He stood. "We have a lot to do and we have to move fast. No one leaves tonight."

The rest of the day was a flurry of activity.

The implant was being held at a secure location in the main office. A technical team that included Joe and Jeff, as well as a medical team, would safely remove the cyanide and double check communication. When they were ready, Mali would be escorted there for the implant to be inserted.

With the help of the team in France, Kirsten had successfully located a list of operatives in the U.S. She brought the list to Jake and Mali, and all three perused it.

"I can't believe the massive number of people helping her," murmured Kirsten as they scrolled down the list. It was alphabetized and broken down by state.

Mali shook her head. "She has help in roughly twenty states with easily more than five hundred operatives in each one."

"…double that in larger states like California and New York. They probably cross-over to other states as needed," said Jake.

"DC has four hundred and twenty-five," noted Kirsten.

"Kirsten, let's assume for now Simpson will need assistance from those here in Manhattan. I want as many rounded up as possible."

"That will take hours, Jake, if not days."

"I know. Agent Hernandez is aware of our plan and has made resources available to us. Use them."

Felix, who had joined them at the table, jumped into the conversation. "If we knew who she was going to select, we could nab them and go in their place."

Jake sat up straighter. "Hmmmm…Kirsten, is there any way to identify which operatives were used for the murders that occurred here in Manhattan? That would be Frank, Daniel Matthews, and perhaps even Thomas Martin."

"I believe there is. Let me check." She rushed off to contact the team lead in France.

"Won't she recognize everyone here?" asked Mali. "She's obviously been watching us."

"We can task other agents," offered Felix.

Kirsten returned ten minutes later. "Simpson's staff was nothing if not thorough. They listed the operatives used for each event. The number of operatives used for each was different depending on how elaborate it was. Only the names were listed, not their roles. For Frank, only four were used, Matthews eight, and Martin seven.

They needed a whopping ninety for James Adams." She took a sip of water. "I cross-referenced the list for Frank, Matthews, and Martin. Two operatives were used in all three murders."

"Great work, Kirsten."

Felix leaned forward, resting his elbows on the table. "So do we replace them with our agents?"

"Without knowing their role, it would risky. Let's locate them and have the ghosts trail them," responded Jake.

Everyone nodded in agreement.

"We're on it," stated Kirsten as she and Felix left.

Dinner was brought in, a simple meal of fried chicken, fries, and coleslaw. Despite the circumstances, there was laughter and animated chatter as everyone ate. The feeling was they would soon catch Simpson and Butcher.

Two things happened just after seven that evening. The two operatives were located, ghosts were deployed to track them, and they got the call that the implant was ready for Mali.

* * *

Richard Thorpe's residence
Monday, September 28, 6:30 a.m.

RICHARD THORPE WAS a man who was used to creature comforts and to getting his way. He didn't get where he was in life by sitting back and waiting for things to happen. He made them happen, and he never let anything or anyone get in his way. Certainly not the two annoying agents who were supposed to be protecting him. They'd been with him for two days now, their asses parked in his foyer, but he had not allowed them to cramp his style.

Which is why, after he finished his shower, he was going to return to the adventurous blonde in his bed. They had met a couple of weeks ago and had been hooking up when she was in town ever since. She had called last yesterday afternoon wanting to get together. When he told her about the agents and being stuck in his house, she had giggled, suggesting he sneak her in so they could have fun right under their noses. He had laughed and readily agreed. She made him feel like a kid. While he usually enjoyed much younger women, girls actually, she was a refreshing change, and most willing to try anything he wanted.

As he reached for the lever to turn off the shower, he felt her hand touch his back before sliding down to squeeze his butt. He groaned, sure she had squeezed his manhood instead, for it had grown substantially and was twitching. He grasped himself with one hand as he grabbed her hand with his other and pulled her close. She rubbed her breasts against his back, pushing his hands out of the way to take over stroking him. He leaned forward until his forehead rested against the shower wall. The hot water poured down on them both from the rain shower head, urging them on. When he could stand it no longer, he turned around and picked her up, wrapping her legs around his waist. Flipping around so her back was against the wall, he ground his mouth on hers at the same time he entered her. He pounded into her, saying repeatedly, "Yeah baby, yeah baby."

Dropping her legs to the floor, she sank to her knees and took him in her mouth. His surprised laugh at her move turned into a whoosh of air. "Shit, baby, you're killing me." His head tipped back as he gripped her head with both hands. He moved against her with increasing urgency. When she pulled away and stood, he looked at her with glazed eyes.

"Do you want to finish this, darling?"

He growled again and reached for her.

Laughing, she swatted his hands away, walked out of the shower and sashayed into the bedroom, dripping wet. She climbed onto the bed as he watched her from the shower. Kneeling, she faced him and rubbed herself with one hand, pulling on her nipple with the other. Groaning, he flipped off the shower and rushed out of the bathroom.

He was so intent on getting to her that he was completely blindsided when a man stepped out from the closet and punched him in the gut. Gripping his stomach, he dropped to his knees, sucking in air as best he could. Before he could catch his breath, he was punched in the face, which sent him flying onto the carpet. Dazed, he looked up and watched as the man walked to the bed and kissed his woman.

"What took you so long?" she asked huskily, still in the throes of passion.

"I figured you'd want your fun."

"You were right, although my fun isn't over."

He laughed, unzipped his pants, and climbed on top of her.

Thorpe, who was still on the ground trying to breathe, was thoroughly confused. One thing was clear, though, he needed those agents. Struggling to get to his knees, he winced in pain. His face was on fire, and he tasted blood in his mouth. He didn't think about the two on the bed, his only focus was to get help. He opened his mouth to scream but a strange gurgle was the only sound. He crawled to the nightstand and was reaching for his cell phone when his hand was crushed in a huge paw.

"Argh!" he croaked out.

"Now, now, Dick," she said. "Let me have my fun. We'll get to you in a minute."

"Longer than a minute," the man on top of her growled.

She laughed and moved under him.

The man punched Thorpe in the face again before pushing him to the ground, never missing a beat in his activities on the bed.

Thorpe half-crawled, half-shimmied to the wall. He turned over and sat up, his back hitting the wall with a thud. The effort exhausted him. He blinked rapidly a few times, trying to dispel the dizziness. Through slitted eyes, he watched the two wondering what the hell was going on.

When they finished, the man stood, zipped up his pants, then handed her a cigarette and lighter.

Staring at her, Thorpe asked, "What the hell is going on? Who are you?"

She inhaled deeply before blowing smoke out through her nose. She studied the red glow of the cigarette. "I needed this." Glancing at Thorpe, she said, "You can call me Justitia."

CHAPTER TWENTY-FIVE

Special Unit Warehouse
Wednesday, September 30, 11:00 a.m.

THE TEAM WAS confused and losing patience. Everything was in place, but nothing was happening. The implant was successfully inserted behind Mali's ear, the pain a dull ache at this point. The memories it brought back were harder to dull. The two operatives had been located, and the ghosts were monitoring each. But no word from Janet, and no activity on #JusticePrevails other than a few comments wondering who the next pedophile was and when the next kill would take place. Everyone was allowed to go home Monday and Tuesday nights, but security was tighter than ever. Jake had stayed at Mali's every night, sleeping on the couch. Tensions were high.

"This waiting is killing me. And by the way, how is she going to nab me if I'm always surrounded by people?" Mali paced back and forth.

"It would be a little too obvious if you just sat on the corner waiting for her. She has to realize we're planning something," replied Jake.

"Yeah," said Felix. "We've taken down so much of her operation, she's probably scrambling to get the help she needs." He laughed. "God, I love what we do!"

Jeff threw a tennis ball he was tossing up and down, hitting Felix in the head.

"Hey!" he laughed as the ball bounced away.

Jake shook his head, smiling. "Let's review this again. Joe, the implant is working, and we can track Hoop as well as listen to her?"

"Yes, Jake. As we've discussed the past two days, every night we tracked Hoop heading home, whether she was in a car, an elevator, or on the subway. Communications are coming through loud and clear. That last message was really cute, by the way." He smirked, looking at Mali.

She stuck her tongue out at him. "I…"

Mali's burner cell rang and everyone stopped. "She couldn't have this number, right? It's a new burner."

"No," replied Joe.

She walked to the conference table where she had left it and answered.

"Father," she sighed in relief. It was short-lived.

"Jasmine, Richard Thorpe is missing."

"What?" Mali's eyes shot to Jake in alarm. "Hang on, I'm putting you on speaker."

Everyone rushed to the table.

"Are you sure he's missing?"

"Richard and I were supposed to meet here at the house, about thirty minutes ago, to discuss a new branch we're considering. He didn't show and he didn't answer his cell. I tried calling his cell again about ten minutes ago. Still no answer. That is totally unlike him. I mentioned it to the agents here. They're contacting Richard's security team now. They said they'd call Jake as soon as they discover anything."

Jake's cell phone was ringing before Charles finished the sentence. Jake excused himself to take the call.

Mali spoke with her father for a few more minutes. Just as she hung up, Jake returned to the group.

"I just spoke with Art Jonas, one of the agents protecting your father. He just got off the phone with Thorpe's security team. Thorpe wouldn't allow the agents to be anywhere in his house except the foyer. That's where they've been all morning. When Art called them, they went upstairs to his bedroom. It was very wet but empty."

"With blood?" asked Kirsten.

Jake shook his head. "Water. And there were women's clothing on the floor. Nothing else. The two agents had no idea there was anyone else in the house. If he snuck her into the house, he could easily sneak out with her. Thorpe was pretty irritated at having security, he's used to having his way. The agents aren't convinced he was taken."

"So they think he snuck out with someone?" asked Mali. "Highly unlikely, especially if he had a meeting with my father. He'd never stand up his partner."

"A forensic team is on the way and may be able to shed some light on what happened."

Mali resumed her pacing.

Jake watched Mali with his eyes. Finally, he said, "Let's assume he was taken until otherwise told."

"Why would Hoop's father's business partner be taken?" asked Susan, with a frown. "He's not on the list."

Kirsten snapped. "I told you this was personal." She glared at Mali.

Mali spun around. "Hey, don't yank my chain. We put security on everyone we believed would need it. We even added security for Thorpe. I don't like the man but it's not my fault he's so egotistical to think he doesn't need protection and plants his security as far away from him as he could." She was huffing by the time she finished. She glared at Kirsten.

"Now is not the time for this," stated Jake, his words hard and clipped. "Everyone is concerned for Hoop as well as all of our loved ones. Take a few minutes to call your families and make sure they keep close to their security detail for the time being."

Mali turned away to call her father again.

"Is Mother there with you?" she asked without preamble.

"Yes, she's upstairs."

"I'd feel better if the two of you would stay in sight of the agents. For now anyway."

"Jasmine…"

"Please, Father. I would feel better if you would just do it. And take an agent with you wherever you go in the house, just to be safe."

He sighed. "Your mother won't be pleased and, I can assure you, she'll draw the line at the restroom, but we'll do it."

It was Mali's turn to sigh. "Thank you. I'll call you as soon as we hear anything about Richard."

Jake pulled Mali aside. I just called Agent Hernandez. She's on her way here. We need to tell her about your relationship with Thorpe and what he did to you.

* * *

Special Unit Warehouse
Wednesday, September 30, 7:30 p.m.

"The two operatives are on the move. Our ghosts are with them," said Jeff.

Jake nodded. "Good. Bring them up on screen."

Two of the screens flickered and they watched each one. The ghost was following one already in a cab, the other was walking down the street. He hailed a cab and was soon pulling away from the curb.

"It's dark, don't lose them," said Jake.

"There's a lot of traffic and the headlights are making it difficult," was Felix's reply. He was controlling the second ghost.

The ringing phone jolted everyone.

"Call for you, Hoop," said Susan.

Mali answered it on the first ring.

"Delta Flight 119 out of La Guardia. You have one hour to make it. You'll get more instructions along the way. Don't bother wearing a wire. You'll be checked before you board. If you miss the flight, your buddy, Dick, dies."

Click.

Mali took a deep breath as she hung up the phone.

Jake said, "Find out where that flight is going and book a ticket for me." He picked up his keys. "We can make it if we hurry. Get the satellite up and track Hoop. I want the ghosts ready to deploy at…" The elevator closed before he finished the sentence.

They hopped in Jake's car and took off. No words were spoken as Jake navigated the streets, weaving left and right, honking his horn to get past people and cars.

When the phone rang, Mali answered via CarPlay so they could both hear.

"Jake, the two operatives are headed to La Guardia," stated Kirsten. "They are also booked on Flight 119. It departs at eight-ten and is a non-stop flight to Atlanta arriving at ten-forty. It continues on to San Antonio at eleven-fifteen."

"Damn it. With them on the flight, we can't risk me being on it as well. And we have no idea if Hoop stays on the plane, changes planes for another destination, or is taken from the airport in Atlanta."

"The operatives change planes. They catch flight 934 to Las Vegas, also non-stop departing at eleven-fifteen, arriving at twelve thirty-five in the morning."

"The operatives going to Vegas could be a diversion," suggested Mali.

"I know." Jake took a deep breath. "Okay, we need agents at the airport in Atlanta as well as San Antonio. Give them pictures of Hoop and the operatives. Book me the quickest flight to Las Vegas. I believe the operatives are needed to ensure Hoop does what she's told. I'm counting on her being on that flight. I need to get there before her plane lands."

"We're on it, Jake. We'll call with specifics when we have them. We're tracking Hoop. As soon as she exits the airport, we'll be able to determine what she's doing." They ended the call.

When Jake and Mali arrived at the airport, he stopped at the doors leading to the departure area.

"Be careful. I plan to be in Vegas before you."

"I hope that's where they go."

"Same here." He kissed her then nudged her out the car.

She was walking to the ticket counter when a man stepped up to her and grasped her elbow.

"Look ahead and keep walking." He pushed a large envelope into her hand. "Here is your ticket and a burner cell. Give me your phone."

Mali dug in her purse and handed it to him.

"Go straight to the gate. You don't have much time. Someone will meet you in Atlanta." The man disappeared.

Mali rushed through security, and ran to the gate, dodging people left and right. Even at this hour, La Guardia was busy. She arrived just as they were issuing a last call. She reminded the team she only had the ticket to Atlanta and someone would meet her there.

The flight was uneventful. Not knowing who the operatives were, Mali didn't speak to anyone except the flight attendant. After drinking some water, she dozed off and on until the plane began its descent.

As she exited the plane at gate A25, another person approached her from behind.

"Don't turn around." He handed her a ticket. "You are on flight 934 to Las Vegas. Go to baggage claim when you arrive. The plane departs in twenty-five minutes from gate B2, and the doors close in fifteen. I suggest you run." His gritty laugh made her shiver. She glanced behind her, but he had melted into the crowd.

Not wasting any time, Mali raced down the hall, jumping over a toddler who wobbled into her path, waving an apology, and shoving people out of the way who were walking too slow. She ignored the angry shouts and kept going. They were closing the doors just as she arrived, out of breath. With a smile, the attendants allowed her to board saying she had just made it. *Ya think!?!*

Mali's throat was so dry, she barely managed to choke down the snacks the airline provided. Water didn't help. She drank it anyway then tried, unsuccessfully, to sleep.

When the plane landed, she went to the restroom, stopping to buy a bottle of water and some trail mix before continuing.

The burner cell she was given rang.

"You're wasting time, Agent Hooper."

"I'm not going to justify going to the bathroom to you, Janet."

"I expect you downstairs in less than five minutes." She hung up.

Mali frowned as she continued moving forward, walking faster as she followed the crowd. She stepped onto the escalator to go down to baggage claim and glanced at the people around her, stiffening in surprise and disbelief. Riding the escalator beside the one she was using, two rows back, was Jake. He was wearing jeans, a navy sweatshirt with What happens in Vegas, Stays in Vegas splattered across the front, and a navy blue baseball cap pulled low to cover his face. And he was wearing glasses and a fake mustache. He winked at her then continued to talk to the woman in front of him.

Turning quickly to face forward, Mali almost laughed at loud at his disguise. She had no idea how he arrived before she did, she only cared he was there. She stepped off the escalator with a decided bounce in her step, no longer tired.

The burner cell rang again as she neared the baggage claim for the flight she was on.

"Exit the last set of double doors and look for a white Dodge van. Thirty seconds, Agent Hooper."

Running, she muttered, "White dodge van, last set of double doors."

She stepped outside. The windowless main body of the van concerned to her. When she approached it, the side door opened. Her mouth dropped open when she saw what was inside.

"Get in," said Janet.

Without looking behind her, Mali climbed inside. A man followed her in, closing the door behind them.

CHAPTER TWENTY-SIX

Thursday, October 1, approximately 1:00 a.m.

"Inside," the man who entered behind her said, pushing her around to the front of the enclosure, then shoving her inside. Mali bent low to get into the contraption and stumbled over the lip. She bounced off the single chair, landing on her knees with a grunt. Grasping the seat of the chair, she pulled herself up, turned, and sat. The enclosure looked like a rectangular silver foil tent. It was held up by metal poles, similar to a pop-up canopy like those seen at craft fairs. Three sides were solid, the fourth being the opening she had just entered. She studied the enclosure, a slight frown forming between her brows.

"Do you know what you're sitting in?"

Mali was facing the front of the van and recognized Drake Butcher in the driver's seat. She looked to the right and stared at Janet, who was sitting in the front passenger seat.

"Janet! I'm surprised you're here. I can't see you very well, but I can smell you. You really should stop smoking, it's bad for your health," stated Mali, as the van pulled away from the curb. She smiled when heard Janet's swift intake of breath and her hiss. "Not enough operatives, so you had to come yourself?" she asked with a forced chuckle.

Janet shifted in her seat to better look at Mali. "Oh, Agent Hooper. You have no idea how easy it is to hire the right people. Money talks." She laughed. "Well, maybe you do have an idea."

"That doesn't mean you can trust them. Trust would have to play an important part in your operation."

"I have enough people remaining who I trust, enough to take your...friend...and bring you to me."

"Oh, I didn't come for Richard Thorpe, Janet. I came for you."

"Yeah right." She snorted. "I asked you a question."

"You mean this cute little tent? It's nice and warm, thank you. I was cold on the plane."

"Have you ever heard of Michael Faraday?" She didn't wait for Mali's response. "He was an English scientist and inventor back in the 1800s, arguably one of the greatest. He created cages that could shield the contents within from static electric fields. Today, it acts like a radio frequency interference device, an RFID (you know what that is, right?). It also protects against electromagnetic pulses. While it protects devices inside, the beauty of it from my perspective is it prevents hackers, thieves, or government agencies like the FBI, from tracking whatever may be inside. It blocks everything from Wi-Fi to GPS. Amazing, right?" She giggled. "I constantly amaze myself!" She laughed again, tossing her head back and clapping in her delight. "I was going to check you for wires and what-not, but when Drake suggested this as an option…" Mali watched her rub his thigh, "…I couldn't resist."

A chill went down Mali's spine when she realized the team wouldn't be able to track her. She lifted her chin, putting up a brave front. "You wasted a lot of effort on this one, Janet. I'm not wearing a wire. I came alone and of my own accord."

"You're hilarious," Janet said without humor. "Do you really think I don't know your boyfriend is in Vegas right now?"

Mali paled.

Janet's voice hardened. "Like I said, you have no idea what I'm capable of." She looked at the man outside the tent, nodding slightly. "I'm bored with this conversation." She sighed and turned toward the front. Staring at the darkness outside the window, she lit a cigarette, dismissing Mali completely.

At a ripping sound, Mali looked up just as a piece of duct tape was slapped across her mouth. The man retreated then returned with something in his hand. Leaning toward her, he grabbed her arms and twisted them behind her back, securing them at her wrists with a zip tie. Again he retreated, this time closing and securing the door, leaving Mali in darkness.

She heard Janet say, "Don't worry, Agent Hooper. There is plenty of ventilation. I don't want you dead…yet."

* * *

Jake had arrived a mere twenty minutes before Mali's plane landed. Two local agents had met him at the gate with a bag of clothing and other sundries inside. Quickly changing in the restroom, he had rolled his eyes he found the mustache before placing it above his lip. They were in place when Mali walked off the plane. Jake was standing with his arm around the shoulders of the female agent two gates down, the second agent was further down. They had tailed Mali and, wanting to reassure her, he had winked when she spotted him on the escalator.

They knew she was headed to a white Dodge van but by the time they ran outside, it was pulling away.

"Did anyone get the plate?" asked Jake.

Both agents shook their heads.

Agent Barker said, "I'll get footage from airport security. I'll call when I have the info," he called out over his shoulder and ran back inside.

Agent Whitby, who was with Jake, said, "Our car is further up, let's go." They raced to the other end of the departure area, climbed into the car and peeled out of the airport.

"Talk to me, Joe." Jake had the team on speaker phone.

"They're headed north on Paradise Road. Turn left on East Tropicana Avenue. They're headed toward the Strip. They're approximately two miles ahead of you."

"The ghost is following the van, Jake," added Kirsten.

Agent Whitby was at the wheel. She turned left on Paradise Road.

"The van is stolen," said Agent Barker, who had called Jake's team and was patched through, conference-call style.

"No surprise," muttered Jake.

"Whoa," said Joe.

"Damn!" exclaimed Felix, who was controlling the ghost.

"Oh no," cried Kirsten.

"Wha…" began Jake.

Jeff interrupted him. "We just lost her signal."

"What the hell do you mean you lost her signal?"

"Four white Dodge vans joined the one with Hoop in it. They just turned right onto the Strip, and they're all weaving around each other," stated Felix.

"Like a shell game," blurted Kirsten.

"It just dropped off. Our system is operational, not sure what's going on," stated Jeff.

Jake glanced at Agent Whitby. "Christ! Put the other ghosts on them, Slick." Jake's nickname for Jeff slipped out without notice.

"It's too late. They're already splitting off. One flipped a U-turn, two turned left on West Flamingo. That's the next major street you come up to. They could be going to Interstate fifteen or may stay on surface streets. The fourth one is now turning right on Sand Avenue. And the last one is staying on the Strip. Without the lights on the Strip, it's going to be harder to see them."

"Which one should I follow?" asked Felix.

Silence from the team.

Jake shook his head and took a deep breath, blowing the air out in a puff. "Stick with the one on the Strip."

Agent Whitby, who was on her cell phone, hung up. "All agents are activated and ready to assist."

Jake shot a look her way and nodded. "I also want a helicopter on standby."

Agent Whitby sped along the Strip, as much as was possible given the amount of people walking around. Jake didn't notice the colorful lights coming from the casinos they passed nor the people who were still flooding the sidewalks as they walked from casino to casino, even at this hour. The beautiful Mediterranean blue lake in front of the Bellagio, with its spectacular ballet of water, warranted just a passing glance.

"Following this van is a waste of time," he muttered, smacking his fist on the dashboard.

"Jake," said Kirsten in a rush. "Richard Thorpe owns a property about twenty minutes outside of the Strip, on Scenic Ridge Drive. I'm sending you the address right now."

"Shit," said Agent Whitby. "That's in the opposite direction, and from here it's about thirty minutes away." Tires squealing, she flipped a U-turn and sped down the Strip the other way.

"One of those vans was headed in that direction." Jake leaned forward in his seat. "Send the ghost to the house, and send the local agents there ASAP. Approach quietly. I don't want them to realize we're there. We're on our way."

CHAPTER TWENTY-SEVEN

MALI SPENT MOST of the drive on the floor of the Faraday cage after the van made a hard turn and tipped her over. At one point, she had rolled onto her knees then managed to get to her feet, remaining in a crouch, to try to look out of the vents on the sides. The flap covering the vent only allowed her to look downward. But she was able to listen to Janet and Drake talking, Janet periodically asking how much longer until they arrived. Drake apparently found her repeated requests funny because he always replied, "Five minutes from the last time you asked." Eventually, Janet didn't ask anymore. When the van took another sharp turn and she tumbled to the floor again, landing hard on her side, she stayed put. She shimmied to the side so she could lean against one of the poles supporting the cage. She was grateful for that because she was able to stretch her legs out in front of her in the small space.

Tonopah Airport
Thursday, October 1, 4:40 a.m.

MALI WAS JOLTED out of her slumber when the van rumbled to a stop. She was sweating profusely after being in the cage for such a long time. Her cheeks and upper lip itched from the tape, her arms ached from being behind her so long, and her derriere was numb. She was actually surprised she had slept at all.

The driver and passenger doors squeaked as they opened. Moments later, the side door opened. Her gasp was muffled when the cage was flipped around so the opening faced the side door. But when the cage door was opened, she gratefully sucked in the fresh air through her nose, appreciating the cooler air on her skin.

It was still dark outside, but from the lights on the building next to them, she could tell they were at a small airport. She had no idea where they were.

"Get her out of there and untie her arms," instructed Janet. Drake eased her to the side so she was sitting on the edge of the van, her legs dangling toward the ground.

Leaning toward Mali, Janet continued. "If you promise not to speak, I will remove the tape. If you say one word, it goes back on. Understood?"

Mali nodded.

Janet ripped it off as Drake snipped the zip tie. Mali simultaneously cried out due to the pain on her lips and groaned when her arms dropped to her sides. Intense tingling ran from her shoulders all the way down her arms to her fingers, before it changed to pins and needles. She shook her arms, trying to dispel the pain.

An engine revved up. The outline of a helicopter caught her eye, just as Janet said, "Time to go."

Drake handed the man an envelope and told him to wipe down the van before ditching it.

Grabbing Mali's arm, he turned and ushered first Janet then Mali into the helicopter. The seat she was told to sit in was infinitely more comfortable than where she was before. She closed her eyes in appreciation.

The ride in the helicopter was shorter than the first leg of this journey. They arrived at their destination at twilight, the night sky just beginning to lighten, when they slowed and descended to a lit helicopter pad in an open field. She still couldn't tell where they were, but she could make out the shapes of trees, as far as the eye could see. There were no city lights.

Richard Thorpe's house, 30 minutes south of Lake Tahoe, CA
Thursday, October 1, 6:45 a.m.

EXITING THE HELICOPTER, Janet led them through the trees, via a dirt path, about eight hundred yards. They left the trail and climbed up a long, winding asphalt drive. When they rounded a corner, Mali trailed to a stop, taking a quick breath as she stared at the house before her. She would recognize it anywhere.

The cedar siding and native stone, coupled with the black metal roof, gave the sprawling six thousand square foot home a rugged charm. Floor-to-ceiling windows and the wrap-around decking provide uninterrupted views of the Sierra at Tahoe Ski resort. A three-car garage was attached to the home, and there was a detached four-car garage approximately fifty yards from the house, with a two-bedroom apartment above it.

It was a house she would never forget. It was Richard Thorpe's summer cottage, as he liked to call the grand structure. They were in California, south of Lake Tahoe. And his house was sitting in the middle of fifteen very private acres.

"Ah, you recognize where we are." Janet had stopped and turned around when she realized Mali was no longer walking. Eyes narrowed, she studied Mali.

Mali's eyes moved from the house to Janet. She shrugged.

Janet cackled. "You're not as unmoved as you would have me believe. If I'm not mistaken, based on what you previously said, this is where Thorpe made a move on you all those years ago. What you may not know, is how he brought his business associates…" When Mali's eyes grew round, Janet grinned. "Not your father, so relax." She had lit a cigarette and took a deep drag, holding the smoke in her mouth before blowing it in Mali's face. "He usually brought a few of the Vice Presidents from other branches, along with clients, here. Always waiting were four or five girls, anywhere from twelve to fifteen years old. Shall I go into detail what they did to those girls?"

Mali was breathing rapidly. She could feel her heart pounding in her ears. She swallowed repeatedly as she shook her head. "I don't believe you."

"Really? Deep in your heart, you don't believe he's capable of that?"

Mali continued shaking her head and took a couple

of steps back. Drake's hand on her shoulder stopped her. "How could you possibly know this?" she whispered.

Her voice dripped with disdain. "I told you…and yet you refuse to believe me, you have no idea what I'm capable of, or the resources available to me." Dropping the cigarette butt onto the ground, she crushed it with her shoe. "I'm not discussing any details. You'll have an opportunity to hear it from the horse's mouth. Now shut up and walk." She turned and continued walking up the drive.

Drake gave Mali a little shove. She shot him a quick glare then trudged ahead.

The main living space looked the same as it had all those years ago. She walked down the steps from the foyer into the dining room and kitchen. Understated elegance was how Mali described the kitchen with its wood beams above, stainless steel appliances, granite counter tops, and a mix of stone gray and antique white cabinets that complimented the backsplash and counters.

"Down here, Agent Hooper."

Mali turned to her right, to the lower living area below and the wide expanse of windows with its spectacular view beyond. As she reached the four steps leading down, a movement caught her eye. She looked to her left, her breath catching in her throat.

Richard Thorpe was sitting in a leather chair that faced the stone fireplace. He was dressed in jeans and a white t-shirt. His feet were bare and there was duct tape across his mouth. Around his neck rested a noose attached to a rope which had been tossed over the wooden beam above. The other end of the rope was then tied to a contraption beyond the rail on the second floor, which opened to the living space below. It was pulled taut so he couldn't move far. His hands were tied behind his back, his hair was mussed, and it appeared as though he had been there for awhile.

When he saw Mali, he started speaking unintelligibly, the words muffled because of the tape. Frustrated, he glared at Janet and Drake.

"Hi Dick! I hope you've been treated well while we were gone. I'm sure you recognize Agent Hooper," said Janet.

Drake walked to Thorpe and pulled the tape off his mouth. Thorpe winced but said nothing.

"Nothing to say to your business partner's daughter?"

He turned his glare on Mali. "Are you a part of this?"

"Of course I'm not," she retorted. "I was brought here because of you."

"Have a seat on the hearth, Agent Hooper. We're about to begin."

"I have to take a piss," said Thorpe, grumbling.

"Too bad." She looked up and nodded to Drake, who had walked upstairs and was now standing at the contraption Mali could now identify as a winch.

Drake pressed a button and the rope jerked upward, pulling a surprised Thorpe up and forcing him to scramble to his feet. He cried out as the rope tightened around his neck.

Mali made a move to go help, but Janet stopped her. "That's far enough Agent Hooper." Mali looked at Janet and froze, staring at the gun pointed at her. "Sit. Back. Down."

Never taking her eyes off Janet, Mali sat. "Stop this, Janet."

Squirming and standing on his tiptoes, Thorpe coughed and gasped.

Janet ignored him as she lowered the arm holding the gun. Drake loosened the rope enough for Thorpe to stand flat-footed on the ground. He coughed a few more times.

"Are you ready to answer a few questions, Thorpe?"

He glowered at her.

"No?" She looked up at Drake.

His voice croaking, he whispered, "No, please." He begged. "I'll answer your questions."

* * *

"Excellent!" She paused, looking at Mali. "Move to the sofa."

Having seen the video camera, Mali shook her head.

Drake had walked downstairs and was standing next to Mali by the fireplace. He smacked her on the side of her head to encourage her to move.

Mali cried out in pain, cupping her hand over her ear.

Janet narrowed her eyes. Stomping to her, Janet yanked her arm down. Drops of blood covered Mali's fingers.

"Argh!!" Janet screamed as she moved Mali's hair out of the way. "You're wearing my implant?"

Mali managed a smile, shaking off Janet's hold and gingerly covering her ear again. "It was your brother's implant, actually."

Janet huffed, "Everything Anthony did was because of me! And I was the one who nurtured the relationship with Simone, she developed the implant because of me!"

"Blah, blah, blah. You really are full of yourself, Janet, and quite boring in your predictability."

Janet was shaking in her rage.

Drake pulled her aside and whispered in her ear.

"There's no way they can get here in time, even with the GPS in the implant," was Janet's reply.

Drake's lips thinned and his right eye twitched. He looked skeptical from Mali's point of view.

"Agent Black and the team will be here soon, Janet. This place will be swarming with agents. Stop while you still can," Mali rushed in to say.

"Shut up!" Hands on hips, she looked at the ground, breathing heavily. "The helicopter is ready to go and security is in place?" She looked at Drake, who nodded. "Good, then let's proceed."

Drake grabbed Mali and shoved her onto the sofa before positioning himself behind the video. He nodded at Janet when he pressed record.

Mali smirked. "Can't do a live feed?"

Janet glared at Mali briefly before smiling. "Oh, we'll post this later, and everyone will see exactly who your father's business partner was. Are you worried people will wonder if your daddy likes little girls too?"

Mali paled. "You bitch."

Janet laughed in delight before turning to look at Thorpe.

"State your name."

"Richard Thorpe."

"And your position?"

"I am CEO and co-founder of Hooper and Thorpe Investments."

"Do you like young girls, Dick?"

Thorpe shook his head.

"Now, now, Dick. I expect the truth. Isn't it true you inappropriately touched Agent Mali Hooper on many occasions, including right in this house when she was approximately ten years old?"

Thorpe peeked at Mali. She sat stone-faced as she stared, unblinking, at him. She was trying to fight the old feelings of anger that were threatening to surface.

"Answer the question, Dick."

Lips thinning, Thorpe's chin jutted out. "I never touched her inappropriately. If I occasionally kissed her, it was because she wanted it."

Mali fumed at his lies. "You're lying, you son-of-a-bitch." She stood, body rigid in her anger. Janet was forgotten.

Thorpe looked at her. "Jaz…"

"You might have touched me and kissed me in the presence of other people, including my parents, but you were very adept at hiding what was going on. Rubbing my chest, patting my bottom, kissing my neck and even my mouth, you wouldn't leave me alone."

"Quit acting so innocent, Jasmine. I know what girls want, what they do and say when they're looking for action."

Mali gasped.

"Now, now," Janet's lips curled in disgust. "There is much more to discuss, and we have no time to waste. Sit down, Agent Hooper."

Mali took a deep breath and sat back down.

"So, Dick, is that why you brought the girls here, to have fun with your friends because you knew what they wanted?"

Thorpe didn't answer, although he was looking down.

"How old were the girls? And how did you find them?"

Thorpe licked his lips and swallowed. In a low voice, he said, "They were usually twelve years old, sometimes a few years older. Children are easy to find, especially when you grease palms."

"What was that? I didn't quite hear you."

He repeated his words.

"And what did you and your friends do with these girls?"

Thorpe shifted from foot to foot, his eyes looking wild. "We…"

"Isn't it true you raped those children, passing them around between you and your associates? That you laid them on the pool table and took turns with them every time you sunk a ball?"

Defiant once more, he growled. "We did much more than that, and they liked it. They did whatever we asked, whenever we asked them to do it. The pool, the hot tub, hell, even on my motorcycle in the garage. They never complained, never cried, and they always welcomed the money we gave them."

"So just because they didn't cry and they took your money, that makes it okay?" Mali couldn't put into words the disgust she felt, how sickened she was. She frowned when she noticed Janet was looking at her with approval.

Janet continued. "Isn't it also true you provided these girls to clients if they joined your firm with an initial investment of five hundred thousand?"

Mali gasped.

"Once in awhile."

"How often did this go on?"

"It hasn't stopped. And it began when Jasmine was ten."

Mali shot off the sofa again. "Whoa! What the hell do you mean by that?"

He lifted his head to stare at Mali and sniffed, not realizing tears had formed and were rolling down his face. "You were so cute, Jazzie. I just wanted to hold you and take care of you. When you rejected me that weekend we were here, I realized I had to move on. But women don't smell the same as little girls, the sweetness is gone."

Mali's hands were clenched at her sides. "So you're blaming me for your deviant, disgusting behavior, and for raping young girls!?!" She wrapped her arms around her middle, taking a few deep breaths, trying to calm herself.

"As entertaining as this is…" Janet lit a cigarette and threw the match in to the empty fireplace. She sneered at Thorpe. "You are a repugnant human, no, not even human. You are a cockroach that deserves to be squished. The question is how?"

Thorpe, realizing what was about to happen to him, begged Janet then Mali to spare his life.

Janet ignored him. "Hmmmm…should we castrate you and let you bleed out? Or perhaps we should hang you. The rope is already around your neck, after all." She took two short puffs then tossed the cigarette to the floor, stomping on it with her shoe. "Justitia has the perfect solution."

Pulling the gun out of her pocket, she turned it this way and that repeatedly, admiring its dark beauty.

She walked to Mali and held out the gun.

"YOU are going to kill Thorpe."

CHAPTER TWENTY-EIGHT

MALI STOOD TRANSFIXED, staring at the gun in Janet's hand. The childhood anger, fear and confusion rolled off her in waves only to meld with these new feelings she was experiencing. She was appalled by all she had learned about Thorpe, appalled and horrified. How anyone could be capable of those atrocities was beyond her. She swallowed repeatedly, not sure if she was going to be sick.

Rubbing her stomach absently, Mali remembered that ten-year-old girl. She had been constantly confused by the kind words he used, but the kisses he gave and the rubbing of her shoulders while leaning down to smell her hair, all contradicted what he said. She was uncomfortable around him, but her parents just laughed it off to shyness. She was scared but unable to verbalize her feelings. And she was angry with her parents for not seeing what was happening.

Her therapist in Chicago had helped her through those feelings but they were bubbling to the surface, and she was having a difficult time setting them aside.

She had no idea of Thorpe's sick proclivities. She

had assumed he was that way just for herself. She barked out a humorless laugh. How arrogant of her, and how bizarre there were traces of disappointment within her. Why would she be bothered that she wasn't the only one? What the hell was the matter with her!?!

Smoke wafted her way, breaking the semi-trance she was in. She glanced at Janet, who was still holding the gun in one hand, a cigarette in the other. But her eyes... they glowed in their intensity as she studied Mali.

"Take it, you know you want to."

Mali shivered. Janet was right. She wanted nothing more than to pick up the gun and shoot the bastard. And why not? She'd be justified in doing so. How many children had he abused because he had the power and money to do so? How many lives were forever changed because of his actions? How many lives would undoubtedly be saved if he wasn't in the picture anymore?

She looked down at the gun.

"Do it," urged Janet.

Mali took the gun from Janet and pointed it at Thorpe.

* * *

Drake suddenly put his finger to the earpiece in his left ear. "They're here."

Without taking her eyes off Mali, she said, "Take care of it."

Moving quickly and quietly, Drake left the room.

"What are you waiting for?" Janet asked. "Do it! Do it!"

Thorpe was pleading with Mali, begging her not to shoot him, repeatedly saying how sorry he was through his sobs.

Mali expelled a breath she had not realized she was holding.

"Shoot him!" screamed Janet.

Time seemed to stand still.

Finally, Mali blinked, knowing what she had to do. She slowly shifted the gun so it pointed at Janet. "No. Even scum like Thorpe don't deserve to die this way. He has a right to face his accusers in a court of law."

Janet was completely still except for her mouth, which had dropped open. Snapping it closed, Janet pressed her lips together. "We'll see about that." Without warning, she turned to the mantle, grabbed a remote and pressed a button then slammed it onto the stone hearth, shattering it.

Thorpe yelped as the rope pulled him upward. The automated winch slowly churned, winding the rope up.

Startled, Mali looked at Thorpe, which gave Janet enough time to hurl herself at Mali. The gun was knocked away as the two fell to the ground. Mali grunted when Janet landed on top of her but immediately rolled to the side, throwing her leg across Janet, giving her momentum to carry her over. Now straddling Janet, she grabbed one arm, pushing it above Janet's head as she tried to get hold of her other arm.

"It's over, Janet," she gritted through her teeth.

But Janet twisted from side to side and thrust her hips up, managing to grasp some of Mali's hair with her free hand. Yanking down hard, Mali cried out as she released the arm she held to grab the hand in her hair. With her now free hand, Janet swung and connected with Mali's jaw, sending her sprawling onto her back.

Thorpe struggled, gurgling and choking as the noose tightened and he was lifted first onto his tiptoes then completely off the floor, all of which went unnoticed by the two fighting on the ground.

On her knees now, Janet threw herself onto Mali, panting and screaming, her face contorted into one of pure loathing. "You bitch! It isn't over. Justitia will live forever, fighting for justice." She clamped her hands around Mali's throat, applying pressure with her thumbs.

Mali gasped for air as she turned her head from side to side, trying to dislodge Janet's hands. At the same time, she grabbed onto Janet's wrists in an effort to pull them off her neck. Gasping for air, her face turned red and she felt like her eyes were bulging. The gleam of triumph in Janet's crazed eyes gave her renewed energy. Reaching up with her hands, she grabbed Janet's head. Placing her thumbs on Janet's eyes, she pushed with all her might. Janet shrieked and released Mali as she fell back.

Coughing and gasping for air, Mali turned on her side. She spotted the gun a few feet from her hands and struggled to her knees. She managed to crawl a couple of feet and was reaching for it when Janet grabbed her ankles and pulled. Mali's knees slid out from under her, and she flopped onto her stomach with an oof, but successfully snatched the gun. She jerked her knees up under her and kicked back, catching Janet in the face. As Janet was thrown back, Mali flipped onto her back and half sat up, gun aimed at Janet. Scrambling into a low crouch, Janet screamed that justice would always prevail and launched herself at Mali.

A single gunshot sounded, the bullet striking Janet squarely in her chest. The force tipped Mali onto her back. She saw shock cross Janet's face right before Janet landed on top of her.

CHAPTER TWENTY-NINE

THE FRONT DOOR slammed open and multiple footsteps rushed into the house.

"Mali," yelled Jake. "Christ!"

She sputtered in Janet's hair, trying to spit it out of her mouth. Her arms flailed as she tried to push Janet off her, to no avail.

Suddenly, Janet's body was removed, and Jake was there pulling her into his arms.

"Oh God, are you alright?" Just as quickly, he pushed her away to look at her. "You're bleeding."

Mali looked down at the red stains on her shirt. She shook her head. "It's Janet's blood, not mine."

He pulled her back into his arms, breathing heavily. "When I heard that gunshot…"

"I'm alright, Jake, except my face feels like it's on fire."

He looked down at her. "That's one hell of a shiner." He smiled his relief. "Let's get you up."

As he stood and brought her up with him, keeping his arms wrapped around her, she noticed Thorpe for the first time.

"Oh God!"

Thorpe was hanging about fifteen feet in the air, the winch having wound the rope completely to the top of the rail. His neck was at an odd angle and his empty stare was looking toward the floor. His arms and legs hung limply at his sides.

"Sit down and put your head between your knees," instructed Jake as he sat her on the sofa. He held her head down while she took deep breaths.

"Better?"

Mali nodded then sat up.

"Take it slow."

Tears were sliding down her cheeks. "I hated him, but he didn't deserve to die that way."

He pulled her to him in a fierce hug. "I don't want to leave you…" He squeezed her shoulder. "…but I need to take care of things."

"Go." Mali waved him away as she leaned back and closed her eyes, listening to the conversations of the agents around her. She listened to the creak of the rope that told her they were lowering Thorpe's body to the ground. People were talking all around her and she heard the table and other furniture around her being moved. She knew the exact moment they removed Janet's body. Sounds of the scene being secured filtered through her mind but she didn't open her eyes until she heard the click of the video camera being turned off.

"Janet planned to distribute the video later. It wasn't a live feed, thank God."

Jake nodded as he removed the camera from the tripod.

"What happened to Drake Butcher?"

"Dead." Jake didn't elaborate. Mali didn't ask.

She was about to close her eyes when a bottle of water appeared before them. Her eyes moved from the bottle to the woman holding it. She took it, thanking the agent with a smile.

"I'm Agent Whitby, Angela. I've been with Agent Black, and the team in New York, since Vegas. This has been quite a night. I was sure Agent Black was going to jump out of his skin when we were listening to what was going on through that implant."

Mali managed a smile. "Let's just say, I'm glad it's over."

"Thank God you're okay, Agent Hooper." She leaned down, handed her a shirt, and whispered, "This is my shirt. I'm wearing my FBI jacket and can keep it zipped. I thought you might like to change out of the shirt you're wearing. You don't have to, but it's yours if you want it.

Mali gratefully accepted it. "It's Mali, and thank you so much, Angela, for this and for all of your help."

Agent Whitby smiled and excused herself to assist, and to make arrangements for their return.

Mali stood and motioned to Jake she was going to change. When she walked into the powder room, she got a good look at herself and sighed. Definitely not look-ing her best. She leaned in and touched her eye, wincing a little. It was now a lovely shade of purple and getting swollen. She turned her head to the side and lifted her hair so she could view the stitches where the implant was. They were still intact, although a thin line of blood trailed part-way down her neck. Her hair looked like a rat lived inside it. She removed the bloodied shirt, splashed her face with cool water, gently patting it dry. Next, she pulled a washcloth off the open shelf, ran cold water on it and wiped the blood off her neck then dabbed the stitches as well. She ran her fingers through her hair then shrugged. Feeling better, she walked out and looked for Jake.

"The authorities will be here for hours, but we're done. We're flying back to Vegas with Agent Whitby then we'll catch a flight to New York. Given the time we return, and everything you've been through, Agent Hernandez plans to come to your place tomorrow morning at nine for a debriefing. She said to tell you everyone is glad you're alright."

"Thanks." She took a deep breath. "I have to call my father and tell him Richard is dead." Jake opened his mouth. She put her hand on his arm to stop him from saying anything and possibly objecting. "I won't give him any specifics, but I need to be the one to tell him."

"The FBI will have to question him."

Mali nodded. "I'll tell him to come in." She borrowed Jake's phone and walked out onto the patio to make the call.

By mutual agreement, they didn't discuss the case at all as they flew first to Vegas then on to New York. Mali was content to hold on to Jake, and she was grateful just to be alive. Details would come later.

* * *

Mali's apartment
Friday, October 2, 8:20 a.m.

Despite the late hour arriving home last night, having arrived a few minutes before midnight, Mali felt refreshed. She had Jake to thank for that. He had held her most of the night, sleeping on top of the covers. She wasn't sure when he left but she had found a note on her dining table an hour ago saying he'd return between eight and eight-thirty.

Now sitting on her balcony, Mali sipped her coffee, enjoying the activity on the Hudson. She laughed as two ducks scurried out of the way of a pontoon, quacking all the way, clearly irritated. Not a cloud was in the sky and the cooler weather suited her.

When the doorbell rang, she glanced at her watch. She rushed to the front door, opening it with a big smile. Jake stood there with a brown bag in his hand, a larger black bag on his shoulder, and a matching smile on his face.

"Good morning." He used his free arm to pull her to his side and kiss her.

With one arm around his waist, she reached for the bag with her other as they kissed.

"Hey!"

She laughed. "I know what you brought and I'm hungry!"

Chuckling, he handed her the bag and she looked inside as they walked to the kitchen.

"Yum!" She pulled out two chocolate croissants and handed him one. "Coffee?"

He nodded as he sunk his teeth into the delicious treat.

"What time did you leave this morning?" she asked as she handed him his cup.

"About four."

"Geez."

He smiled.

They enjoyed the peace of the moment as they finished their croissants.

At ten minutes to nine, the doorbell rang.

Jake walked to the door, welcoming Agent Hernandez in. As they walked to the dining room, Jake picked up the black bag he had set down.

"Good morning, Agent Hooper," Agent Hernandez said. "How are you today?"

"Feeling much better, thank you."

"That's quite a shiner you've got. Any other injuries?"

"Just a few scratches."

"Good. I've made arrangements for the implant to be removed this afternoon at one, Mount Sinai Hospital."

"Thank you. I'm ready for it to be out." Mali smiled.

Agent Hernandez sat. "Let's begin."

For the next hour and a half, Mali and Jake described the sequence of events from each of their perspectives.

Jake looked grim when he spoke of losing contact with her. "Her signal just dropped, and we had no clue why. Jeff kept saying the system was working."

"They put me in a Faraday cage when I landed in Vegas." At Agent Hernandez's questioning look, Mali described what the cage did. "Janet said they couldn't check me for a wire at the airport and opted for this."

"That's brilliant," acknowledged Agent Hernandez.

Jake continued. "To top it off, they brought in four other white Dodge vans and played a shell game with us. We lost you." He turned tortured eyes to Mali.

Mali reached across the table and squeezed his hand, letting go to pick up her coffee. Agent Hernandez's eyebrows shot up, but she said nothing.

"Thorpe has a house in Vegas, and we were sure you were there. We wasted almost an hour at that location, would have spent even more time there but your signal suddenly appeared."

"That's probably when we arrived at the airport. They took me out of the cage to get on the helicopter."

"As soon as you headed north, I recalled you telling me about Thorpe's summer home in Tahoe and realized you were heading there. I got the address of his home from your father."

Agent Hernandez looked at Jake. "You have the video?" Jake nodded.

Mali swallowed hard as Jake pulled the camera from his bag and set it up. Turning it on, they all watched in silence.

As Janet described the things Thorpe did, Jake hit the pause. "We heard Simpson tell Hoop her father was not a participant when they were walking from the helicopter to the house. That recording is at the warehouse.

file was also left in the house with the names of the vice presidents in his company and the clients who did participate. We will bring each in for questioning and arrest those who were involved."

Agent Hernandez nodded and motioned for Jake to continue with the video.

When Drake left the room, the video remained on Thorpe. They observed Mali and Janet fighting as they watched Thorpe hang. Mali rubbed her stomach, feeling nauseated. She would never forget Janet's cackle or watching Richard die.

All were silent when the video ended. Mali was taking deep breaths. Jake looked grim.

Agent Hernandez looked up at the ceiling then at Mali and Jake. "I'll never get used to cases like this." She shook her head. "We'll need to speak with your father."

"I understand. He should arrive here at eleven. He will cooperate in any way needed."

"Good. We'll take him to the office to discuss the events that occurred."

Mali nodded.

At precisely eleven, there was a knock on Mali's door. When she opened it, her mother took one look at her and teared up.

"I'm alright, Mother," Mali said as they hugged.

"Every time I come here you are injured in some way." She sniffed and her mouth dropped open when she noticed the implant.

"Before you say anything, Mother, we put the

implant in this time so Jake could track me. It saved my life."

Willow sniffed again. "Well, in that case, I'm grateful."

"Hello Father." Mali hugged a grim-looking Charles.

"I'm glad you're alright, Jasmine." Looking at Jake, who had walked up to him, Charles shook his hand and said, "Thank you for saving Jasmine, Jacob."

"I'm sorry about Richard Thorpe."

"Yes, well…" He cleared his throat. "There is much to talk about."

"Indeed there is, Mr. Hooper." Agent Hernandez joined the group and introduced herself. "I'd like you to accompany Agent Black and myself to our office for our conversation. This shouldn't take more than a few hours. We'll have you back to your hotel in no time."

"Of course."

"Get some rest this weekend, Agent Hooper. I expect you back at work on Monday."

"Yes, ma'am."

The three left after Jake packed up the video camera to take with them.

Willow accompanied Mali to the hospital at one for the removal of the implant. Afterward, they picked up lunch and returned to Mali's apartment to eat.

"This is a sad day," murmured Willow as they both sat on Mali's balcony with a glass of wine and their salads.

"I'm sorry about Richard, Mother."

She shook herself like a cat. "Yes, well…it's also a

y happy day and that's what I intend to focus on. w hat time are Jerry and Heather due to arrive?"

"Jake said they'd all be here at five."

"Wonderful!"

Mali squeezed her mother's hand, smiling as she leaned back in her chair and took a sip of wine.

CHAPTER THIRTY

Mali's apartment
Friday, October 2, 5:10 p.m.

MALI'S MOTHER HAD returned to the Ritz shortly after lunch to shower and dress for dinner. Mali took the time to do a Zoom call with Kirsten, Sara, and Jen to tell them she was alright and to explain some of what had happened. They had cried a little and then expressed their gratitude that Mali was safe. After promising to get together the following weekend, they had said their good-byes.

She took a long, hot shower and emerged from her bedroom wearing a black knit midi dress in a sleek rib-knit design. The long sleeves, off-the-shoulder and open back completed the look. She wore red stiletto patent leather heels that were open-toed with adjustable straps. They were a bit of whimsy with a maxi flower on the right side, but she was feeling light-hearted knowing the stress and horrors of the past few weeks were over.

She answered the door on the first ring, smiling broadly when her parents, Jake, Jerry, and Heather all arrived together.

"Where's your purple eye? Daddy said you had something called a shiner and it was purple." Heather stood on tippy-toes trying to see Mali's face, a cute pout on her face. Laughing, Mali leaned down to better accommodate her.

"Makeup does wonders at times!" She winked then hugged Heather. Holding her by the hands, Mali stood back to look at her. "You look very pretty tonight. I love your hair. Did your daddy fix it for you?"

Heather beamed as she turned her head this way and that, showing off her french braids. "No way can daddy do this. Papa worked his magic. Oooh, look at the lights outside!" She raced past Mali to the windows, talking non-stop.

"You look gorgeous." Jake pulled her in for a kiss.

"Jake!" Mali blushed afterward. "My parents…"

Charles and Willow both laughed as they, too, hugged Mali. Mali looked closely at her father. He looked sad to her, and he was a little pale, despite his laughter.

Seeing her concern, Charles patted her hand. "Tonight is a night to celebrate. Tomorrow, we will talk about Richard's actions against you, something we are deeply sorry about, and I will deal with the changes to come for the company." Willow slipped her hand into Charles' hand and squeezed as Mali leaned in to kiss him on the cheek.

After ushering everyone into the living room, Mali walked into the kitchen to grab the bottle of wine chilling in the refrigerator as well as a strawberry pouch drink for Heather. Pouring five glasses of wine, she placed them on a tray, along with Heather's drink, then walked into the living room and set the tray down on the coffee table.

"I thought you'd like to try this Sauvignon Blanc, Father. It's a two thousand nineteen from Twomey Cellars in Napa Valley," said Mali as she handed Willow a glass before turning to give one to Charles.

Charles made appreciative noises as he smelled the wine, while Mali handed glasses to Jake and Jerry then joined Heather at the window. With a flourish, she handed the pouch drink to her.

"Ooooh, strawberry is my favorite."

Returning to the sofa, Mali sat next to Jake and picked up her own glass.

Charles raised his glass. "A toast. To the safe return of our daughter and…"

Interrupting him, Willow said, "…and to saying goodbye to the security detail that's been hovering over us."

After a round of cheers and laughter, everyone sipped their wine and settled into a lively conversation.

Heather, who was still watching the boats chug down the Hudson as she finished slurping her drink, suddenly stopped and turned to look at her dad. When he nodded, she jumped up and down then ran to Mali.

Mali was so taken with this sweet child. The happiness on Heather's face brought Mali immense joy. She looked at her parents and Jerry, then at Jake in wonder. The people in this room had become the most important people in her life. She felt so blessed.

"A-hem!" Heather stamped her foot, eliciting a laugh from all the adults as she drew Mali's attention back to her.

"Oh, I'm so sorry, Heather."

Heather took a deep breath then got down on one knee. Startled, Mali glanced at Jake. He, too, was on his knee. Her free hand flew to her mouth, and she teared up. She didn't notice when Willow plucked the wine glass that was in danger of dropping to the ground out of her other hand.

Jake took her hand in his. "Mali, I love you. I have since the day I saw you on that video screen. I can't…" He looked at Heather and smiled, "…we can't imagine going through this life without you. I've learned these past few years something that was reinforced yesterday. Was it just yesterday?"

Mali smiled through her tears. Jake smiled too as he squeezed her hand.

"I've learned we can't wait on life. People think they have time but that's not always the case. We have to make the most out of every moment on this journey we call life. And…"

Heather stomped her foot again. "Daddy, are you done yet? You said I could ask!"

Everyone laughed.

"I guess I'm done." Jake tugged on Heather's french braids with his free hand.

"Finally!" Heather grinned and kissed her daddy. Placing her hand on top of theirs, she asked, "Mali Hooper, will you marry us?"